KILLING ME SOFTLY

SHEILA QUIGLEY

burgess books

www.theseahills.co.uk

First Published in 2017 by Burgess Books
Copyright © Sheila Quigley 2017
All rights reserved
The moral rights of the author have been asserted

British Library Cataloguing in Publication Data:
A catalogue record for this book is available from
the British Library.

ISBN-13: 9780992878443

Printed and bound by
RECREATE MARKETING, Durham, England

Burgess Books
Houghton-le-Spring
United Kingdom
www.theseahills.co.uk

DEDICATION

for Ann Peel

ALSO BY SHEILA QUIGLEY

THE SEAHILLS NOVELS:
Run for Home
Bad Moon Rising
Living on a Prayer
Every Breath You Take
The Road to Hell
Lady in Red
The Sound of Silence

THE HOLY ISLAND TRILOGY
Thorn In My Side
Nowhere Man
The Final Countdown

To find out more visit:

www.sheilaquigley.com

KILLING ME SOFTLY

Prologue

They met at the prearranged time and place. Dressed in black leather with his black hair gelled and combed back over his head, he looked her up and down.

His dark eyes slowly raked over her body taking in her dull grey appearance, from her mousey coloured hair tied in a tight bun at the back of her head to her grey checked blouse along with the grey trousers. *Hell even her fucking shoes are grey.* He thought. *This one really needs some colour, whatever she says. Pink I think, yes a bit of pink will be good, bring out the colour in her cheeks.*

He grinned. For a small time. although maybe red would be even better.

Yes defo red.

She was nervous at first, fidgeting with the two gold rings on the fingers of her right hand and refusing to look him in the eyes. But he soon charmed her and had her confidence.

'You look lovely.'

She blushed. 'Do...Do you think so?'

'Oh yes.'

'So,' she asked after a minute of awkward silence on her part. 'Have you got everything I asked for?'

'Have you got everything *I* asked for?' He held out his hand. Slowly she placed a brown envelope in it.

'Thank you, and yes, of course I have everything.' With a smile, he put the envelope in his breast pocket then opened the boot of his car. She returned the smile, although a bit shaky, when she saw the contents of the boot.

He lifted two glasses out, handed them to her then picked the champagne bottle up, the cheapest brand on the market, and pleased that he's guessed rightly that she wouldn't know the best from the cheapest rubbish. All the time his eyes never left her face and his mouth kept smiling at her.

Opening the bottle he filled both glasses, and watched as she quickly drank a large mouthful. He touched his glass to his lips his eyes never leaving her face as she finished the drink and asked for more.

Giggling she said. 'This is the first time I've ever tasted champagne...Do you like it?'

'Very much it's all I ever drink.'

She peered at him sideways, for a moment with her head slightly tilted; his voice seemed to have changed. '*No, it's just me, feeling a little dizzy.*' She held her glass out for more champagne. Slowly he filled it to the brim.

When she was half way through the second glass and actually flirting with him through her eyes, he threw his glass untouched to the ground. With a tinkle the glass shattered.

For a moment she was in shock at his action, then slowly she looked up at his still smiling face, for a moment she was confused, then she recognised the smile for what it was. Her heart skipped, fear replaced the contentment she had been starting to feel in as long as she could remember.

'No.' slowly she started to move away. Her legs began to wobble as she backed into the car.

'Oh yes.' His voice was gruff as his smile grew ever wider when he reached for her, resting one hand on her shoulder and gripping tightly so that she wouldn't fall, he ripped her grey blouse wide open.

'No,' her voice was slurred as she said it again, the drugs he had earlier put in the champagne began to kick in. 'No...No. This is not how we planned it, you know what I want...please no, don't do this.' She tried to struggle but her limbs felt heavy and useless. 'Please.'

'Trust me...Nothing in this life is ever how you want it to be,' he replied, the knife held high as he smiled at her. 'Never.'

'Please don't do this. Please.' She begged. 'This isn't what I wanted...You promised.' She managed to raise her arms level with her waist, but that was all the resistance left in her slowly they fell by her side.

With a sigh he brought the knife down and placed it on her throat, gently he caressed her trembling skin with the blade. Up and down, up and down.

'Pity we can't all have what we want isn't it.' he said slowly. 'Such pretty skin you have...Really you look much better than your picture, and as for colour you will look so much better my dear, when I change your lipstick to red. Trust me; I just know you are going to suit it.'

Her eyes closed, and then flicked open, showing her fear as her heart pounded with fright. 'No,' she tried to scream, but nothing came out of her mouth except blood as he stuck the blade in to her throat and viciously twisted it.

Her legs gave way and she fell to the road.

He stared at her. Before taking her legs and dragging her into the bushes. Quickly he ran to his car, grabbed up everything he needed from the boot, and was back in seconds. Carefully he applied the bright red lipstick, sitting back on his heels he took a precious moment and admired his work.

The tiny night creatures frantically scrambled over each other to find a way in through the heavy silk shroud towards the smell of blood; as the moon faded and the sky lightened, they disappeared. The body cooled slowly. By morning, it would be as if life had never lived there.

CHAPTETER ONE

He threw his cigarette out of the car window, then turned the radio up, after a moment he changed the station from a country and western channel to a heavy rock. For the last half an hour the motor way had been empty. His late night journey from the South to the North after his latest job meant he had been driving for four hours and urgently needed a sugar fix.

It was just after four o clock in the morning and Meatloaf was belting out the words to 'Bat Out Of Hell.' When he left the motorway and drove into the Wetherby service station car park- at the same time as a dark red Fiat. Although there was plenty of room in the car park, the Fiat pulled up alongside of him. As he got out of the car, the owner of the Fiat also got out of his, a tall thin man wearing glasses, he was also holding onto the leader of a large German shepherd dog.

When the dog spotted him it started barking and tried to jump up, as his owner apologising, dragged him away. 'Bad dog Misty, Shut up...come on.'

He scowled at the dog, which still kept turning around and alternatively kept barking and snarling at him.

'Sorry,' the owner said again over his shoulder after yawning loudly. 'Don't know what's got into her...She's not usually like this, she's always very friendly with people.'

He shrugged at the dog owner, and still scowling watched as he and the dog walked away.

After using the facilities he went into the cafe and ordered a large coffee, and a thick slice of chocolate cake, he put six sugars into the coffee, and stirred it slowly, as he debated with himself whether to sit in one of the booths, or go back to his car.

Deciding on the latter he turned and bumped into a young blonde woman, who was well under five foot and wearing a very low black dress, she apologised, even though the blame was more his than hers, he scowled at her then headed back to his car. Watching him the woman shuddered.

The dog was already in the back seat of the Fiat and again started barking at him. 'Fuck off.' He snapped, which made the dog bark even louder.

Scowling at the dog he opened his car door and placed the coffee and cake on the passenger seat, before looking quickly around at the almost deserted car park as he moved to the boot of his car. 'I'm going to kill you, bastard.'

Still looking around he opened the boot and took out a heavy wrench, and walked round to the other side of the red Fiat so that he could see the doors of the cafe. By this time the dog as if sensing what was about to happen, was howling.

He lifted the wrench high above his head, 'Trust me you're going to suffer, and what's left will be fed to the rats.' He was about to smash the window in, when a movement caught his eye. Another car had pulled in close to them.

'Shit!' He was so angry and his grip so intense on the wrench that his fingers spasmed, he felt no pain as he quickly hid the wrench and pretended to be checking his tyres.

The dog hiding on the floor kept on howling as two teenage boys, both intently checking their phones, got out of their car, and without once taking their eyes off their phones and oblivious to the noise the dog was making, they headed towards the cafe.

Jumping up he grabbed the wrench and once more aimed for the window just as the owner walked past the two youths on his way out. 'Fuck.' Quickly he threw the wrench onto the back seat of his car and grabbing his keys out of his pocket jumped behind the wheel.

Revving the engine up, he read the number plate and yelled. 'Lucky dog this time bastard. But I'll fucking well find you.' As he took off into the night.

CHAPTER TWO

Lorraine Hunt opened her eyes, stretched her long slim body, turned her head and looked at the alarm clock. Half six and semi dark already, it seemed only weeks since it was daylight at this time. *Won't be long before the clocks move now, I guess winter is just around the corner.* She groaned loudly as she slapped the top of the alarm clock to stop it going off later.

She was dreading the winter months arriving. Especially since Carter, one of her young officers had decided as well as being a history buff, he was now a long range weather forecaster and was predicting a violent snow filled winter to come. But at the same time, she was pleased that she had woken up before that bloody noisy pigeon this morning, which had somehow taken up residence in the neighbourhood this year and lived as close as he could get to her window.

Luke was in the middle of a deep snore, so the small noise she had made, hadn't disturbed him. Knowing she wouldn't be able to get back to sleep at this time, because even though today the opportunity was there, as she and Luke were both on late shifts, but because of the damn singing pigeon, who she swore must be the happiest bird on the friggin planet, and would pretty soon be starting his own damn dawn chorus. With a heavy sigh, she got out of bed and dressed, wondering as she did most mornings, just what today would bring.

Yesterday had been a good day, a disgruntled snitch, had finally helped them to clear up a case of recent pub robberies, which would put the mastermind, one they had suspected for months, behind bars for a long time. But as good as yesterday had been, today was another day, and anything could happen.

Ten minutes later, wearing a pale blue track suit and white trainers, her long blonde hair hanging free, she pulled up outside of her mother's house, taking the house key out of her pocket she quietly opened the door. Tiptoeing along the passage way she entered the kitchen where Duke the dog was snoring nearly as loudly as Luke had been.

'Some bloody guard dog.' She muttered quietly as she stared fondly at him.

Duke opened his eyes, and tail wagging hard, he jumped out of his bed and quickly ran to Lorraine- just as Lorraine felt a tap on her shoulder. 'Shit,' she spun round fists high in a Karate stance, to find Peggy standing over her holding a cricket bat in the air, with a grin covering her face.

'Peggy!' Lorraine relaxed. 'You frightened the life outta me. When the hell did you get back?'

Peggy was best friends with Lorraine's mother, had been since they were toddlers, and she was also Lorraine's Godmother. Peggy had lived with Lorraine's mother, Mavis, for a good few years now, only disappearing on and off when a new man appeared on the scene.

Peggy dropped the arm that was holding the bat, with a huge smile she said. 'Very late last night my lovely,' she tucked her hair behind her ears, cocked her head to one side and raised her eyebrows as if in a question.

'So what the hell are you doing up this bloody early on a morning then?' Lorraine refrained from mentioning the colour of Peggy's bright bottle red hair, in fear that she wouldn't ever get out of the house for hours and hours, knowing full well that Peggy, as usual, was fishing for a compliment.

'Couldn't sleep a wink pet.' Peggy replied as she flicked her hair behind her ear again.

'Me neither...Jet lag with you?'

'Aye got to be something like that pet.'

'And just what the hell do you think you were you gonna do with that bat, if I had been a six foot burglar, built like a brick shithouse?'

'Give the thieving twat a nice bump on the bloody head, that's what I'd do, you know that, and to hell with the stupid ignorant PC brigade, who as well with a lot of other stupid idea's like not giving your kids hand a slap if he tries to put it in the fire, now seem to think it's not right to defend your own bloody property, friggin idiots.'

Lorraine shook her head, knowing that's exactly what Peggy would have done, even though she would have probably ended up biting the burglar's ankles. As for the PC brigade she knew exactly where Peggy, was coming from but it was too early on a morning to listen to a Peggy rant.

'Thought you weren't back until next week, those down in Australia sick of you already?' Peggy had been away for a month visiting her sister Millie, who she wasn't too keen on anyhow, wrong gender for Peggy, along with an aunt who she somehow sort of liked.

Peggy screwed her face up. 'The other way round more like, I managed to catch an early flight, way to hot down there for me mate, not used to such bloody weather, couldn't flaming well breath half the time. Honestly couldn't take any more of that friggin heat.' She fanned her face with her hand.

'In which way I wonder.' Lorraine said with a smile as she clipped Duke's leader on, thinking, *I wonder whose wife she's managed to piss off this time*, but saying. 'Right then, I'll catch you later Peggy.'

'You sure will. Err, what did you mean by which way?' Peggy played with a lock of her hair again and smiled sweetly as Lorraine, with Duke leading the way, walked out of the door. If Lorraine had looked back she would not have been the slightest bit surprised to have seen Peggy still fiddling with her hair.

Lorraine decided to walk up to Houghton and head in the direction of table rock. *A long time since I've watched the sun come up from there*, she thought as she passed the library on her right and reached the Gentoo offices on her left. She was about to turn left and cross over the road towards Halo's hairdressers and Recreate Print, when looking right she saw two youths who were undoubtedly trying to break into the library. Quietly she slipped over the road.

Dropping Duke's leader, who although growling softly, immediately sat down, she grabbed the right arm of the one dressed all in black with his hood up, and twisted his arm up his back. He squealed like a girl. Lorraine pressed his head up against the shutter and stuck her foot out as the other one tried to run. He ended up sprawled on the pavement. Suspicious, Lorraine pulled the hood down off the one she had against the shutter.

Her hunch was right. 'So Christie Bales up to your old stuff again, eh girl?'

'Don't know what you mean. And you're friggin well hurting me.'

'Tough...And I guess you were caught in the act this time alright,' she looked at the one lying on the floor, whose hood still covered his face. 'And I just bet that's your very best mate Wayne Barret!'

Barret, who underneath his hood, had longer and thicker black hair than his partner, was hugging his left leg, he looked up and glared at Lorraine. 'I'm having you for this copper, 'cos you've only gone and broke me friggin knee, haven't you...Pushed me onto the ground with excessive force and tried to rape me...Its sexual harassment, as well as overdue force.'

'Yeah right, you wish.' Lorraine said, remembering just how many times the scumbag who was Barret, had tried to pull that stunt on a number of officers, and Evan Delany a very promising young officer, who unable to go on anymore, had left the force because of Barret's false accusations. Claiming that he couldn't take any more of Barret's friends on the street, calling him pervert, among other names in front of his wife and two children and the knowing looks from others, who didn't know the full story or how much of a liar Barret was.

Delany had always been a liked and respected officer and just about everyone from the top brass to the beat coppers had tried to talk him out of it, but to everyone's disappointment he had been adamant he couldn't go on. He now worked as a postman, his dreams shattered because of Barrets evil ways.

She reached for her phone, only to realise she had forgotten to pick it up. *Damn.*

Looking up, then down the street, she found it totally

deserted. Bending over, her face a few inches from his, and resisting the urge to gag, she said, 'Sorry but it looks like you're gonna have to hop all the way to the police station, dick head.'

She quickly straightened up when he replied with his breath stinking of pickled onion crisps. 'Fuck off...I'll go to the papers, tell them everything you did to me, this is cruelty as well as attempted rape, and undue force...I have rights you know, human rights.'

'Yes you do have rights, number one being the right to crawl back into the filthy hole where you belong, arsehole, move it now, I haven't got all day to waste on the likes of you.'

'We weren't doing anything wrong,' Christie Bales snapped, as Lorraine moved her hand to the top of Christie's right arm. 'And that hurts.'

'I so believe you. Delicate little angel aren't you.' Lorraine looked down at Barret. 'I said move it.'

'Are you thick or what copper. I already said that I can't fucking walk,' he moaned loudly as he rocked back and forth, this time holding onto his ankle. 'I'm in terrible pain through you. I'm fairly having you done for this.'

'That's alright Barret. I'm pretty sure your mate Christie will carry you,' Lorraine smiled at Christie, who glared at her. 'Won't you Christie...I just know you'd really love to help your mate out. Come on there's a good girl, you can't just leave him lying there, pick him up.'

Barret spat towards Lorraine's feet.

Steeling herself Lorraine, took a couple of deep breaths as she stared him out.

'I'm not carrying the fat twat.' Christie said as she and Barret scowled at each other.

Barret, making a big show of effort, slowly stood up. 'Well give is a hand then cow face.'

'Fuck off.'

'Now girls,' which brought an even bigger scowl from Barret, this time along with a growl that was directed at Lorraine. 'Let's just hop along.'

'Me ankles killing me,' Barret, moaned. 'You thick or what copper. I can't fucking walk... I'll have you done for this as well as attempted rape. Just watch me.'

'Yeah whatever...By the way scumbag, I thought it was your knee?'

'Err, em...It's both.' Barrets hands hovered between his knee and his ankle.

Lorraine laughed. 'Sure it is...Move it, and no funny business because, trust me, any false moves and this dog will bring you straight down.'

Barret glanced nervously at Duke who wagged his tail at him, with a sneer, he said. 'What?'

'You heard.'

'You mean that friggin ugly useless thing?' Barret tutted then laughed sarcastically. 'It looks as soft as shite! Probably run away from a rabbit.'

Picturing Duke running away from a rabbit, which he had done more than once, and not about to tell him that Duke was really as Barret suspected, basically as soft as shite, or even softer, Lorraine said. 'Well that's for me to know and you to wonder isn't it creep.'

He spat on the floor.

Lorraine glared at him. 'And as for running away from a rabbit isn't that just the sort of thing you do?'

He glared back at her.

'According to your so called mates, that is.'

'Least I've got some.' He spat again.

'Yeah right and enough of this it's becoming boring. I'll tell you one more time that's all... Move it now.'

It took more than ten minutes for them to reach the station, with Barret exaggerating every step and stopping to rub his knee every minute or so, stretching Lorraine's patience to the limit.

When they finally got there, Lorraine handed the pair over to the duty sergeant, after telling him what she had caught them doing, he raising his eyebrows and said, 'Hmm, Shiney Row library was done over night before last, along with Hetton, bunch of computers nicked from both, you two happen to know anything about that?'

'It wasn't us man, fucking coppers, pin the blame on innocent victims all the time,' Barret rubbed his knee and winced as if he was in severe pain. 'We were just minding our own fucking business until she came along,' he looked Loraine up and down with a sneer. 'And also...I want to make a complaint about her for sexual harassment. 'Cos I've got a witness,' he looked at Christie. 'Haven't I Christie love?'

Christie looked at the far wall, pretending that she hadn't heard him.

'Haven't I?' He demanded again as Christie continued to ignore him. 'Go on tell her.'

Christie shook her head as she transferred her gaze to the floor.

'Bitch.' Barret snarled.

'What, got nobody to back you up creep? Now that's a bloody

shame.' Lorraine smiled at him.

Glaring at her Barret muttered something unintelligible under his breath.

'What?' Lorraine asked, the corners of her mouth twitching.

'Nowt.'

'OK then...I wonder just what we'll find in your flea ridden flat, or perhaps your mother's posh house. You must be such a big disappointment to her.'

Mrs Barret was known by most of the locals, as the biggest snob in the North East, and very few people had been surprised when her son who many considered to be nothing more than a spoilt brat, had turned out the way he had. Way too busy with her own advertising company, Wayne had more or less been left to his own devises, relying on his mother to defend him, which right or wrong she always did.

'Waste of time...There's nowt to find.'

'You sure of that?' Lorraine grabbed his hand and slammed it on the counter. 'Finger prints don't lie, and yours will be matched, thicko.'

'We wore gloves.'

Lorraine laughed. 'Did you now?'

'Yes we did.'

The officer barely able to keep a grin off his face, looked up at Lorraine as she went on. 'Yes maybes on the inside of the buildings, but not on the outside. Which I'm certain the CTT camera will verify.'

'But...' Barret was silent for a moment, realising that he had just put his foot right in it.

Shaking her head, Lorraine said to the officer. 'Make sure a search warrant is issued on both their and *his* mother's properties while they are both still under arrest. I'll be in later to interview them, very much later.'

'We not stopping in here all day,' Barret stamped his foot. 'You can't keep us till you decide to turn up, lazy bitch.'

As Lorraine and the officer ignored Barrets last statement Lorraine winked at him, with a smile he said. 'Sure will boss.'

Lorraine left them with Barret finding his voice and loudly protesting their innocence, and insisting on a doctor and his solicitor.

Five minutes later, as the sun was bravely trying to make an appearance through the many dark clouds, Lorraine was walking through the Seahills on the way to her mother's house. The streets were very quiet, a few cars leaving for work, but a lot of the curtains still closed, she could see Mr Skillings pottering around in his garden further up the street, other than that the streets were pretty much deserted.

Just before she reached Mr Skillings house she saw Kerry Lumsdon coming out of her gate. Slightly amused that Kerry was also wearing a pale blue track suit, she gave her a wave as she jogged past her on the other side of the street. Kerry, out for her early morning run, smiled and waved back, when suddenly two youths wearing dark green hoodies and looking as if they were up to no good at all, ran past her. She stepped to one side quickly before they had a chance to knock her over.

Turning, Lorraine frowned at their backs. *Who the hell?* She didn't recognise them at all.

Reaching Mr Skillings she stopped to say hello, the smell of freshly turned soil in the air, mixed with the last of the summer flowers was strong, she smiled when he said. 'Well if it isn't my favourite copper.'

'And good morning to you Mr Skillings,' she turned to look back at the two youths who were now at the bottom of the street and just about to turn the corner; turning back to Mr Skillings she asked, 'Do you know those two?'

'No, never seen them before. Looked in a bit of a hurry though didn't they.'

Lorraine shrugged. 'They did that.' She had already taken on board every item of clothing the pair had worn, right down to the identical pale blue Nike trainers.

Mr Skillings rubbed his back. 'How's your mam and Peggy getting on?'

'Both good Mr Skillings, and how are you?'

'Not bad for twenty five.'

Lorraine laughed. 'You wish.'

'Haven't seen them around for a while.'

'Well, Peggy's just got back from Australia, and mam's struggling with the flu that seems to be just coming back and back. I'll tell them you're asking after them.'

'Right my love, I'm just full of the usual aches and pains today my dear, terrible when you get to twenty two.'

Lorraine laughed. 'You've just lost three years, guess the scientists will just love to meet you...Well got to move on, Mr Skillings, have a good day.'

'You too Mrs Copper.'

Lorraine smiled. It was people like Mr Skillings that made her job worthwhile, gave her something to get up on a morning for, knowing she was helping to protect them.

She reached the corner shop, to see the new owners standing outside looking around. The previous owner had died of a heart attack and the shop had been empty for the last few months.

'Is there a problem here?' she asked the tall Sikh man who was standing with his hands on his hips frowning in the direction she had just come from and looking really frustrated.

'Pardon me but who are you?' He asked with a gentle smile.

'Detective Inspector Lorraine Hunt.' She held out her hand, gently the man shook it.

'Baldev Singh,' he said in perfect English with a Manchester accent. 'Pleased to meet you, this is our first day and I think we have just been robbed,' he turned to the other man, who looked young enough to be his son. 'Don't we?'

The young man looked at Lorraine. 'Yes we do.' He nodded then went inside the shop.

'You think?'

'Well, we have just opened half an hour ago, and not had much time to do a proper stock take seeing as we just arrived last night, but two young boys have just been in and I'm certain they filled their pockets with bars of chocolate and ran.'

'Do you have CT cameras?'

'Not getting fixed up until later today.'

'Would you recognise them again?'

'Not really as they were wearing those daft hoodie things, flaming toe rags.'

'OK, anything about their clothing, or anything else you can remember?'

'Only their bright blue trainers.'

'Right, they actually ran past me...Problem is I've never seen them around here before either. But, we will keep an eye out for them...One thing don't mention the colour of the trainers to anyone.'

She had just remembered that Barret and Bales had been wearing bright blue trainers as well, and figured it was either a gang sign, which she hoped not, or someone had knocked off a warehouse full of the damn things.

'Right then I'll send a PC down to take your report, and good luck with the new business, trust me they aren't all like that on the Seahills, and I doubt very much if those two even belong here, I've certainly never seen them before.'

'Thank you.' Mr Singh smiled as he turned to go back into the shop.

A few minutes later Lorraine was dropping the dog off at her mother's house.

Using her mother's phone, she dialled the station and asked to be put through to Dinwall.

'Hi,' she said when the connection was made. 'Twenty minutes ago I arrested Wayne Barret and his side kick. I was going to make them sweat it out but I have a feeling they should be being questioned about now.'

'Right Boss.'

'I need you to find out where he got the blue trainers they are both wearing.'

'OK, any reason why?'

'Just a hunch, but dig deep.'

'Will do.'

'See you later then.'

'OK Boss.'

After saying goodbye, Lorraine went into the kitchen, to find Peggy and Mavis sitting at the table both nursing a cup of tea. There was also a can of diet coke on the table.

Sitting down Lorraine opened the can took a swallow, and

then placed the can back on the table.

'Saw Mr Skillings earlier, he was asking after both of you.'

Mavis smiled as Peggy said. 'Is he after some pale blue trainers like?'

'What?'

'I heard you saying on the phone about pale blue trainers. Just wondering that's all.' Peggy ran her fingers through her hair.

Lorraine tutted. 'That wasn't him on the phone,' she drank some more of her pop, then stood up. 'I'm off.' Picking her can up she waved as they both said goodbye.

CHAPTER THREE

Twenty four hours earlier

With shaky but very quick fingers, she pulled out the rollers in her mousey brown hair, carefully brushed it into a style she liked, then applying her makeup, she changed the colour of her lipstick twice, from pale pink to red. All the time, in the mirror she could see the reflection of her computer sitting on her desk behind her. The screen blank but beckoning as if it was waiting for her, downstairs directly below her, she knew her parents were talking about her again. It was all they ever seemed to do, constantly.

'Go away,' she whispered. 'For God's sake just go away...It's my life mine, mine, mine...And I will do what I want with it, not what youse two want me to.' She bit into the middle finger of her right hand, deep enough to draw blood, dabbing at the blood with a tissue, she held it for a few minutes until the bleeding stopped then started chewing the nail, quickly spitting a piece of nail out when she tasted the blood.

Staring into the mirror she decided she didn't like the colour of this lipstick either, not the look she was after, she wanted to look vibrant, sexy for once, not dull and dowdy, not the look that everyone thought was her. It would be her stage and she would play the part she wanted. Rubbing her lips with a tissue, she picked a darker shade of red.

Finally satisfied with her reflection, she tilted her head from side to side, a rare smile crossing her mouth.

Yes, this is it.

Picking at her ragged nail, she walked over to the computer and typed in the address of the website, she wanted-needed. She had heard about the dark web, but had never been really sure if it existed, or if it was just people's imaginations at work; until she had gone looking. Now she was about to find out if her needs could be met.

He smiled when he checked his bank balance, and again a few minutes later when she came on line, a handsome dark haired man, his face slightly flushed as if he had been in a hurry, and he smiled again when she posted her picture. After they had talked for a few minutes she fell silent, he frowned, then a fresh rush of words from her came on the screen causing him to smile again.

'Will you be gentle?'

'Of course I will...Very gentle. I promise. Everything will be as you ask.' He replied with a smirk she couldn't see, loving the colour of her lipstick, which reminded him of someone else and caused his heart to flutter with excitement.

'Quick?'

'Very quick. Trust me.'

She hesitated a moment before saying with a soft smile. 'I do trust you, very much.'

With a happy sigh he closed the connection, this new contract meant that he would have to travel north for the first time ever, but he was quite happy with that, from the pictures he'd seen, it looked a pretty remarkable place, and he so loved his countryside rides in the car, one of his few pleasures. He nodded. *About time I started spreading my wings.*

Going over to his wardrobe he took a black holdall out of the bottom and started to pack. Black shirts, five of them, black trousers, black jeans. Two black jumpers might be cold up there in the north. 'Yes it is autumn time.' He said to himself, as he pulled the zip closing his holdall.

With a contented smile he went down stairs and made a cup of tea, barely feeling the pain as he spilt some of the boiling water over his hand, he scooped four spoonfuls of sugar into the cup, hesitated a moment then added a fifth. Taking the cup into the sitting room, he used the downstairs computer to search for hotels in County Durham. It took him less than five minutes to find the one he wanted.

After booking a room, he drank the rest of his tea, washed the cup, and then looked around to check that everything was in place, the way he liked it, he hated coming home to a messy house. His mother used to say quite frequently, 'A place for everything, and everything in its place.'

Satisfied he put his black jacket on. Running his hand over the soft leather, he looked in the mirror. *Perfect*, he thought, for the angel of death.

Grinning he put his hand over his mouth as he pictured a pair of wings peeping over the top of his shoulders.

CHAPTER FOUR

Present day

Early morning and still dark when he checked into the hotel, he took his bags upstairs and decided to take a look around.

He drove around for a while and noticing a sign which said Ancient town of Houghton le Spring, he decided to pay a visit.

He loved nothing more than wandering around in the dark, targeting certain houses and passing through the next day to see if there was anyone living there who took his fancy.

Leaving his car by the side of the first house he took a slow walk around the Seahills.

Smiling to himself as the residents, totally unaware of the evil that walked among them; dreamed on.

CHAPTER FIVE

'Don't be too long Dale.' His mother shouted, from upstairs as Dale slipped his dog Skip's leader on. 'Don't forget the dentist this morning, before school. We can't miss this appointment like we did last weeks, remember love.'

'As if I could forget.' Dale groaned, picturing the dentist chair with him lying in it and the dreaded mask hovering over his face. That was the part he hated the most! He shivered as he slammed the door shut behind him, loud enough to wake the late sleepers in the Seahills and beyond.

I so hate the dentist. He was about to stamp his foot when suddenly, a moment later he was nearly pulled off his feet as the dog spotted next door's cat crouching near the gate. Hearing the dog before he saw him, the cat hissed his defiance, before taking off at lightning speed up the street.

'Bad dog.' Dale yelled, pulling hard on the leader, Skip's tail immediately fell between his back legs, as he attempted to cover Dale in dog kisses. Managing to calm the dog down they carried on their way up through the new estate, which was once the Homelands and now a building site, as more new homes were being erected, and towards and past the swings and the school where he would turn right and go up through Grasswell.

Dale scratched the back of his dark head, wondering if he'd caught anything from that new kid Abby, and then felt ashamed at even thinking that, Abby was his friend. Some of the other kids had been nasty and were bullying her just because they could, saying she had dicks in her hair and that she was fat, which she wasn't, plus other nasty stuff. But Dale liked her, she loved to draw things like he did, and she didn't look scruffy like they said she did, and her hair was very nice and shiny. When he told his mam about them she had said they were probably just jealous of Abby, and nasty little bitches. Dale guessed his mam was right.

He scratched his head again and found another spot, which were starting to appear regularly these days. His mam said it was normal for his age and not to worry. But the more he thought about it the more he wanted to scratch; he shook his head, but still couldn't resist one more scratch.

The white van crawled along the narrow back lane in Grasswell which was only wide enough to allow one car at a time. The lane was at the top end of Grasswell with the sign for Newbottle being only a foot away.

'Here, stop here, this is where he comes with the dog every morning.' The bulky teenager said, as he pulled the black balaclava down, hiding most of his face.

'You sure he's always alone?' The driver of the van asked. The driver, a thick set middle aged man with a totally bald head, who went by the name of Mick, though no one knew if this was his real name or not because he had never given any one his surname. He had a thick welsh accent and had only been on the scene for three months.

'Double sure, the little toe rag is always here, mostly about this time.'

Mick quickly looked around, when he was satisfied that the place was deserted he pulled his own balaclava down as he jumped from the van, at the same moment a young boy of about eleven years, wearing his school uniform came around the corner holding a blue leader, on the other end of the leader was a young Collie cross Retriever not yet a year old, mostly black in colour the dog had distinctive gold hairs on his front legs and a silver muzzle. The dog wagged its tail when he spotted both men.

In a flash before he registered the balaclavas covering their faces and realised what was happening, the dog's leader was snatched out of the boy's hand. The van door was opened and the young one, named Vincent jumped into the back with the dog, Mick slammed the door behind them, and ran to the driver's side, jumping in he started the engine and quickly took off.

The boy terrified, in shock and heartbroken, started screaming and ran on to the main road after the van as it headed towards Newbottle, shouting for Skip, over and over.

Adam Glazier, on the way up to Houghton to be first in the queue to collect his dole money was riding his bike down the hill in Grasswell, on the other side of the road he spotted Dale, who's father had been a cousin of his mother, run into the middle of the busy road, and quickly checking for traffic, he swerved his bike and headed across to Dale.

'What the hell's the matter with you, running in the middle of the road like that?' A lorry from the nearby quarry skirted round them, the driver blasting his horn. Adam stuck his middle finger up and turned back to the boy. 'You're gonna get yourself killed, frigging idiot.'

'They...' he gasped for air. 'They nicked my dog, Skip...Them, look them in the van.' Tears streaming down his face, he pointed up the bank.

Adam looked up just in time to see the van turning right into Newbottle village which led towards the A19. He whipped his phone out and rang the police, then his right hand guiding his bike and the other around the boy's shoulders he led the distraught boy down through the alley way, past the school towards the Seahills.

'It's alright; the coppers will be at your house in minutes... Well as soon as they can.'

Wiping his nose with his sleeve, the boy looked up at Adam. 'Will they Adam? Will they get Skip back?'

The sheer pain in Dale's eyes struck Adam's heart, and not really knowing if they would or not but suspecting that the dog was gone forever. Adam reassured him that they would be doing their best to find him soon.

CHAPTER SIX

Vanessa Lumsdon switched the iron off and pulled her blue dressing gown tightly together over her red and white striped pyjamas as she shivered. Handing the white school shirt over to her sixteen year old son Darren, she said, 'Don't know about you son but I'm bloody freezing this morning. Feels like bloody summers never happened this year.'

'Thanks mam,' He said, as he put his shirt on and fastened the buttons up.

'Brrr, didn't you hear what I said?'

'It's not that cold Mam.'

She frowned at him, then for a moment she was taken aback, although not as dark skinned as his father, he was turning into the double of him, as well as sounding like him. His father had been, or so the low life had told her at the time, a very promising law student who had suddenly disappeared overnight, hours after she had told him she was pregnant.

Shaking herself out of her reverie, she went on. 'Right son, now you just make sure you make me really proud today, and remember we'll all be there watching you...Not that you don't always make me proud,' she quickly added. 'You always do son, you always will. There isn't anybody prouder in the whole world.

You believe me!'

Darren groaned. 'Please, no shouting at the ref or the other players... Or even the other parents. Please Mam.' He practically begged.

'Who me?' Vanessa grinned as she clapped her hands, and just stopped short of dancing. 'As if I would,' she laughed. 'I'm so, so excited, you'd think it was me gonna score all the goals today, you really would Darren. Honestly.'

Shrugging his blazer on, Darren said. 'I've just had a great idea Mam.'

'Yes and what would that be?'

'Put the heating on.'

'Yeah right quick fix, at what cost. You know we can't afford to have it on most of the day, the price just goes up and up and the fat cat's, who can afford whatever they want...Just keep on letting it...You've got a hell of a lot to learn about this world son.' She smiled as she patted his arm. 'Most of them up there just look after themselves, and that's the flaming truth. The rest of us can just rot in hell for all they care.'

Darren shrugged as Vanessa's mind drifted back to her youth. *If only*, for a moment she was quiet as she stared out of the kitchen window, thinking back to a different time, a different place, when she was Darren's age and so full of hope, until she was lured into drugs and drink by the very people who she thought cared about her, but in reality only cared about lining their own pockets. Then she shook herself.

Don't go there.

It's over.

'Mam?' Darren looked oddly at her. 'You alright?'

'Yes, yes I'm fine son...I used to be really good at sport you know, I mean it, really, really good...Honestly I'm kidding you not. You just go and ask Sandra...That's where you and our Kerry get it from, me,' she nodded her head. 'Defo me. Because I was good you know, in fact I was better than good. At one time I was the best high jumper and runner in the whole damn school.'

'Mam.'

'What?' She smiled at him.

Seeing how happy she was, Darren shook his head. 'Nothing, it's nothing.'

'OK, see you at the game son.'

'Yeah...Bye Mam.' With a shrug Darren felt in his pockets and checked that he had everything. Satisfied, he shot her a quick smile and left.

She watched out of the window as with his navy holdall containing his Sunderland football gear slung over his shoulder, he left for school. Blinking the tears back, she again thanked God for the second chance she had been given. She was high on life now and needed no stimulants in the form of alcohol or drugs to get there. If only she had realised from the start. If she hadn't been so naive and so bloody stupid. She shrugged. *If only. If only. If only...*'Stop dwelling on the past,' she whispered to herself. *My children are my life now, what's done is done. I'm so lucky to have been given a second chance.*

And a few months ago at Robbie's twenty first birthday that fact had certainly been driven home with a huge hammer, it turned out to be a day no one would ever forget.

The emotions of that day ran through her again, from intense pride to horrendous fear, pride in her children who against all the odds had turned out fine, each and every one of them. Deep sadness that it had taken her so long to realise just how precious her kids were...and the fear on that day, that they would soon all be dead, had actually nearly stopped her heart.

They say pride is a terrible sin, but it well and truly won that day alright. She had the newspaper in a large frame hung on the sitting room wall for everyone to see, proclaiming both of her sons as hero's of the day, unknowingly she stuck her chest out, why wouldn't she be proud, *from the gutter to the stars*, she smiled, no she grinned, as humming her favourite Bee Gee song, 'Jive Talking,' softly to herself, she switched the iron back on and carried on with the rest of her ironing.

CHAPTER SEVEN

Just up the street, her best and lifelong friend Sandra Gilbride, stepped slowly out of the downstairs shower room, wrapping the green towel tightly around her body she hugged herself...For a long moment she stared at the cold white tiles on the wall.

When she had finished dressing, she went up to her bedroom, her husband was at the top of the stairs, home from one of his frequent trips to Germany, with his job as a long distance lorry driver. Smiling at her he said, 'Just popping out for an hour or two love, thought I just might get a haircut,' he ran his fingers over the top of his fair coloured hair. 'Getting a bit long now like isn't it. You reckon so?'

He was very surprised when she muttered 'Fine,' and went into the bedroom without giving him a second glance. At the least he had expected her to go off on one, instead 'fine' was all he had got. *Defo not Sandra like*, he thought, at the bottom of the stairs as he put his black jacket on.

Something must be up. He searched his mind. Everything had been good when he came home last night. They had stayed in, watched a film she loved, one which he hated, for probably the tenth time, and had a Chinese take away. Sandra had gone up to bed first and fifteen minutes later when he'd followed her she had been sound asleep, so if anything was bothering her then, no way would she have been asleep. I know how she worries over the slightest thing. By this time he had reached the front door, with the keys in his hand ready to open the door he froze.

No way!

Shit.

She can't know.

No, she would have killed me by now.

Taking a deep breath he opened the door, he needed to get to the bank now, he quickly headed down the path. Guiltily he looked back at the house expecting her to be watching him out of the bedroom window. But there was no quick flick of the curtains which were still closed, that alone was puzzling as Sandra was extremely house proud and would never dream of having her bedroom curtains still shut at nine o clock in the morning.

He got into the car and headed in the direction of Houghton Le Spring, stopping the car just up the street to let Mr Skillings cross over the road, the old man waved his cane in a thank you gesture. He smiled at him, before driving on.

Vanessa Lumsdon spotted Mr Skillings coming up the garden path and went into the kitchen to put the kettle on. She heard his regular two knocks before he opened the door, and his usual shout. 'Hello it's only me.'

She shouted back. 'I'm in here love.'

He tapped his way into the kitchen, with a groan he sank down into the first chair he reached.

Vanessa turned from the kettle. 'You alright Mr Skillings?'

Slowly Mr Skillings shook his head. 'Not really love...It's this bloody arthritis pet, getting worse by the day, by the minute even.

The sun might be shining now, but bet you anything you like it'll be pouring down later.'

Vanessa looked out of the kitchen window. 'Surely not?'

He rubbed his knees as Vanessa put a teacup and a saucer in front of him, before sitting down on the seat opposite. 'Oh it will, trust me; arthritis is a bloody good indicator of the coming weather I swear.'

'Well, my aunt used to say the same thing.' Vanessa sipped her tea, and offered Mr Skillings a ginger snap biscuit.

'Thank you, don't mind if I do...And all them bloody doctors do is pump you full to the brim with chemicals, not good for you. Trying to kill us off well before our time, just to save bloody money if we die quicker, and to make them money if we don't. Win win.'

Vanessa frowned trying to work out just what he meant, then shaking her head, said. 'Really! Anyhow I thought you were gonna get a knee replacement?'

'Changed me mind.'

'What? Why?'

'Cos, don't want one, heard too many tales, a mate of mine got his hips done, and yes he can walk better, but he can hardly bend. I might not be able to play bowls anymore. What would I do with me self then?''

'But it's gotta be better than being in pain all the time. Think about it'

'Well I suppose,' he hesitated for a moment, then went on. 'And to be honest its days like this when I sort of do reconsider,' he shook his head. 'I don't know.'

'Look, let me make an appointment for the doc to talk this through with you.'

'He already did that.'

'I'll come with you, maybes you didn't take in everything he said, 'cos I'm sure I've heard others say the op was fantastic and they never felt better...Alright.'

'Well, that would be very good of you. Seeing as my own wallet munchers, don't seem to have the bloody time of day for me anymore.'

'Now I'm sure that's not true, in fact I know it's not. And you know how busy they are with their jobs and the kids. They both come to see you at least once a week, and they always phone, and it's not as if they live next door is it?'

Mr Skillings nodded. 'Yes you're right, it's a nightmare getting out of Newcastle after work, and Darlington...Ignore me, it's just this bloody pain...Makes me a grumpy old sod and feeling sorry for myself...Poor Jim at the bowling club never see's his three from one month to the next...I remember my old Aunt Maud saying about one of her friends who never saw her kids from one day to the next either. If one mam can look after five kids how come five kids can't look after one mam...Mind you she was a miserable old bugger, never spoke to a soul in her entire street if she could help it, and never had a single kind word for anybody either, probably the nastiest human on the planet if the truth was known.' He thought for a moment, before saying. 'Guess I'm really lucky then.'

'Guess you are...And you know calling in the doc's is no bother at all love. I've got to go up to Houghton this morning anyhow, so I'll call in then and make an appointment and we'll get this sorted, once and for all.'

Mr Skillings sighed. 'Alright then, and by the way the kettles boiling its arse off.'

Laughing Vanessa jumped up. She was about to refill their cups when she saw Sandra coming up the path.

Mr Skillings was just about to thank Vanessa again, when the door opened and Sandra walked in.

Noticing right off that Sandra's auburn hair was hanging loose instead of being tied up in the long plait that nearly touched her waist, Vanessa's eyes moved to Sandra's very pale face, as she pulled a chair out. 'Sit down Sandra, what's up?'

'I...I...' she looked at Mr Skillings.

Realising by Sandra's face that she wanted to talk to Vanessa alone about something private; he looked at his empty cup waiting to be filled with tea, and sighed as he slowly got up out of his chair. 'Guess it's time for me to go, I'll catch you later then ladies, be good now.'

Sandra nodded, and Vanessa said. 'Yes we will, and I'll pop over when I get back from Houghton. And, it's your turn for the bacon sarnie's, don't forget.'

He grinned. 'As if...Twelve o clock on the dot pet.'

When he had gone Vanessa looked at Sandra, fearing she had got into grief again with the loan sharks, because Sandra loved nothing more than spending money on her home, even though things had been tight for the last year or so because her husband had had to take a cut in his wages.

'What is it, them thieving shit bastards bothering you again? Because this time. You mark my word, we off to the coppers. Time the bastards got what was coming to them.'

'No...It's not them, they're all paid off, and don't worry I learned my lesson, I'll never go near them again ever, even if I'm starving to friggin death...I...I,' she reached for Vanessa's hand, looked into her eyes and blurted out, 'I don't know what to do, help me Vanessa.'

Vanessa frowned. Her mind buzzing, if Sandra didn't know what to do then she didn't know what to think, Sandra was the strong one, she always had been, all of their lives Vanessa had relied on Sandra, and looking at her now, Vanessa was becoming increasingly worried, she knew something was definitely up here.

'What do you mean?' she stared into Sandra's sad eyes, and the fear began to build.

'Sandra for fucks sake, what's up?'

'I...I think I've got cancer.' Sandra blurted out, grabbing tightly on to Vanessa's hand.

'What?' Vanessa yelled. 'No fucking way. How? Where?' By now her face was as pale as Sandra's.

'Just now in the shower...' For a moment Sandra froze, then the fear she was feeling leaked from her eyes as she whispered. 'I found, I found a lump on my breast.'

'Aw shit man...For God's sake!'

Sandra slowly nodded; she grabbed Vanessa's hand again, and said. 'Yes love...My right breast. It's cancer I know it is. I just know,' her voice raised to a high pitched squeal as she stared into Sandra's eyes. 'I don't know what to do.' she sobbed. 'Please help me Vanessa. The boys, John, how can I tell them? What will I do, I know its cancer?'

'Oh Sandra,' Vanessa stood up. 'Give me two minutes to sort myself out love. We'll go to the drop in centre now.' She rushed to get her clothes on.

Sandra sat staring at the wall, she felt a small sense of relief and a bit easier now that the words had spilled out and she had told someone, but just a tiny little bit, because in reality she was actually terrified to death of what the doctor would say and had contemplated not telling anyone, not even Vanessa. Hoping that with a bit of luck it would just go away and tomorrow she would wake up and there would be nothing there.

But common sense had won; she knew that really every lump should be checked out. *And it's probably just a fatty lump, aren't most of them*, she reassured herself.

Course they are.

She stiffened her spine. *I'm worrying for nothing!*

But what if?

What about my boys?

What will they do?

No, don't even go there.

She was wiping the tears from her eyes when Vanessa came back, wearing black jeans and a black jumper.

Is that an omen? She thought, biting down on a sob.

'Come on then, we'll get the bus up.' Gently Vanessa took hold of the top of Sandra's arm. 'It'll be fine, stop worrying. No fucking sense in it till we find out what's what. And,' she raised her right hand in the air with her fingers crossed. 'I just bet anything you like that its nowt.'

Suddenly Sandra caught her breath, remembering quite a few years ago saying the same thing to a friend of theirs who had found a lump in pretty much the same place as hers, six months later the friend was dead. And she had only been eighteen.

'Look I know who you're thinking of,' Vanessa said, feeling a lump rising in her throat at the memory of Linda, as they waited for the bus. 'But that was a long time ago, they are much better at finding these's things fast now, and much better at treating it. So again no need worrying yet and probs not at all.'

'But what if?'

'What if nothing! You're gonna be friggin worrying yourself to death and making yourself really ill over something that's probably nothing. Like I said, they are much better at mending cancer than they used to be.'

Sandra sighed. 'I know your right, and I'm probably worrying for nothing, but still...'

'Look here's the bus; we'll be there in minutes.' Vanessa held her arm out for the bus to stop.

They were just about to sit down when they saw Adam Glazier with his arm around young Dale Wilson who was sobbing his eyes out, pass the bus stop.

Throwing Sandra a puzzled glance Vanessa said, 'Wonder what's up there?'

Sandra shrugged, 'Probs fell over, or something. You know that Dale's a clumsy kid, always has been. Remember that time nearly the whole of us on the Seahills went on a bus trip to Redcar, who ended up in the hospital out of all those kids?' Sandra knew she was babbling but it gave her a certain comfort dwelling on the mundane rather than face the fear.

Vanessa nodded. 'Oh yes clumsy little bugger...'

'He is that. I mean who out of the whole bus trip could have an accident but Dale?'

'I know, lovely kid though.'

Changing the subject, and raking her brains to think of something to keep Sandra's mind occupied. Vanessa said. 'Do you think I'll suit my hair blonde? Never had it that colour before, and you know what they say, a change is as good as a rest. Maybe's one of those blue silver tints that's all the rage these days, might even bag me a new man.' She laughed.

The look of surprise on Sandra's face encouraged Vanessa to

keep talking about anything that came into her mind, all the way to the walk in centre door, she kept babbling on. By which time she had gone from hair colour, to nail varnish, to football, then to spaceships.

'You and your bloody conspiracy theories .' Sandra laughed as they walked through the drop in centre door.

CHAPTER EIGHT

After bringing a practically hysterical Dale home, who was now clinging onto his mother, and after also assuring her that he had already informed the police, and they would defo be coming soon. Adam patted Dale on his back. 'Chin up kid, they'll find him. I know they will, so try not to worry, yes.' Then after saying goodbye to them both he quickly mounted his bike and rode as fast as he could up to the post office.

He passed Len Jordon, an old friend on the way, *Shit,* he thought, quickly looking in the opposite direction, hoping that Len had not seen him.

Reaching the post office he was relieved to see that the queue was for once practically nonexistent.

Just a couple of oldies, thank God, he thought. *Be out soon.* That was until the man in front of him suddenly collapsed to his knees, holding on to his chest and moaning in pain.

'Shit! You alright mate?'

By this time the old man was stretched out on the floor gasping for breath. Adam yelled at the cashier to get help as he placed the old man in the recovery position- loosening the tie that was tight around his neck, and praying that the old geezer who Adam knew to be a heavy cigar smoker, didn't need mouth to mouth. *But no,* he thought, with relief, *thank God the old buggers breathing has settled down.*

It was fifteen minutes later after being congratulated by the ambulance team and those in the post office for saving the old man's life that he drew his dole money, and was back out on the street, he rummaged in his pockets for his shopping list.

'Shit.' He muttered, realising that he had either lost it or forgot to pick it up in the first place. Trying to remember what was on it, he pushed his bike along the street to the butchers.

Pork chops? Lamb chops? He stared in the window.

Fucking hell. No way could he remember, all he could picture was her yelling at the top of her voice, 'NO FUCKING CARROTS.' He only knew that his best option was to go home and hopefully find the list, rather than face the flack, because if he went back with the wrong meat there would be hell to pay.

Mounting his bike he headed for home, hoping that she had gone to visit her friend or even her aunt again, even though she'd slept there last night and the night before, and that he would have time to nip in and grab the note, do the shopping and make the dinner, and have everything done before she got back.

Praying that he had left the note in the house and not lost it, he rode home as fast as he could.

CHAPTER NINE

Across the wooden kitchen table, and resting her chin on her hands, Lorraine Hunt pulled a face at her partner Luke Daniels, as he poured another spoonful of sugar over his cornflakes. They had shared Luke's house for over three months now and Lorraine was still surprised at how well things had turned out.

'What?' He pulled a face back at her.

'You know what.'

Finishing the last spoonful, Luke smacked his lips. 'You know I have a sweet tooth darling.' then leaning over the table he kissed Lorraine.

'Gross.' Lorraine wiped her mouth with the back of her hand, 'I can taste the friggin sugar...Not good for you...Not good at all. Bloody hell.'

'But you're so sweet my love. I'm surprised you can taste any other sweetness.'

'Err, you after something with all the slavering Mr?' She smiled as she tilted her head. 'Really not your style.'

'Who me?' Luke smiled. 'As if,' the smile turned to a grin. 'Actually my love I was just thinking, we could do with a few more of these late shifts, a night or two in a nice hotel. Maybes you could wangle a few?'

Playfully she punched his arm, 'Now that would be very nice indeed. If only the bad guys would behave themselves for a week or two...Hell even a day or two would do. But I guess that's just a bit too much to ask isn't it babes?'

Luke nodded. 'Like that's gonna happen. The bad guys behave, 'cos the coppers need a break. Wow!'

Then he jumped as she yelled a moment later, 'Shit what the hell!' when next door's cat, resting on his favourite spot, the wall between the houses, suddenly squealed as a passing seagull swooped very close to him. 'Nearly frightened the bloody life out of me, I swear they are getting bigger by the day I'm telling you, a few more years and they'll be the size of an albatross, it's all the junk food they are scavenging, sky rats that's what they are, rats with wings that's all they are...'

'The farmer must be ploughing the fields up Grasswell, that's what brings them here, that and the flaming tip.'

And about to remind her that she'd said this before about the size of the seagulls, more than once, probably because Edna, Scottie's stand in mother says pretty much the same thing constantly, since she was attacked by them once in Whitley bay as she was eating fish and chips, which they nicked right out of her hand, and something she often reminded them of. Luke, dark skinned, tall and handsome, kept quiet when Lorraine's phone suddenly rang.

'Quick,' she said a moment later as she snapped her phone shut and headed for the stairs. 'We're needed at the Angel of The North, soon as.'

Rising from his chair Luke frowned. 'Any idea why?'

'Some cat walker found a body.'

'Cat walker?'

'Yeah, that's what I thought,' pulling her clothes off as she ran for the bedroom, she yelled, 'Ouch,' as a strand of her long blonde hair caught in a button on her blue pyjama top, then shouted from the top of the stairs as she unravelled the hair from the button, 'Maybes if next door took their cat out on a leader it might not get attacked by the friggin gulls,' she laughed, then went on. 'Give Carter a ring; tell him to get round here double quick.' She opened her wardrobe and grabbed a black trouser suit out. 'Fuck.' Luke heard her shout.

'What's the matter?'

'Bloody zips burst.' Quickly she pulled a similar suit out, this one dark gray in colour. Matched it with a white blouse and hurried down the stairs.

Luke whistled as she stood before him. 'Very nice indeed, and I better phone, your mother as well, tell her we can't get down to walk the dog.'

'Already walked him.'

'What?'

'Yup, while you were snoring your friggin head off.'

'Who me?'

'Yes you!'

'Then you went and threw your pyjama's back on and slithered back into bed?'

'Something like that.'

Shrugging his jacket on, Luke replied. 'My but you're one devious lady.'

'Gotta be in my job. Also caught them two creeps Christe Bails and her mate Barret trying to break into the library, and looks like it might be those two creeps who have stolen computers from other libraries in the area.' She finished off, as she walked back into the room.

Luke looked suitably impressed. 'That's my girl...Mind you do get about while I'm sleeping.'

'You mean snoring.'

Luke shrugged. 'Whatever.'

'Yes, and guess what, the ugly git had the nerve to say that I tried to rape him, as if.'

Luke laughed. 'Comes with the job love, and he's got history of that sort of evilness, the dirty swine, remember?'

Lorraine cut him off before he could say more. 'Yes I know the horrible git. And I think there's a scam going on concerning blue trainers that I'll tell you about on the way.'

About to say something Luke was suddenly overcome with a bout of heavy sneezing.

'That's all we need, friggin man flu.'

Luke looked at her and shook his head. 'It's just a bloody sneeze, must be dust or something.'

'Are you saying I don't do the dusting?'

'I'm saying nowt.'

Quickly they finished getting ready, and waited at the door for Carter, who arrived in a few minutes.

CHAPTER TEN

First in the queue at the library the man hurried to the computer unit, shoved his backpack under the desk and quickly started the computer.

As the page he had opened quickly flooded with words, he typed in. 'Slow down.' Before fervently looking around to see if anyone was watching.

'Sorry,' came the reply, 'I'm just so excited you're coming on board. It's been a long time since we met up. Bring back the old days, eh mate.'

'No thanks. And I have not said I am yet.'

'Am what?'

'Coming on board.'

'But I thought.'

'Yeah jumping the gun as usual.'

'It's money in the bag mate.'

'So you say.'

'But it is, meet me and I'll show you the proof.'

'Not sure.'

'Come on mate...It's nothing you haven't legally done before.'

'That's completely different.'

'Same result though.'

'Erm not really.'

'Yes it is, and you can do whatever you want before and after, they won't know.'

'I'll know. And that's what I'm not too keen on. And why the hell did you think I would.'

'Because.'

'Because what. I'm not like you and I never have been. I wish you had never contacted me.'

'What about that guy in Afghanistan?'

'He deserved what he got.'

'Want to see some pictures.'

'NO.' He typed in capitals, before quickly shutting down the computer. He shuddered as he looked out of the window. Torn in half, because what his once old friend had suggested in earlier posts and knowing it was against anything he believed in, or anything he could do, and totally uncertain as why he could ever think that he would want a part in it. He knew he should report it, but even the idea went totally against the code. He picked his back pack up and left the library.

CHAPTER ELEVEN

As the police car sped north along the A1, the occupants, DI Lorraine Hunt and DS Luke Daniels, driven by PC Carter, stared out of the window at the beautiful red and gold colours of the autumn trees lining the motorway.

Lorraine smiled as she looked at Luke. 'I love this time of year, the trees are beautiful, and this stretch of motorway...'

'Is just fantastic, and out of this world,' Luke finished for her. 'How many times?'

Lorraine narrowed her eyes at him. 'So what Mr Grumpy, if I've said it before, it's true.'

Luke shrugged and grinned as his eyes scanned the trees, thinking, how right she was they weren't just beautiful they were truly magnificent. But looking at her out of the corner of his eye he couldn't help but wonder why she seemed to be so preoccupied lately, and why she kept repeating herself.

'Anyhow what's up with you this morning Mr Nitpicker, like you never repeat yourself?'

'Who me?' Luke shrugged, sneezed, just managing to catch it in a hanky quickly grabbed from his pocket before saying again. 'Who me?'

Lorraine poked his arm, 'It's all the bloody sugar you eat, its making you hyper.'

'Aye, you just might be right about that.'

Lorraine pulled a face at him and turned her attention back to the scenery.

Behind the wheel, Carter grinned, he loved it that Lorraine and Luke were so happy together, they were his two favourite people in the whole world.

The turn off for the Angel of the North came into view; Carter eased into the left hand lane, took the slip road off the motor way then turned right, then right again at the roundabout. Just a few minutes later they were pulling up in the Angel of the North car park.

A few yards away a man was arguing with a young woman PC, with dark red hair, who Lorraine had never met before, getting out of the car Lorraine, followed by Luke and Carter, walked over to them. The jacket of the grey suit Lorraine now wore, because of the burst zip on her other suit, had a habit of riding up, pulling at it as she neared them, she also swung her head irritably flicking her long hair out of her face, because in their hurry to get here she had forgotten to tie it up. Showing her badge she said to the PC, as she looked the man up and down. 'Got a problem here officer?'

'You bet there's a problem,' the man, tall, early thirties, dark haired, wearing a black polo neck jumper, practically shouted as he stepped in front of the PC.

Lorraine turned to him, 'And you would be?'

Looking her up and down with an arrogant stare, he said. 'My name, for your information is Mr Steve Jonstone. And I have driven all the way up from Stockport to take pictures, and this,' scowling he swung his head back to the PC. 'This woman will not let me pass.'

'Tough, Mr Steve Jonstone, obviously you can see that *this* woman, is a police officer doing her job. If you can't see that, I suggest you buy some extra strong glasses.'

'Spec savers are good.' Luke put in. Only to receive a glare of irritation from the man.

'Oh yes they are,' Lorraine raised her eyebrows at Luke, her eyes sparkling with a hidden smile, before turning back to Mr Steve Jonstone, and with another smile said. 'And now that you know where to go for the glasses, the officer will now escort you back to your car, where you will immediately get the hell away from here and drive all the bloody way back to Stockport. Where trust me, I'm pretty damn sure the good people of Stockport certainly won't have a welcoming committee waiting for you. OK Mr Steve Jonstone...Officer.'

Trying but failing to hide a smile the officer reached for the man's arm, shrugging her off he yelled. 'Get your filthy hands off me bitch.'

Lorraine took a step forward as Luke tapped the man on his shoulder, spinning round with a nasty sneer on his face the man quickly stepped back, narrowly missing Loraine's toes, when he saw Luke staring down at him.

'You want somebody to yell at bitch, try me, come on. Yes? No?'

When the man said nothing, Luke went on. 'Just what I expected from you...All right then mate, you have less than a minute to apologies to my officer or the cuffs go on.'

Steve Jonstone held his hand up. 'OK, all right. I'm out of here,' looking at the PC, he muttered, a sarcastic, 'Sorry.' then at Luke, he muttered. 'You're not my mate.'

Luke took a step forward, turning Steve Jonstone headed

swiftly for his car. His body was stiff with anger as he opened the door and got in. Luke's face was burned into his brain, he needed to get the anger out, he knew this or his next job would not go according to plan.

'Arse hole.' Lorraine muttered, as she, Luke and Carter made their way up the incline to the base of the Sculpture. Half way up she stopped and frowning looked down at the car park. 'Hmm, did anyone see a camera in his possession?'

'Now that you mention it, no I certainly didn't.' Luke said.

'Me neither.' Carter frowned.

'So what was he doing here then, and why say he was taking pictures?'

Just then Mr Steve Jonstone's car took off at top speed out of the car park.

'Looks to me like he's in a desperate hurry, or he's in the huff and behaving like a spoilt bitch.' Luke stared at the retreating car, knowing at this distance you would need a pair of binoculars to read the reg, and guessing rightly that would be the next thing that Lorraine would ask.

'Any one get his reg, yes, no?'

'No.' Both of them said.

'OK, could be something or nothing,' she glanced at her watch. 'Let's get a move on.'

As they started to walk, Carter said. 'Did youse two know that the Angel of the North was created by Sir Anthony Gormley; also it's believed to be the biggest Angel Sculpture in the whole world,' Carter stared up at the sculpture. 'It's actually twenty meters tall, with a total wingspan of fifty four meters. Magnificent...Massive. And...'

Lorraine rolled her eyes at Luke, who shook his head with a

smile. 'Oh, there's Scottie and his gang,' she said, a moment later, as Carter was about to sound off again. She hurried down to meet them, Luke and Carter following quickly behind her.

Scottie and his team had beaten them by ten minutes and set up just inside a large copse of trees, where the path meandered to the north of the Angel.

'Hi lovely...And youse two.' Scottie said with a smile when they reached him.

'How you doing Scottie, looks like you've finally got rid of that damn flu bug that's been haunting you this last couple of months or so.'

Luke started to cough, Lorraine groaned inwardly as they all glanced at him, Scottie went on. 'Yes at last. Of course Edna swears it's her flu cocktail that's finally done it.'

'Oh yes, what's in it?'

'God only knows, and she's not saying. Could be rat's blood for all anybody knows.'

Lorraine laughed. 'That's true...So what's this about a cat walker finding a body, gotta be a first?'

'Oh you'd be surprised love; it's been known to happen. Actually I know three cases where they've been out walking a cat and found a body, but to be honest it is rare...Think it actually happens more in America than here though.'

Lorraine looked amazed. 'You mean to tell me that some people actually walk a cat like it's a dog?' She looked at Luke and shook her head. 'Seriously!'

Scottie nodded. 'Oh yes...Nowt stranger than folk.'

'Right then,' she shrugged. 'Guess it takes all sorts. So, run us through it Scottie.'

Scottie nodded and gestured with his right hand for them to

follow him.

When they reached the tent, they dressed in the white coveralls with Lorraine grumbling all the time, especially when she got her leg stuck and managed to rip a hole in the suit she hated the things. She scowled at Scottie as he handed her another one, and she had to go through the process again.

When they were ready Scottie lifted the flap on the tent, and one by one they followed him through. 'OK guys, we have a white female early twenties, the strange thing is, that there is no sign whatsoever of a struggle.'

Lorraine gasped. The young woman was lying on a thick white silk sheet, the sides pulled over and covering most of her body. Blood covered the lower part of the sheet- her head rested on a pillow of the same material-her long dark hair had been fanned out over the pillow and a bunch of eight white roses lay at her feet, each rose lay about an inch apart from the others and every one had a snapped stem. Her bright red lips were slightly parted, as if she was ready to smile; from her neck hung a thick silver chain with a silver angel lying between her breasts.

'Has she...Has she been raped?' Luke asked quietly, as he slowly walked round the body, studying it from all angles.

Heaving a huge sigh Scottie said, 'We won't know exactly until we get the poor soul back to the lab. Because of cross contamination it's best not to open the sheets here, though somehow I dread to think what we are going to find.' He looked over at his assistant, a question in his eyes.

Sam, whose Chinese linage showed in his usually smiling face, shrugged, as he took a last picture. 'I'm all done here so we can move her whenever you're ready.' With a respectful nod to everyone there, he lifted the tent flap and left.

Lorraine sighed; she was remembering a pretty nasty case last year when the murderer had left flowers. *Must be the fucking in thing*. She thought, as she squatted down close to the young woman's head.

'You're right Scottie, she's defo early twenties...If that even, so flaming much to live for.' She stared at the dead face for a few moments.

It was Luke who answered. 'Damn shame, wonder why? Has she upset the creep in some way or is it a random kill? Or maybes a stalker?' He looked at Scottie, who heaved another sigh as he held his hands out palm up.

'That's just it, there's a suicide note.'

'What!'

Scottie sighed again. 'Yes.'

'But it's obviously murder.' Lorraine said.

'I know.' He took a plastic bag out of his pocket and handed it to Lorraine.

With Luke looking over her shoulder, Lorraine opened the bag and shook the note onto the palm of her hand, together they read it.

Sorry, mam and dad, please forgive me, it's not your fault. I love you. But I just could not take it anymore. The note was signed. Caro.

Lorraine looked at Scottie, then down at the body, then back at Scottie, as she said. 'What the hell?'

'Beats me.'

Lorraine stared at the dead girl once more. It was times like this that she wished she had a total office job, even if it meant listening to Carter rabbit on all day about local history or even Sanderson and Dinwall getting there digs in at each other, anything but this.

'Right then,' she stood up. 'We'll pop over to the morgue later, in the meantime we'll see if the foot soldiers have come up with anything...Youse two have a closer look round here, in case they've missed anything, before we go back to the office and see if a Cara has been reported missing,' she waved at Scottie as she headed out side. 'Catch you later mate.'

'You will that pet.' He gave her a salute and a smile.

Outside of the tent Lorraine stripped her coveralls off, as did Luke and Carter, before going to have a quick look around the back of the tent.

Lorraine walked over to the nearest constable, a young Asian woman who she knew. 'Hello Labuki, anything?'

Labuki shook her head. 'Sorry boss but it doesn't look as if even a blade of grass has been disturbed around here.' She looked further down the path at two officers who were searching the area with large sticks. Cupping her hands over her mouth she yelled. 'Anything yet?'

They both looked up and shook their heads.

'No footprints?' Lorraine looked back at Labuki.

'Not human, couple of prints that could be dogs or foxes, but even those are more than a day old.'

'Are they around the body?' she frowned, knowing she herself had not seen any.

'No, over there,' Labuki pointed to another copse of trees down the slope to the right hand side of the narrow footpath. 'That muddy patch down at the bottom.'

Luke, who with Carter in tow had just arrived back, and hearing what the officer said, looked to where she pointed then turned to Lorraine. 'Totally clean around the back boss, we'll have a look down there, come on Carter.'

'Ah,' Carter said as they reached the spot the officer had indicated. 'Defo dogs, and foxes.'

Knowing he would regret it, Luke still asked. 'How do you know the difference?'

'Well,' Carter rubbed his hands together as he went on. 'There is a much larger space between the toes and the heels of a fox than a dog. Also...'

'Got it.' Luke stared at the prints. 'So those are dogs and these over here are foxes, right?'

'Pretty much...'

'Good, let's look around.'

'OK Boss.'

Fifteen minutes later they were back on the A1 heading for Houghton Le Spring. 'So the only prints found anywhere were animals?' Lorraine looked at Luke.

'I would love to say otherwise and that we lifted a full shoe or trainer print, which would make life a damn sight easier, but sorry nothing.'

'Actually more foxes than dogs. Did you also know that the foxes are in decline while the deer population is on the increase?' Carter put in from the driver's seat. Having recently plucked up the courage to tell his mother that he was gay, Carter was feeling much more at ease with himself, although having not said anything to his colleagues he guessed that they already knew, after all his mother had said she had known for years.

'Really...Well you learn something new every day...Wonder why those broken roses were placed there?' Lorraine said.

Luke shrugged, 'Could be any amount of reasons. Some crave

the attention when the bodies are found and leave actual clues for their big day when they are caught, some love the thrill of the chase, though hope never to be caught. Some take trophy's some leave them. How can we really understand fully how their minds work? I suspect even the experts struggle at the best of times.'

'Maybes because they were her favourite flowers?' Carter added, slowing down as the traffic in front began to build up.

'Which would suggest that he knew her. And statistically more murders are carried out by people who know the victim, than strangers, aren't they?' Lorraine answered.

Luke, snacking on a bag of his favourite fruit, strawberries, was about to answer when they were suddenly hit with a loud frightening crunch from behind them.

Lorraine was flung forward banging her head on the back of the driver's seat and twisting her shoulder, as Luke nearly choked on a strawberry and the blood running down his throat from where he had bit into his lip. A split second later they were shunted with lightening speed into the car in front.

CHAPTER TWELVE

'Aw for fucks sake stop bloody whinging Len,' Danny Jorden glared at his cousin Len. 'If it's not one friggin thing with you, it's another, every bloody flaming day.'

The cousins had lived on the Seahills all of their lives, and were much alike except in height and temperament, Danny usually had a smile on his face where as Len always looked like he'd lost a pound and found a penny.

They had met up with their friend Jacko Musgrove, outside of the White Lion on the corner of Newbottle street, chewed the fat on the park seats facing the church for a while, and Danny had gone on and on about a certainty that he had for the two o clock race this afternoon. They were now contemplating going to the betting shop.

'What's he on about now?' Jacko glanced at Len, as he fiddled with his eye patch; while Len kept on muttering, then Jacko turned to Danny with a questioning frown on his face.

'Aw man, the friggin daft tit's moaning on yet again, 'cos believe it or not, he flaming well only had to pay five pence for a carrier bag this morning, sick of hearing about it, gone on for months he has.'

Jacko grinned. 'Really'

'I swear I'll strangle the skinny git if he doesn't shut the fuck up about it.' He turned and glared at Len, who shrugged as the three of them rose and headed for the betting shop.

Seeing Jacko's grin Len tutted, 'Well I'm only saying mate if you'll all listen properly. It's not really on like is it. Bet anything youse like, that the bloody Queen doesn't pay it.' He nodded his head, with the pure belief that the Queen didn't pay for her carrier bags. 'Just saying like.'

'Unbelievable.' Danny muttered.

Unperturbed Len went on. 'Aye man her and that greedy penny pinching government lot. It's alright for them, bloody loaded the lot of them. Fat cats, that's what they are, nowt but greedy fat cats. No worries with that lot about where next week's flaming rent's coming from...Or even tomorrows friggin dinner. I ask you, is there now?'

Jacko stared open mouthed at Danny just before they fell into the betting shop laughing their heads off.

Len didn't believe in gambling and very often told his cousin that it was a mugs game, even though he knew he was wasting his breath, the problem was that Danny was pretty lucky now and then, and sometimes won against all the odds. He lived with the dream of many, that the big win was just around the corner, even though Len had forgotten how many times he had bailed Danny out, as Danny had also forgotten.

Len watched with a look of distain covering his face as Danny and Jacko put their bets on, surprised that Jacko, who rarely gambled had fell for one of Danny's certainties.

He dusted his jacket sleeve with his hand, and dusted it again to make sure there were no more bits of hair left on it from one of Danny's dogs. Danny's wife bred German Shepherds, and when visiting them Len always took a brush with him, which he used with vigour in his yard when he got home.

He had forgotten how many time's Danny had tried to off load one of the puppy's on to him, and although he really did like dogs, well, some of them, Len couldn't stand the mess they brought with them.

'Must have picked these hairs up in the van.' He muttered as the betting shop door opened, and a stranger, all dressed in black walked in. For a moment the stranger surveyed the room in front of him with an arrogant stare. One more full circle and he spotted the counter, slowly he headed towards it.

The stranger looked Len up and down with the same arrogant look that he had walked into the betting shop with, as he walked up to him on the way to the counter. Reaching Len he made no move to go around him, and Len had to practically jump out of his way. At the counter the stranger took out a pile of notes which made Fat Alice who worked there raise her fake black eyebrows to the limit, in shock.

He placed an already filled out betting slip beside the notes. As he waited for his slip to be returned, he opened a bar of nut flavoured chocolate, snapping off a large wedge he put it in to his mouth, without a thank you to the still wide eyed Fat Alice, he picked the copy of his betting slip up, turned and walked out.

Quite a few of the regulars had noticed him, and when the door closed behind him, Tom Davidson, who lived up Hall Lane and who Len so very much envied because he owned a vintage car, said to Len. 'Who the hell was that?'

Before he could answer Fat Alice piped in, 'Dunno but I could defo manage a bar of choc right now.' She smacked her lips and grinned.

Len looked at her and resisting an urge to lick his lips at the thought of chocolate, shrugged, turning back to Tom Davidson he said 'Never seen him before...The last of the big spenders, you reckon?'

'Aye you're right there mate, had to be a grand or more he put on there like.' He whispered as Fat Alice moved along the counter to serve another punter.

'Well over a grand.' Jacko said in Len's ear.

'Aw man!' Len jumped.

Grinning, Danny said. 'Come on let's get outta here.'

Frowning at Jacko's back Len followed them both out of the betting shop. Outside and fancying a bar of chocolate Len tried the paper shop door only to find it locked. 'Aw man.'

'It's flooded.' Danny said.

'What's flooded?'

'The friggin paper shop.'

'How do you know that?'

'Read the bloody notice right under your nose.' Jacko said.

'Aw right...So are we gonna pick those bags of soil up for me allotment?' He asked Danny, for the third time that day.

'Might as well mate, B and Q?'

'Aye.' Len clapped his hands together as they walked towards the van, muttering to himself. 'About time an 'all, only been asking all day.'

As they drove up through Grasswell they ended up behind a white van that ran through a red light at the top of the hill.

'Typical,' Danny said. 'Where the fucks the coppers when some other twat does that?'

'I know.' Len said. 'Shocking isn't it, if it had been you, you would of been caught.'

Not knowing if Len had actually cracked a joke for the first time in his life. Jacko nevertheless laughed.

'You know what Len,' Danny said. 'You're like a fork in a bowl of tomato soup. Fucking useless.'

Jacko laughed even louder, while Len again frowned at his cousin.

CHAPTER THIRTEEN

Carter opened his eyes and moaned, slowly he turned his head and looked in the back of the car, it was empty but both of the back car doors were wide open. Just then, startling him, the door at his side was pulled open.

'You alright mate? And what's your name?' A gruff male voice asked.

Carter didn't answer his eyes wide open and staring, were locked on a stretcher being carried past him, the person on the stretcher was obviously dead as the sheet was covering the face as well as the whole body, but hanging down were strands of long blonde hair.

His heart beating heavily, sank like he had never felt it sink before. 'No...No...It can't be,' he gasped, then suddenly screamed. 'Please God...No...No...No,' he wanted to be sick, as he felt the tears streaming down his face. 'I'm sorry boss,' he muttered. 'I'm sorry. Really I am.'

The ambulance man leaned in and began checking him over as Carter sobbed.

'Right then mate. Where does it hurt? And please tell me your name.' He repeated.

'Ca...Carter,' he stared at the ambulance man. 'I...Mostly my foot. And my ribs are bit sore and err...Down there,' he pointed between his legs with a shaky finger.' Where shards of glass from the side window covered him from the waist down, then managed to ask between sobs. 'Where, where is Luke?'

'The bloke who was in this car?'

'Yes.'

'He's in the ambulance with your other passenger.'

Oh no. He thought, as his body froze and his mind filled with fog. *No... Both of them dead.* For a moment he couldn't think as the grey fog swirled ever deeper.

Then reality kicked in. *Both of them.* His mind screamed at him, as the blood drained from his face. All he could think of was how good both Luke and Lorraine had been to him, and now they were dead.

Was it my fault? He wondered.

Was I going to fast to stop?

It must have been me.

Oh God...I killed them.

No please no.

He could barely breathe and started to sob more loudly, and gasp for breath between sobs.

'It was my fault.' He managed to say.

'No it wasn't son, so don't go blaming yourself, you were caught in the middle.'

'No it was me. It had to be.'

Feeling sick to his stomach he leaned forward and vomited over the ambulance man's arms, it splashed down onto the road and over his shoes.

'S...Sorry. I'm really sorry.' Carter tried to brush the tears off his face but they were coming thick and fast.

'It's alright son, I've had worse than that, trust me. Do you think you can stand up?'

Slowly Carter nodded. 'I...I'll try.'

'Come on then, let's get you out of here and into the ambulance. They'll sort you out in the hospital.' Lost for words, Carter could only nod again.

When he was on his feet he could feel blood trickling down his legs, slowly he looked around at the devastation. He suddenly felt dizzy and started to shake, at least seven or eight cars had been involved in the pile up, there were four ambulances and two fire engines, people were being cut out of the blue car that was two in front of his, which looked like it had been shunted to the left and ended up on its side. He could hear more than one child crying for their mothers and fathers, adults shouting out names of loved ones. Slowly he shook his head and looked at the ambulance man, his legs started to shake uncontrollably, and he fell to his knees.

His last thoughts before he passed out were of Lorraine and Luke smiling at him, the very first day he had met them.

CHAPTER FOURTEEN

He stared at his lap top, with his right hand he reached for his brown snakeskin diary, dropping his pen he knocked his head on the side of the desk as he leaned down to pick the pen up. 'Bastard,' he muttered, as he straightened up and rubbed his head.

Checking his diary he typed in the day, time and place that he would pick her up. Taking extra care to make sure he had the right post code. Being a stranger to the North East, although he did have one or two longstanding friends who lived here, but most of the places he'd took details of, he had never heard of before.

'Yes that's good. Very good.' He smiled when the words came on the screen.

'It won't hurt...Will it?'

'Of course it won't. I will take great care of I you...I truly Promise. Everything will be exactly as you want it.' He made no mention of the hidden extras as he wrote everything she asked for in his diary.

Five minutes after he had said good bye, he popped some chocolate Brazils into his mouth and was talking to someone else on the computer. His heart raced with excitement, he looked out of the window at the green hills behind his hotel.

'I could live here,' he muttered. 'Permanently.' He thought about house hunting as he filled another page in his diary.

'Or even a luxury flat.' He had spotted some the other day by the bridge in Sunderland, facing the river. But first he needed to look for a cheaper place for a few months or so, and maybes curb his gambling for a while. He laughed at that thought, *As if that's ever gonna happen.*

And why not, stay permanently, if the work keeps coming in at this rate, after all what he did was a service to mankind, and so he deserved to be rewarded.

He held this thought as he answered another call, this time to a young male student.

CHAPTER FIFTEEN

Scottie scrubbed his hands, then rinsed them thoroughly, he hoped, prayed that he was right and the young girl lying on the slab had been mutilated after her death, and not before. He was only thankfull that Edna was off work today, with a sprained ankle, or so she said, strange that it somehow didn't stop her from going to the bingo though. He sighed, 'Shit I forgot she's coming back in later today.'

'Who you talking to Scottie?' Madge the cleaner asked as she scooped up the waste and placed it on her trolley.

Scottie laughed, 'Just muttering to myself pet, it helps the mind stay calm.'

'Yeah right.' Madge said as she pushed her trolley back outside. 'Bye Scottie.'

'Bye Madge, same time tomorrow.' He heard her laugh as without turning her head, she waved her hand at him.

Looking back down at the body, his thoughts went back to Edna. If she sees how savagely this girl has been treat, knowing her she'll probably go looking for the brute herself armed with one of her crocheting hooks.

As it was he expected a massive firework explosion from Lorraine; even Sam who usually had very little to say, had slammed instruments around as he had been clearing up, and kept muttering over and over. 'Animal.' Interspaced with a couple of Chinese words, that Scottie had never heard and really didn't want to know the meaning of.

He heard the door slam and looked up just as Sam practically ran back into the autopsy room. 'Jesus Scottie, you're not going to believe it,' he was shaking as he hurriedly went on. 'There's been a massive accident on the A1, just seen Carter being wheeled into the emergency department. Couldn't get much sense out of him but he's babbling on about Lorraine and Luke.'

'You mean...Have they been hurt?'

Sam just stared at him.

'Sam!'

Slowly Sam shook his head. 'I...I don't really know for certain, he just kept talking rubbish over and over, I think...' He sighed. 'He's high on the morphine, he's crying then babbling.' Sam shrugged his shoulders. 'It really doesn't sound good Scottie. He...He keeps saying it was his fault...And that they're dead because of him.'

For a moment Scottie stared open mouthed at Sam, then shaking his head muttered. 'No...No way...No.'

Before Sam could say anything else Scottie was out of the door and taking the stairs two at a time up to the AE, quickly followed by Sam.

Bursting through the doors into the AE, Scottie and Sam stopped dead and stared. It was practically pandemonium, the corridor and the whole of the area was taken up with stretchers, with more arriving constantly. Children were screaming for their parents, parents screaming for their children. Under staffed and over stretched nurses, were running in different directions. Two stretchers were wheeled past them, their occupants both obviously dead, with more stretchers coming down the corridor.

Taking a deep breath Scottie caught the arm of a nurse he knew. 'Do you have a list of the casualties please Linda?'

Linda shook her blonde head. 'Sorry love, but I'm sure someone will have one shortly...I've really gotta go Scottie.' Quickly she squeezed past him.

'Sure.' Scottie watched her retreating back then turned towards the desk.

Followed by Sam, he quickly walked over to it, bending down on the way to pick up a cuddly toy that a little two year old girl dressed all in pink had thrown from her pushchair. He handed it back and the little girl screamed and threw the doll away. Scottie shrugged picked it up again and handed it to her mother who seemed locked in her own hell, silently she took it from him and muttered an automatic, 'Thank you...' For a moment she stared at him, then asked. 'Have you seen David?' Before turning away again to stare into space.

'Who's David?' Scottie asked gently. Praying it wasn't a child.

'My...My husband.'

'Sorry no.'

She looked at him again her face a total blank, and then turned her head back to the window.

Sadly, and guessing rightly, that he would be seeing the young woman's husband later in the morgue, Scottie turned to the receptionist who only had eyes for Sam.

'Hi Sam.' Katy, the pretty young girl with coal black hair behind the counter winked at him.

Red faced and unable to meet her eyes, Sam muttered a quick.

'Hello Katy.'

If Scottie's mind had not been so preoccupied he would have laughed at Sam's red face which was very nearly a match for the T-Shirt he wore. Instead he said. 'Hello Katy love, can you tell me if someone by the name of Lorraine Hunt has been admitted, and Luke Daniels? They were involved in the crash on the A1'

'Yes,' she nodded without looking at her half complete list. 'They have, I know them, they live up my Aunt's street in Houghton,' leaning over the desk she pointed to a room on her far left. 'They were taken in there.'

CHAPTER SIXTEEN

Vanessa ran up the stairs and started collecting the washing from each of the bedrooms.

'Just finished one bloody pile, and here I go again. It never friggin ends.' Continuing muttering to herself she moved from room to room.

Tripping on an empty can of pop in Darren and Robbie's bedroom, she managed to put her hands out to break her fall. 'Shit, shit.' She yelled, rolling about in agony as she clutched her left wrist.

Fifteen minutes later, after downing a couple of painkillers and her left wrist strapped up, and using only her right hand, she was putting clothes into the washing machine.

She then went into the kitchen and made a cup of tea before wandering into the sitting room and looking out of the window. Staring at the empty house opposite she wondered not for the first time, who her new neighbours would be. The last lot had been really snooty at first, but Suzy had become very friendly with the little girl, and though they were on the posh side, they had turned out to be really nice people in the end, and Vanessa had been sorry to see them go. But Suzy still kept in touch with them and they had even visited a few times which was nice of them, and Suzy stayed over at their house in Gosforth now and then.

She turned her gaze left, to look at the house next door to Mr Skillings, which had just had a To Let sign, put up this morning. It used to belong to the Davidsons, but when the last of their kids left home they moved to a bungalow round the corner, where late last year, within a month of each other, they died. And now their oldest son having failed to sell it, had decided let it out.

Vanessa had noticed a couple of other such signs up on the estate, mostly on a house who's family's had lived there for years, which the younger ones left behind when parents and grandparents had died had decided to sell them off, and wondered where people got the money from to buy these houses in the first place then let them out or sell them. She shrugged. *Guess it's a fast changing world these days.*

Just then, two cars pulled up. A youngish woman with short brown hair got out of the first one. Vanessa didn't recognise her, neither did she recognise the man, who wore dark clothing and had slicked back black hair. Together the pair of them walked up the path. Smiling at the man, the woman took a key out of her back pocket and they went inside.

'Hmm,' Vanessa said. 'Wonder if it's both of them, or one's just showing the other one around.'

She saw Mr Skillings curtains twitch and smiled.

'Nosy.' A voice suddenly said behind her.

Vanessa jumped, even though she recognised one of her daughter's voices; she had not heard Kerry come in, nor had she even seen her.

Turning round she gently slapped Kerry's arm. 'Bitch you frightened the life outta me.'

Kerry laughed. 'You shouldn't be so nosy then. Honestly it's hard to tell who's the nosiest on this bloody estate.' She grinned. 'Out of the whole lot of you.'

'Listen who's talking, I've many a time heard you wandering around in the middle of the bloody night if there's a noise outside...Anyhow what you doing home this early?'

'There's only gone and been a flood.'

'What! The paper shop's flooded.'

'Yep, burst pipe up stairs, and the ceilings nearly fell in. Good job the shop was empty except for me and Natalie. Although there's been a lot of stock ruined.'

'Never.'

'Yes we locked the doors and scarpered out of there double quick, and took a little trip to Sunderland, Natalie was after some new shoes.'

'Friggin hell youse could have been drowned.' Dramatically Vanessa clutched her chest.

'Err...I don't really think so mam. Anyhow we waited for the boss before we left, he's there now trying to sort things, but it looks like I'll be off for the rest of the week,' she dropped the bag she was carrying. 'Guess I'll go for a run...Hang on a minute, what have you done?' She stared at Vanessa's wrist.'

'Bloody well fell over. Them two lazy gits, it's their fault, to flaming bone idle to pick empty cans up.'

'That'll be our Darren...Bet it was one of those energy drinks, really mam they aren't good for you. Anyhow shouldn't you go to the doc's? It might be broken?'

'No, it's not broken, look I can wiggle me fingers, probs just sprained. It'll be fine in the next day or two. It's happened before, must be my weak spot.'

'You sure?'

'Yes, don't worry about it.'

Five minutes later Kerry closed the door behind her. Reaching the gate she looked up just as the people across the road on the way out of the house reached their gate. The woman smiled, but as she turned away the man who had been behind her stared at Kerry and kept on staring.

Feeling self conscious Kerry started to run, but for the rest of the day she couldn't forget the predatory way he had looked at her. She had seen that look before.

CHAPTER SEVENTEEN

'Thank you.' Scottie said to the receptionist. They both hurried over to the room she had pointed too. Outside of the door he turned the handle, dreading what he would find inside.

A moment later he stepped back quickly in shock-when he saw Lorraine and Luke, both sitting up, Lorraine on the bed and Luke on the seat. 'Bloody hell!'

He stared at them in amazement, the very last thing he had expected was to find them both upright, the vision in his head was of both of them lying on the beds covered in a white sheet each. Instead, Lorraine had what looked like a temporary sling on her right arm, and a slight bruise on the side of her face, while Luke had a collar round his neck, plus what looked like a very swollen and sore lip.

'What's up Scottie?' Lorraine said, throwing an empty can of diet coke into the waste paper bin, as she smiled at him.

'It's Carter, he's distraught, he only bloody well thinks youse two died in the friggin crash.' He blurted.

'What...No way, poor bugger,' Luke got slowly up from his seat. 'Where is he?'

Scottie blew air out of his lungs in a sigh of relief and said. 'So did I mate. Can't bloody begin to tell youse what a shock it was...Don't know where Carter is though. It's flaming well like a battlefield out there.'

Lorraine stood up and took a couple of steps towards Scottie, with a smile she patted his cheek, 'We're fine Scottie love, just a couple of bumps and bruises that's all, nothing at all for you to worry about.'

'So do you know how it happened?'

'Well...I do know there was a bloke in a big red Vauxhall car weaving in and out, at high speed as well, don't know yet if that prat was the actual cause of it though.'

'Hmm probably was him, for the sake of gaining an extra five minutes or so, look what havoc the selfish git has caused...Have you any idea where Carter is?'

'I'm guessing through there.' Scottie stepped away from the door, and pointed up the corridor to his right, as Sam leaned into the room and smiled at them.

'Hi Sam.' they both echoed.

'Good to see you all.' Sam smile grew larger.

'Actually we were thinking about going to find him when you popped in.' Luke said, leaving the room and passing Scottie he lead the way to where Scottie had pointed, which was the emergency room.

After asking a few nurses where Carter was, one of them finally told Scottie which cubicle Carter was in. He turned to Lorraine and Luke. 'I think it's best if I go in first and tell him your both alive, probably get the shock of his life and have a heart attack if youse two just walk right in. The daft bugger will think he's seeing ghosts.'

'Yes you're probably right, go on in, we'll wait here,' Lorraine her arm linked through Luke's, nodded towards the cubical. 'Go.'

Wasting no time Scottie swished the curtain back and entered the cubicle. Carter was lying on the bed looking totally devastated; he gave Scottie a weak smile.

'Have you heard?' He murmured.

Scottie moved over to the bed and put his hand on Carter's chest. 'It's alright mate you got it wrong- the pair of them are alive and kicking, you made a mistake.'

'What!' Carter struggled to sit up, and groaned before he grabbed Scotties arm. 'You sure?'

'Yes.'

'We're both fine Carter.' Lorraine said as she and Luke walked in.

'Oh my God!' Carter's face was filled with relief. 'I...I thought I had killed you both,' he brushed his knuckles across his eyes. 'I really, really did.'

Lorraine squeezed the top of his arm. 'It wasn't your fault Carter we were caught in the middle, trust me there was nothing you could do. Nothing any one could do.'

'Are you really sure?' A smile chased the grief from his face, as he let out a heavy sigh.

'Yes we are,' Luke said from the other side. 'If you hadn't been so quick to stop...I don't know what would have happened to us. You did the right thing Carter.'

'Thank you.' Carter said, slowly he looked from one to the other as the tears flowed down his face. Then back at Luke. 'Does that hurt? He pointed to Luke's mouth.

'Well, guess it does a bit, mostly when I talk.'

'Well stop talking then.' Lorraine raised her eyebrows at him.

'I'll just sneeze instead.'

Lorraine looked up at the ceiling.

'Well seeing as my three favourite coppers are fine, we'll head off, come on Sam. Looks like were gonna be very busy. Bye guys. I'll look in on you later Carter.'

'Yes we best be going as well,' Lorraine said, before Carter had a chance to thank Scottie. 'Does your mother know what's happened yet?'

'Yes.' Carter sighed. 'The hospital phoned her.'

'Right then I'll get Dinwall or Sanderson to pick her up. So don't go worrying about anything, right.'

'Thanks boss.'

When they left Carter lay back on his pillows. 'Thank you God.' He muttered, he knew he would never have been able to live with himself if they had both died, whether it was his fault or not.

CHAPTER EIGHTEEN

The police car pulled up outside of Dale's house, he, and his mother Jayne had anxiously been waiting at the window for nearly an hour. Twice Dale had gone out of the house, walked up and down the street shouting Skip's name in the hope that the dog had somehow escaped from whoever had him, and made his way home. Only, to come back in the house feeling worse than he had when he'd left.

'Open the door Dale...Quickly, now, they might have some good news about Skip.' Jayne said, smiling through the window at the two officers.

Dale ran from the window, opening the door he showed the two officers into the sitting room. 'Please sit down,' he said politely. 'Would youse both like a cup of tea?' He looked at his mother, who smiled at him.

'Not for me thanks,' the first officer a tall fair haired woman said as she turned to the other officer. 'How about you?'

'Yes please I'm parched, no milk two sugars.' She smiled at Jayne as they both sat down.

A few minutes later the officer who had declined the tea started to question Dale. 'So, tell me what happened son.'

Between sobs, Dale did his best to tell her exactly what had happened.

'So you have never seen either of those men before?' She asked when he was finished.

'No.' Dale shook his head. 'But they, they had masks on, so, so I might have...I don't know.'

'Was there anything you remember about them, something you might have seen before, try and think, picture what happened in your mind...A tattoo on his hands even?'

For a few minutes Dale was silent, then lifting his head he looked into the officer's eyes. 'No...Sorry.' He sighed. 'They were mostly covered up. 'Will you find Skip for me...Please, please.' He begged as he wiped his eyes.

'We'll do our best son. Now what sort of clothes were they wearing, any distinctive fashion names or marks.'

Dale sighed, again he shook his head. 'Just black, everything was black...But,' his face lit up for a moment, the one who snatched Skip's leader had a big thing on his hand.'

'What sort of thing, a mole, a birthmark, or a tattoo?'

'I think it's called a mole.'

'Good. Now the van, you sure you don't remember seeing it anywhere before?'

Again he shook his head as he stared at the carpet. 'I already said.'

His mother put her arm around him. 'He loves that dog to bits, we all do.'

'Well we'll do our best, but with no number plate and no identification, apart from the well spotted mole. Have you any idea how many white vans there are on the road... I'm sorry, all I can say is we do have a few lines to follow up and if anything comes of it you'll be the first to know.' The tall police woman stood up followed by her partner, who really couldn't bare seeing the little boy cry any more.

She moved over to him and patted his arm. 'We'll do our best son. And by the way, you're mam makes a great cup of tea pet.'

Dale nodded, his lips quivering.

Outside they got into the police car, the smaller police woman punched the dashboard. 'Bastards, hope somebody actually catches them in the act and kicks the shit out of them. Over and friggin over, the bastards.'

'Yes, but these days thanks to the PC lot who are out to destroy the Britain that we know, even though they are guilty as hell, the swine's would probably have the cheek to sue for damages.'

'Yeah probably.' Shaking her head, she drove off.

CHAPTER NINETEEN

'Brilliant news, thanks.' Sanderson put the phone down, relieved that Lorraine and the others were all right, it had been a bit of a shock when he had first heard the news, about the crash and just how many people were in it, and an even bigger shock when he'd found out who was involved. But now he could relax. He sat for a moment, staring out of the window.

Two hundred and three days, he thought, less than a year and this view will no longer be mine.

He shuddered at the thought of what he was going to do to fill the time in. Neither a golfer, nor a fisherman, he racked his brains and could think of nothing at all that he could show an interest in, except his love of horror books, and that was hardly a social thing. *Boredom here I come.*

Turning from the window he pulled a file in front of him just as Dinwall walked in with coffees, muttering a grumpy. 'Thank you.' He took the coffee from Dinwall.

'Your welcome.' Dinwall replied, pulling his chair up to his computer. Dinwall hated wearing suits, his usual attire were jeans and a tee shirt, along with his long dark hair tied in a pony tail he looked more like a hippy who had transported through time from the sixties than a policeman of today.

'You found out anything at all about those blue trainers yet Dinwall?' Sanderson asked, as he stirred half a dozen tiny bags of sugar into his coffee.

Screwing his face up as he watched him, Dinwall said 'No, there was at one time a gang who only wore blue trainers as a sort of badge.'

'Oh, bloody hell, that's exactly what the boss definitely doesn't want to hear. She'll go bloody mental.'

'She's got nowt to worry about; it was in New York in the nineties.'

Sanderson tutted, and a few minutes later walked over to the tea machine, turning back to Dinwall he said. 'You want a cuppa or not?'

'Em, we've just had coffee a few minutes ago.'

'And it's left a bitter taste in my mouth. Don't know why I drink the bloody stuff, does it every time.'

'Bitter taste with all that sugar?' Dinwall shook his head. 'I very much doubt it...You sure it's off the coffee?'

Sanderson pulled a face and turned back to his tea making. 'You want one or not?' he asked again, as once more he added spoonful after spoonful of sugar into his tea. He tasted it and added another.

'Yes milk, one sugar please, I find that's more than enough...Fortify me on my mission to get Carter's mother to the hospital...Thanks.'

Sanderson carried the teas over just as his desk phone rang. 'Here.' He said handing Dinwall's cup over, and quickly grabbing the receiver.

'Hello.'

'Hi Sanderson,' Lorraine said on the other end. 'Anything on the murder victim?'

'We're still digging boss, when we rule most of the flotsam out we'll let you know.'

'OK, how about the blue trainers.'

'Nope, Barret was adamant they got them off the market, couldn't budge him. We've still got him kicking his heels, he might open up to you. Oh, yes boss, and the search warrant for their properties has just come through. Do you want me and Dinwall to follow it up?'

'Yes, ring me as soon as you find anything. Bye.'

Ten minutes later Dinwall and Sanderson with two constables were outside of Wayne Barrets flat in East Rainton, for the full ten minutes, Sanderson had done nothing but complain about the weather, getting out of the car Dinwall said. 'Well let's hope it's hot in here then.'

Sanderson scowled at him as they walked up the path. His face changed when Dinwall knocked on the door and it was opened a moment later and Wayne Barrets mother, who he had known for a long time and never liked, stood there. Her makeup as usual was heavily applied, as she glared at them over the top of her glasses. Strong lily scented perfume wafted out of the door, it took all of Sanderson's willpower not to wave his hand in front of his face in an attempt to get some fresh air.

'I hope you've come to tell me my son has been released?'

'Sorry no.'

'Well how can I help you?'

'We have a warrant to search the premises Mrs Barret.' Sanderson produced the warrant from his jacket pocket.

'You can't do that.'

'Ah but I'm afraid we can Mrs Barret. We also have another warrant to search your house.'

'What!'

'So,' Dinwall put his foot in the door. 'Are you going to let us in peacefully or not?'

Slowly she fully opened the door, as she snapped at them. 'There's nothing to find here, I assure you.'

'Bedroom.' Sanderson turned to the police officers, who both nodded.

A moment later before Dinwall and Sanderson had a chance to enter the small galley kitchen, one of the constables shouted. 'It's all in here boss.'

Quickly Sanderson and Dinwall rushed into the bedroom with Mrs Barret close behind them.

'I knew nothing of this.' Mrs Barret insisted as they all stared at the wall to wall boxes full of pale blue trainers.

'So you've never been in your son's bedroom Mrs Barret?'

'No, why would I.' She stared at Sanderson, her lips curved downwards in a sneer.

Just then the two police officers who had gone outside into the shared garden and looked in the large brick shed came back. 'The same in the shed, wall to wall boxes of blue trainers.'

Sanderson stared at Mrs Barret. 'I take it you know nothing of those either?'

'This is ridiculous, why would I?'

'So what are you doing here?' Dinwall asked.

She clicked her tongue. 'Visiting my son obviously. Now I know that's not a crime.'

'But your son is locked up, as you well know. Mrs Barret.'

'But I ...I.'

'Mrs Barret I'm arresting you...' Sanderson read out her rights as Dinwall produced a set of handcuffs.

'No,' she practically yelled. 'I haven't done anything wrong, there's no need for this...You're just doing this out of spite because I rejected you all those years ago. You've always had it in for me, everyone knows.'

Dinwall stepped back in amazement, and looked in awe at Sanderson.

'Rubbish, not becoming entangled with you was the best thing that ever happened to me.'

'You bloody sly old dog.' Dinwall, said out of the corner of his mouth.

'Shut up. And you too.' Sanderson snapped, turning back to Mrs Barret.

'Huh.' Mrs Barret tossed her head. 'I want my solicitor, and I want him now.'

'You'll get him at the station, now I'm sure you won't want the neighbours to see you making a fuss so get into the car now.'

CHAPTER TWENTY

Tracy Brewer pulled her green blinds up and looked nervously out of her kitchen window. She could have sworn she'd heard the gate open, but no, it looked shut. Frowning she turned away from the window only to scream in fright when she saw the tall thick set man with a heavy black beard standing there.

'You will shut up right now. If you know what's good for you.' Slowly he walked towards her, his eyes boring into hers as she tried to back away, but there was nowhere to go.

'What do you want?' She managed to say. Though she knew full well what he was after.

'You know what I want. You owe money and I'm here to collect it.'

'But I...'

'You haven't got it. Is that what you're trying to say, fucking stupid cow?' Without waiting for her to answer he quickly stepped forward and slapped her face hard.

Tracy screamed.

'Shut up cow.' He yelled his own face now only an inch from hers.

Terrified she stared at him. 'I haven't got any money,' her voice trailed off to a whisper. 'Honest you gotta believe me...Please...Please don't hurt me.'

Once again with the stance of a boxer he pushed his face into hers, she could smell the stale tobacco on his breath. 'You have two days, that's all two fucking days.'

She nodded as he stepped away from her. 'I will, honestly two days. I promise...Thank you.'

He glared at her for a moment, then turning he walked out.

Tracy, put her hand on her chest, her heart was pounding. Feeling dizzy she slowly made her way into the sitting room, where she sat down heaved a sigh and smiled.

CHAPTER TWENTY ONE

With a huge sigh Carter lay back on his pillow, and closed his eyes, he couldn't stop grinning and couldn't ever remember feeling so happy and relieved in his whole life.

It wasn't me.

It wasn't my fault.

The curtain made a loud noise as it swished open then Carter heard Lorraine's voice. 'So Carter, what's the Doc had to say about you then?' Lorraine asked. She and Luke were waiting to be discharged and had decided to come back and spend the time sitting with Carter.

'That he just might be malingering.' Luke gave a lopsided grin at Carter.

'I wish.' Carter grimaced.

Lorraine laughed. 'OK, what did he really say?'

'Probs only be in for a couple of days. Seven stitches in me arm, and somewhere else, though, most in my arm where it went through the side window as it shattered, and a few other bits and pieces. Some plasters and bandages, all the usual things.' He refrained from saying one of the places where he had a few plasters and a couple of stitches, but Lorraine was reading his files and her lips were seriously twitching.

Just then Scottie who had popped back up on a small break, frowned as his phone rang, pulling it out of his pocket with a grand flourish as he reached them, he answered with his usual, 'Hello, you're through to the far side of hell.'

'What?' he blurted a moment later, then, 'No...The rotten lousy bastards. Wait till I get my hands on them.'

Lorraine raised her eyebrows at Luke. Scottie was a big man and usually very placid and easy going, but a man of his build could certainly do damage and Lorraine had never before seen him looking so angry.

'How's the bairn?' He nodded at the answer then said, 'I'll call in on my way home from work. OK...' With a sigh to match Carter's he closed his phone.

'Something up Scottie?' Lorraine asked.

'Something up,' he repeated angrily. 'I'll say there's something up alright, some nasty horrible scumbag, has only just gone and nicked my nephew Dale's dog.'

'When?'

'An hour or so, I think.'

Luke shot Lorraine a knowing look then quickly looked away. Lorraine feeling nearly as angry as Scottie, knew exactly what the look meant. *Not again.*

'Details?'

'Snatched the leader right out of the kid's hand, that's what the bastard did, then jumped into a white van and took off...Just like that.' Scottie snapped his fingers.

Looking back at Luke, Lorraine said. 'We got to catch these swine's, it's happening too bloody much these days...I'm sick to death of hearing about broken hearted old folks and young kids. They never seem to pick on six foot blokes walking a dog who can fight back, do they?'

Carter slowly nodded his head. 'Cowards as usual.'

Luke agreed then looked at Lorraine. 'Yes and you and me both know who's behind it.'

'What!' Scottie erupted. 'You know?'

Dale's father, Scottie's brother in law had died when the boy was only three, having no children of his own Scottie had taken his sister Jayne and nephew Dale under his wing, which had pleased Edna no end to have a surrogate grandson. Quite a bond existed between the two now, yet another reason why Scottie was pleased that Edna was not at work, though he would have to tell her about it tonight.

'Let's say we have a good idea, but the twat managed to walk free a few months ago, on a friggin technicality of all bloody things,' Lorraine turned to Carter. 'We've got to go now Carter, I'll check in on you later love meantime, no heavy lifting and that's an order.'

'That's a sure thing boss.' Carter grinned. 'You go get them kid.' A second later he couldn't believe he'd actually said that to his boss.

Lorraine laughed at his red face.

Luke nodded at Carter with a smile. 'Later mate.'

'Hang on Lorraine, If you actually know the lousy git behind this, what you gonna do about it? From what I hear of these things, you need to be fast.' Scottie frowned.

'As soon as we get back and see if Dinwall has found out anything about Caro, I'll look into it Scottie, and I'll let you know what's what, when we come back about the murder victim. OK...I promise it defo won't be forgotten,' Lorraine gave Scottie's arm a pat. 'I promise.'

Scottie nodded.

'Don't worry we'll make sure it's not shoved to one side.' Luke added.

'Thanks guys.'

When they had gone Scottie turned back to Carter. 'Is there anything I can do for you?'

'No thanks I'm fine, just can't wait to get out already...Oh, yes can you get my mother to bring my lap top in, forgot to ask Lorraine. I'm dying of boredom already.'

'No bother, I'll pick her up, if you want.'

'Cheers Scottie but its sorted, Dinwall's going to pick her up later, but I haven't got my phone, I think its somewhere in the car, must have fell out of my pocket when the crash happened.' He shuddered as the memory came flooding back.

'I'll ring Lorraine she'll sort it.'

'You found anything out about the young girl yet?'

'Yes, it's not good Carter.' Scottie frowned, not wanting to give Carter anything else to worry about, he said. 'I'll see you later OK. You just concentrate on getting better.'

Carter watched as Scottie left, wondering what it was Scottie wasn't telling him.

CHAPTER TWENTY TWO

'Hurry up, and get the fucking bastard out right now.' Mick the white van driver jumped down from the cab and ran round to open the van door. The dog, who had known nothing but kindness and love in his short life, was frightened now; and barking his head off, even as he was cowering in the corner.

The youth, minus his balaclava, was clean shaven dark haired and with a large mole on the back of his right hand, he jumped down with the dog in tow, nearly tripping over the leader he slapped the dogs head, before running into the house. Inside two other young men were playing cards, arguing over the game as they smoked cannabis and drank lager.

Putting his can down, the one with a face full of freckles and pale ginger hair, who was facing the door gave a huge grin when he spotted the dog. 'Ah, hello boy, lovely boy come here. Come on boy, come here...Come to Frecks.' The dog wagged his tail and moved towards him, only to be savagely yanked back by his handler. With a yelp the dog cowered down.

'No need for that man, friggin hell.' Frecks scowled at him as he threw his cards on the table and slammed his bottle down hard, making the table shake.

'Stop being so fucking soft will you, they're here to make

money off, nowt else, sick of fucking telling you. They're only fucking animals.'

Frecks shrugged, 'Doesn't mean you can't say fucking hello does it, misery guts.'

Scowling, the dog handler took a step forward, his fist raised high as Frecks stood up.

'What the fucks going on here?' Mick asked, a second later, coming into the room.

'It's him,' Frecks said. 'Fucking miserable git, that's all he does...Piss's people right off...All he ever fucking does is moan, moan and more fucking moan. I was only talking to the fucking dog for Christ's sake. Shoot me now.'

Mick, looked at Frecks. 'You have no idea how easy that can be arranged.'

'I was...I was only kidding...Honest.' Frecks held his hands up. 'Honestly.'

'He was, he really was.' Greg his card playing friend quickly put in.

'I've told you me self before now haven't I, for fucks sake. Are you fucking thick or what, you stupid ginger bastard?' A second later he slammed his fist into Frecks chin, knocking him to the floor.

Scuttling into the corner, like a spider flung from a bench, Frecks rubbed his chin as his tongue found a loose tooth. Spitting blood out, he said, his voice full of amazement. 'What the fuck did you do that for?'

'Because you just don't get it do you?'

'Get what?'

'Aw for fucks sake, how many times. They're just fucking animals, and like he just said, here to make money off, nowt else, thick twat.'

The dog walked over and licked Frecks chin. Mick raised his foot to kick it in the ribs, but Frecks quickly pulled the dog out of the way. Glaring at Mick defiantly, Frecks gently stroked the dog as he cuddled it to his chest.

'Aw for fucks sake you useless git,' Mick yelled. 'Some fucking fighter it's gonna be...Eaten alive at the first round, through you.'

'What you talking about?'

Ignoring Frecks question Mick went on. 'And get it and the rest of the ugly fuckers fed instead of lying around here for fucks sake, lazy git. Do what you're paid for, 'cos you stupid twat, if the big guy finds out, trust me you'll both be out on your fucking arses. That's if you have any arses left.' Turning, he stormed out and slammed the door behind him.

The handler smirked at Frecks'. 'You know what to do so fucking do it...Now.'

Slowly Frecks without taking his eyes off the door pulled himself up from the floor. Inside he was seething, he looked over at his mate Greg who he'd been playing cards with, but Greg frightened not only for his own skin, but because he knew what Frecks could do if he snapped, mouthed 'count to ten.' then quickly looked away.

Greg had grown up living next door to Frecks, best friends before they could walk. Both sets of their parents had been best friends too, until one night just after Frecks and Greg had turned sixteen.

On their way home from Manchester, where their parents had been together celebrating both of their wedding anniversaries, while Frecks and Greg had stayed at home with Frecks grandmother, a freak storm had practically turned the motorway into a fast flowing river. Eight people died that night, leaving Greg and Frecks orphans. Together with no other family except for Frecks grandmother, they had joined the army.

Greg knew better than anyone what Frecks was capable of. Anyone who didn't really know Frecks thought he was a push over. But the mostly mild mannered Frecks was anything but, and Greg knew he wouldn't let this go, he was a stewer, slow to reach boiling point and when he did finally explode anyone and everyone who was in the way, got it big time.

They had only had this job for ten days or so, both of them like many others who left the services, had experienced a hard time since leaving the army, no luck at all in finding a decent job. Both were finding it really hard to slip back into civilian life. And Greg, knowing how much Frecks loved animals had been wary of telling him about this gig, in case it hadn't worked out; but they were both short of cash and Frecks was his best mate, it was basically, or so they had thought at the beginning, just guarding the dogs, feeding and walking them. Idiot that he was when another mate had told him about this job he had thought it was all legitimate and a proper dog boarding kennels. They were however, slowly learning the truth, and it was a truth neither of them were beginning to like.

And right now Greg was wondering if he should make a run for it, dragging Frecks with him, because he truly did not like what was coming this afternoon, he still had not told Frecks that today was the day when they started to turn the dogs into mean fighting machines, he knew Frecks would freak out, and he wasn't too keen on the idea himself, and he also guessed that it would now happen long before this afternoon.

Again the dog handler jerked the dog towards him, the dog

yelped, and looked back at Frecks, his eyes wide and appealing, this was the catalyst.

Frecks crossed the room in seconds, both fists up, he slammed the left one into the other man's face, the man tried to retaliate, but Frecks was quicker, his second punch knocked the man out, he fell to the floor.

'For fucks sake.' Greg yelled. 'Did you have to hit him so hard...What we gonna do now?'

Ignoring him Frecks bent down and checked the man's breathing along with his pulse.'

'He's alright,' Frecks said after a moment. 'Probably faking it.' He kicked the man's leg. 'Wake up wanker.'

Greg took hold of Frecks arm. 'We gotta get out of here before the other one comes back.'

'No way 'cos I'll give that bastard what he fucking deserves an 'all.'

'No Frecks, we getting out of here now. Come on.' Greg began packing their few possessions into a large navy holdall. 'Come on man...Move it.'

Just then the downed man began to stir. They watched as he pulled himself into an upright position.

'You'll pay for this bastard.' He growled.

Frecks moved forward. 'Oh yes, who's gonna make me... You?'

The man jumped up and without another word headed for the door. Frecks laughed.

'Not funny, what we gonna do now for money.' Greg glared at Frecks.

'Chill man, you've been really edgy lately, something the matter?'

'Not with me!'

Frecks shrugged. Well there might be something. I was talking to someone earlier.'

'Doing what?'

'Tell you about it later, can't make my mind up whether to get in it or not.'

Greg looked at Frecks with a puzzled look, wondering what he might be getting them into. *Whatever it is, it doesn't look good.* He thought.

CHAPTER TWENTY THREE

Vanessa and Sandra left the walk in centre with the promise of a hospital appointment for Sandra, which she had practically begged for, and a reassurance from the doctor that he was very optimistic that it was just a cyst.

'See I told you it would be fine didn't I, so chin up cos there's nowt to worry about...Sorted.' Vanessa said as they made their way down the Burnside to the surgery to make an appointment for Mr Skillings.

'I know, and I am glad I came, and...Really, it's not really that much sorted is it though,' she paused a moment. 'And I'm still a bit worried though. He...He can't see inside me can he, I mean it's not like he's got X ray eyes is it?'

'You're bound to be worried pet, anyone would be...But for what it's worth, I'm sure that the doc's right...And we'll find out for certain pretty soon, from now on its just a precaution, honestly there's nowt to worry about,' she squeezed Sandra's hand. 'So just chill love eh.'

'Yes but remember it could be weeks before I get an appointment through, everything takes so long these days, and there's lots of people complaining about cancelled appointments, what if it comes too late?'

'You're worrying yourself sick over things that might or might not happen.'

Ignoring what Vanessa had just said, Sandra grabbed Vanessa's hand as she went to drop it and squeezed back. 'And anyhow, how do I know he's telling the truth, he, he could just be saying it, couldn't he. Doctors don't really like giving people bad news do they?'

'They tell the truth Sandra, and he obviously thinks it's nothing to worry about. Bet you a tenner he's right and it's most likely just a cyst.'

'But what if he's just saying good things to fob me off...Shut me up even.'

'I already said, why would he do that? I'm sure he wouldn't give you false hope, Doc Marr's not like that is he now. So come on, chin up Mrs, its good news.'

Sandra opened her arms and Vanessa hugged her.

Five minutes later waiting outside of the doctors, Sandra lit a cigarette up, she had chosen to wait outside in case she spotted another doctor who she usually saw in the surgery and broke down in front of everybody and demanded to know how long she had to live, while Vanessa went in to make the appointment for Mr Skillings.

Not really a heavy smoker, less than ten a day, she had already passed her limit this morning. She looked at the cigarette and groaned inwardly to herself. *Should I bin it?*

Will it be too little too late?

She dropped the half smoked cigarette to the ground and squashed it with her right foot.

The boys have been on at me for ages to pack in.

Damn it, gonna give it a go.

She straightened her shoulders just as Tracy Brewer, who lived up the street from them, spotted her as she was heading for the chemist's which was next to the surgery. Sandra frowned. *Surely that's the coat I handed into the charity shop last month?*

No, can't be.

Ah but, didn't she have the same dress as I had on at the summer street party, and also my brown shoes that I gave to the charity shop as well. Now I come to think, she had a pair the same as them a few weeks later.

Now that's weird?

A few minutes later Tracy came out of the chemists and Sandra was listening to Tracy's gossip about Mr Skillings cheating at bowls.

What a total lie. Sandra thought, and was just about to tell her so, when Tracy turned to go, only she stepped back and said, 'I nearly forgot to tell you about Dale's dog.'

'Dale... Me and Vanessa saw him crying when we were on the bus, we were wondering what was wrong with him...So what's happened like?'

'Somebody's only gone and nicked it... Broad daylight an 'all, cheeky buggers.'

'Never.' Vanessa put in, as she joined them.

'No the wonder the poor soul was crying.' Sandra shook her head.

'That's three I've heard of already this past couple of months.' Tracy said. 'My aunts next door neighbour in Ryhope had her American bull dog nicked out of the garden, she lives close to where they put that Christmas tree up for the first time last year.

Anyhow that was two months ago.'

Sandra gave her a puzzled look.

'I mean since the dog went missing, not the Christmas tree put up. Anyhow we've never seen it since, the dog I mean. Lovely thing it was as well, nowt like what you hear about; gentle as a lamb Elsa was, kiss anybody or anything in sight she would... Oh and did you know about Steve Cains?'

'What about him? Vanessa frowned.

'Well people are saying its him that broke into Hetton chemist's last week, horrible toe rag what he is...Anyhow I gotta go. Bye.'

Vanessa and Sandra said their goodbyes. Sandra who without thinking had lit another cigarette up finished it and said, 'What a vicious nasty cow she is, everybody knows Steve Cains has been in hospital for the last two weeks with bloody kidney failure, the poor soul. And God help her if Steve's sisters hear what she's just said.'

'Hu, that goes without saying.'

'Well, I've never heard her say anything good about anybody. In fact that's the first time I haven't heard her calling one of the neighbours.' She didn't dare tell Vanessa what Tracy had said about Mr Skillings as she pictured Tracy with absolutely no hair left on her head.

Looking in the direction Tracy had gone Vanessa agreed. 'Too bloody right, she'll meet a sticky end one day, if she keeps on causing bother, stupid cow. And there's nobody's man safe where the dirty cow is either. She'll have it off with any Tom, Dick, or Harry...Slut.'

'Oh she will defo come to a sticky end.' Sandra decided to catch Tracy herself and warn her off about telling people lies about Mr Skillings the last thing she wanted was Vanessa getting herself into trouble.

'Sandra do you remember when she first moved here and under a month she had it off with Janette Stantons bloke?'

'Yes I do, real nasty piece isn't she?'

Vanessa nodded. 'She's without doubt the nastiest person I ever met, it's like she gets a kick out of hurting other people. Why would she?'

'I don't know how people can do that on purpose.' Sandra shook her head. 'And I know there's a name for people like her, only I can't remember it.'

'Me neither...But also don't forget, it takes two to tango, doesn't it.'

'You're right, but somehow would never have thought it of Jake Stanton. His wife divorced him over it.'

'Do you blame her?'

'Not really, like I said though I always thought he was a goodun. Not many stand up and give you his seat on the bus these days, and I know he does a hell of a lot for charity...He always struck me as a decent bloke.'

'Hu and how many of them are there around?'

'Come on Vanessa there's millions out there...OK, might be thousands...Or,' she cocked her head to one side, screwed her face up, and went on. 'Maybe hundreds.'

Vanessa pulled a face at her. 'Now are you sure about that...Thousands? Hundreds? Really?'

'Well there might be one or two.'

They both laughed, as they headed home. After arranging to meet up later in the afternoon to go and watch Darren play football, and with another hug they went their separate ways.

As Sandra approached her house she noticed that her

husband's car was in the drive.

What can I say? She wondered as she walked up the path.

Should I tell him?

Should I tell the boys?

No. She decided as she reached for the door handle. There's no point in worrying any of them until we know for real.

Taking a deep breath, she slowly opened the door and went inside.

'Is that you?' she heard her husband's voice from the kitchen.

With a deep sigh, she took her coat off and went into the kitchen. Seeing him standing there with his usual smile on his face, she nearly broke down.

But hiding her pain with a matching smile, she walked over to him and kissed him.

CHAPTER TWENTY FOUR

'So how are youse two?' Dinwall and Sanderson asked together, as Lorraine and Luke, minus the neck collar and sling, walked into the office.

'Fine,' Lorraine answered for them both. 'Thought we might be wearing a collar and a sling for a week or two, but no, the doc said we are both alright, and fighting fit.'

Dinwall silently heaved a sigh of relief, knowing Loraine was not the most patient person in the world, and if she had been restricted in any way from doing her job properly, their lives would have been hell. He sent a slight smile in Sanderson's direction, which was ignored.

'Good, how's Carter?' Dinwall got in before Sanderson, much to Sanderson's irritation.

'He's gonna be just fine as well, probs get out tomorrow or the next day...Though he may find walking a bit difficult for the next few days,' quickly she looked over to the window so that they couldn't see her smile, before going on. 'Oh just got a message from Scottie, when you pick Carter's mother up, make sure you grab his lap top will you Dinwall? The poor buggers going stir crazy already.'

'Dinwall looked at his watch. 'Will do, about an hour or so, if it's alright with you Boss?'

'Yes that's fine. Because the poor bugger certainly isn't going anywhere for a while.'

'So he's hurt his legs?' Sanderson asked.

'Something like that.' Luke said, cringing as he looked away, Lorraine had told him on their way back from the hospital, where most of Carters injuries were.

'Poor bugger. Sanderson said. 'I remember when I broke my leg- its damn well painfull...Couldn't get about for weeks, keep having to rely on others. Really frustrating.'

Lorraine nodded at him. 'Yes I remember that...Find anything on Caro yet Dinwall?'

'Couldn't find a trace of her on here, but half an hour ago a Caro was reported missing by her parents. Here they left a picture of her.'

Lorraine took the picture from Dinwall, stared at it for a moment, then blew air out of her cheeks and passed the picture over to Luke, as she said, 'That's definitely her. Do we have an address?'

Luke nodded his agreement, as with clenched lips he put the picture back on the desk.

'Yes,' Dinwall handed Lorraine a slip of paper, 'Just up the road in Grasswell.'

Lorraine sighed. 'I have to say I've never seen her around Houghton before.'

'Give me a look.' Sanderson picked the photograph up from the desk, studied it for a moment, before saying. 'Aw hell, I have. I'm certain she used to go with her mother to Mavis's pottery classes a couple of years ago.'

'She's a bit young for that like isn't she?' Dinwall said. 'I mean come on, a teenager...Pottery, these days. It's all phones and internet with this lot now!'

'Takes all sorts doesn't it, she is...Was a very shy and quiet young girl. Your mother knows Caro quite well, Lorraine, her and her mother, because her mother used to go to the same school as we did, at Newbottle.'

'God that must have been a long, long time ago mate. The spot's being developed into houses now.' Dinwall nodded at Sanderson, who chose to ignore him.

As did Lorraine, as she went on. 'Hmm, 'I don't remember her mentioning her, but Peggy interrupts that flaming much when I'm talking to my mother, grabbing the limelight as she always does, anyhow we're going down for supper tonight. Peggy insists we try her new recipe for God knows what, so I'll let her know the poor girl is dead.'

Sanderson nodded. 'Best coming from you than hearing it on the street. And I take it Australia is just fine now that Lady Peggy is home.'

Lorraine laughed. 'Sanderson; I doubt very much if Australia will ever be the same again.'

'So,' Lorraine said a few minutes later as she finished filling Sanderson and Dinwall in on the actual crime scene. 'As far as we know it's a one off...At the moment.'

'Not so boss.' Dinwall turned from his computer, 'I started checking when you phoned in, and nothings come up so far that matches, apart from one murder a few years ago in Coventry. Actually two years today, and the resemblance was two flowers found at the scene with broken stems.'

'Hmm, it's gotta be him, can't be a copycat because we would have heard about it before now. Also how did it not come up last year in the other case?'

Dinwall shrugged. 'Guess nothings a hundred percent is it. Even the latest technology can be flawed, can't it?'

'Two flowers,' Sanderson scratched his chin. 'And there were eight found at our crime scene. So was the victim treat the same as the others?'

'Male or female? Luke put in.

'The Coventry one was male,' Dinwall scrolled down the screen. 'Peter Howardson. Twenty eight years old. Left the army two years before hand and subsequently suffered from depression... Oh my God, the dirty horrible bastard.'

'What?' Lorraine said.

'The poor soul- he was poisoned with enough shit to kill a flaming army, also,' he shook his head, his face a picture of disgust. 'His penis was cut off and stuffed in his mouth and he'd also been raped.'

'Shit, shit, shit. What sort of friggin nutter are we looking for here?' Luke stared at Lorraine, as he went on. 'So, if he leaves a broken flower at each death and there were eight at the latest it could mean we're looking for a serial killer who has killed at least eight people in two years.'

'But,' Sanderson said. 'What if it's a different sort of count?'

Lorraine frowned. 'What do you mean?'

'Like a different tally for men and woman.'

'So you're saying that up to two years ago he had killed two men and up until last night eight women?' Lorraine's blood ran cold as she asked the question.

He shrugged, 'Could be ten men and eight women, or five men and eight women.'

'Aw for fuck's sake, keep digging Dinwall. Luke we've gotta see if anything's happening about that poor kid's dog when we come back from visiting this Caro's parents. We won't be too long guys.'

'What dog?' Dinwall asked, looking at Sanderson, as Lorraine and Luke left the office.

Sanderson shrugged. 'Don't know, she's a sucker for animals, you know that. I once saw her throw a hell of a punch at this creep when he admitted to cutting his dogs ears off. The soft shite cried like a baby.'

Dinwall laughed, 'Aye, she has some right hook on her.' He turned back to his screen.

CHAPTER TWENTY FIVE

Lorraine's fist was raised to knock on the red door when it was suddenly opened, and a tall very thin woman with bleached blonde hair greying at the roots, and startling green eyes which stared out at her, stood there. The women's eyes quickly flashed to Luke as he started to pull his badge out.

'You've found her?' The woman practically yelled, guessing that they were police officers, even before she had seen the badge. Relief and excitement showed on her face.

'Can we come in please?' Lorraine asked.

The smile quickly diapered from Mrs Delany's face when she saw no answering smile on Lorraine's, as she stepped to one side and ushered them in. The passage way was dimly lit which was not helped by the dark brown wood look alike cladding on the walls. She ushered them into the sitting room which was spotless but equally dim with the same brown cladding, a heavy smell of garlic filled the room which the scent from the numerous vases of flowers failed to cover. 'Please sit down, my husband is upstairs I'll get him.'

As they sat on the green leather settee, Luke threw Lorraine a puzzled look. 'You know what, It's as if she's actually expecting bad news?' he whispered.

Lorraine nodded as Mrs Delany and a man not quite as tall as her, entered the room.

'Hello,' the man, balding with thick rimmed glasses said. 'I'm Caro's father. Simon Delany, pleased to meet you.' His face was stern as he looked at them. 'That hasn't taken long it's only a few hours since we reported her missing.'

Lorraine flashed a weak smile at him as both of Caro's parents sat down, holding tight to each other's hands.

'I'm sorry,' Lorraine said. 'But it's not good news.'

The father glanced at Lorraine, then over at Luke, while the mother staring at the far wall, said. 'She's dead isn't she?' It was a statement and not a question.

Lorraine nodded. 'I'm sorry.'

'She killed herself didn't she?' The mother screamed, as she beat at her chest. Her husband grabbed her arms and held her tightly to him.

'Why would you say that?' Luke asked, frowning.

Mr Delany heaved a long drawn out sigh; Lorraine could see the deep pain in his eyes as he said. 'We've been sort of expecting it for a long time...My daughter, our Caro, has been depressed since she was around twelve years old. Most of it caused by bullying...Small things at first, then it got worse as time went on...We did everything we could. Yesterday morning my wife found her tablets, and we realised that she hasn't been taking them for over a month. That's why we reported her missing straight away when her bed had not been slept in last night...I'm sorry.' He put his head in his hands and started to cry. This time it was his wife who put her arms around him.

'When did you last see your daughter?' Luke asked.

'Must have been around about ten o clock last night,' Mr

Delany sighed. 'I remember because we were watching the news and she came down for a drink of water. My wife asked why she hadn't been taking her tablets and she flew into a rage, saying it was none of our business, stuff like that. She looked tired so we decided to wait until this morning to really have it out with her, because it's really important that she takes them.'

Mrs Delany burst out crying again, only this time it was more like a prolonged scream.

Lorraine felt like crying herself, as she said. 'I'm so sorry to have to tell you that your daughter didn't take her own life...She was murdered.'

Mr Delany froze, after a moment he lifted his head up. Shock, horror, and disgust played over his face. 'No, no way who would do that...Why?'

'No.' Mrs Delany screamed again.

'You have the wrong girl...It's not her. It's the wrong girl.' Mr Delany turned to his wife, begging her, pleading with her. 'Tell them Margaret, tell them it's not our Caro. Tell them. For God's sake tell them it can't be Caro.'

Mrs Delany stared into his eyes as she shook her head. 'It must be her, we knew this might happen.' She looked at Lorraine. 'She...She sometimes wanders around in the dark, in the middle of the night, we've told her over and over about the dangers, but...But she would take no notice...How? Where?'

'She was found near the Angel of the north.'

Mr Delany shook his head. 'She loves...Loves...Loved it there. It's her favourite place, she writes poetry, did I tell you that? That's her favourite place to write, sitting under the Angel writing poetry, I drop her off some days then go back and pick her up later.' He said proudly.

Lorraine smiled at him, understanding his use of past and present tense.

'But why..? Why our Caro?' He sobbed even louder then, clutching onto his wife. 'Who would do it?'

Suddenly he jumped up this time his face full of anger, he shook his fists in the air. 'I'll kill the bastard...Find him, you have to find him.' He leaned forward from his waist and stared at Lorraine. 'Before I do.'

The next minute he was on his knees sobbing into his wife's skirt. Gently, her own tears falling on to his back, she stroked the top of his head.

After arranging a time for Mr and Mrs Delany, to formally identify their daughter Lorraine and Luke left.

'I will find the bastard,' she said clicking her seatbelt on as Luke drove away.

Luke sighed. 'You bet.'

CHAPTER TWENTY SIX

Dale opened the door to find Abby standing there. 'Can I come in please?' She asked, smiling shyly at him.

Nodding, Dale stepped back, he shouted up the stairs to his mother. 'It's just Abby, Mam.'

'OK love.' His mother shouted back.

Abby looked around noticing some framed drawing on the wall that must have been done by Dale. 'They're good, especially that one.' she pointed to a painting of Dale's mother and his dog, before sitting down. 'Is it true about the dog?'

Dale dropped his head and nodded. 'A man jumped outta the van and snatched the leader right outta my hand. He really gave me a fright.' Dale gulped, reliving what had happened, and the fear he had felt.

'Aw, that's an awful thing to do, I would have died. But the coppers will find him, won't they?'

Dale shrugged. 'I don't think they'll be that bothered about a dog.' He was trying hard not to cry, the last thing he wanted was for Abby to see tears.

'Of course they will, bet all the coppers in Houghton are out looking now.'

'How did you know about it?'

'The whole school's talking about it.'

'Hi Abby,' Dale's mother said as she walked in. 'I'm going to make some pea and ham soup, fancy some?'

Abby blushed and put her head down. 'Err...'

'Yes she would, wouldn't you?'

Abby nodded. 'Please,' she looked up and managed a quick lopsided smile.

'Right' pet. Hope you like brown buns we don't do white bread in this house.'

'Yes that's fine thank you.' She muttered as Mrs Wilson went back into the kitchen.

For a brief moment Dale's mind was taken off Skip, as he thought that Abby was becoming even more shy, he sat down facing her.

'Have they been picking on you again?'

She looked up at him. 'Yes,' she almost whispered. 'They threw my PE kit over the fence after they had ripped it to bits, and called me names again, over and over. Then...Then they chased me down the street.'

'Who did this?' Mrs Wilson asked, coming back in from the kitchen, a heavy frown on her face.

Abby didn't know where to look.

'Some nasty kids at school, they won't leave her alone.' Dale put in. 'They're being really nasty, calling her names, nicking stuff off her, things like that.'

'So what do your mam and dad think of all this?' Mrs Wilson asked. 'Have they told the school?'

Abby shook her head. 'I haven't told them. Mam...Mam would go crazy. So would dad.'

Mrs Wilson leaned towards Abby. 'You have to tell them pet,

sometimes a little crazy helps in situations like this...Or at least tell the teacher's, because bullies will just go on being bullies. That's the way they are until stopped. If they hit you, you hit them back harder, whatever they do always return the favour love, it's the only way to stop the little, or big cowards. Because that's all bullies are, quite pathetic really.'

Abby smiled, but it was a false smile only for Mrs Wilson's benefit, she knew full well that she wouldn't know where to start or how to start hitting back. Only a few days ago Scarlet Jhons had slapped her and she'd ran away crying while Scarlet's friends all laughed. She still didn't know which had hurt the most, the slapping, the name calling, or the laughing.

'I'll bring the soup in on trays and youse can eat it in here.' She patted Abby's shoulder.

'Thank you.' Abby looked at Dale and shrugged, as Mrs Wilson left the room.

'She's right you know, a few years ago some of the lads were picking on me, so one day I lost it and I lashed out, it's the only thing that stops it, because it will go on and on.'

'My mam said before to just turn the other cheek and walk away...But she doesn't know how bad it is now.'

'Doesn't work.'

'I know.' Sadly Abby looked at her new shoes, where one side of her left shoe was covered in black paint.

Dale tutted. 'Who did that?'

'Scarlet's friend, Jodie.'

'No need for that like...I know,' he snapped his fingers in the air. 'We'll go and see Emma Lumsdon after school. She'll know what to do.'

'Will she help?'

'Oh yes. She hates bullies as well.'

'You going to school this afternoon?'

'Might as well,' he got up and walked to the window and looked up then down the street then sighed, turning back to Abby he went on. 'Emma's in the next class to us, you don't know her yet- but that lot do. She's alright Emma, she sticks up for other kids...She'll sort it, the same bunch tried it on with her a couple of years ago,' he laughed. 'They run the other way when they see her coming now. In fact I might even see her this afternoon.'

Abby looked interested. 'What did she do?'

'Well and truly sorted it, she'll tell you how.'

Just then Mrs Wilson came in with two trays, one on top of the other, the top tray had two bowls of pea and ham soup, buns and spoons, she dropped the bottom tray in Dale's lap, before putting the other one in Abby's.

Helping himself to a bowl and a bun Dale said. 'I'm going to school this afternoon Mam.' He dipped part of his bun in the soup, tasted it and smacked his lips which made Abby giggle.

'Good lad...It's for the best son, not a lot you can do here. I'll phone the school if there's any news.'

'Thanks Mam.'

Their soup finished and with Mrs Wilson again reassuring Dale that she would phone if there was any news, they headed off for school.

Abby who had been happily talking about their current art project fell silent as they neared the school gates. She ran her hands down the sides of her blue school dress then shoved them nervously into her blazer pockets.

'It's alright Abby, there's no sign of them.

'I know...But.'

'They'll not dare touch you inside the gates, cos they've been in trouble before.'

'That won't bother them...I know cos they're sly and do things where no one can see.'

She was shaking now and Dale wanted to put his arm around her, but knew if he did and that lot saw they would make a big thing out of it.

He wondered not for the first time. Why people were sometimes so nasty to each other.

'Look, in our first lesson you're only two desks down, I'll keep watching, honest.'

'Promise.'

'Yes.' He smiled trying to reassure her.

Slowly after taking a deep breath she took a step forward. She considered Dale as the only true friend she had, but she had not told him just how alone and far down she felt, she hadn't told him that only last night and not for the first time, she had taken a knife to her skin.

CHAPTER TWENTY SEVEN

Having got as much information as they could from the two officers who had attended the missing dog case, Lorraine and Luke were passing one of the interview rooms when Lorraine spotted a familiar face.

'Just the one I wanted,' she said with a smile and trying really hard not to punch the air in glee. Turning to Luke she went on. 'About time we had a bit of luck where that smarmy bastard's concerned isn't it.'

'Yep.' Luke laughed. 'Go get her kid.'

Lorraine looked him up and down. 'Really!'

Luke grinned at her, then quickly pulled out a pack of paper handkerchiefs as he started sneezing again.

'You've been knocking around with Carter too much mate.' Shaking her head, Lorraine knocked on the door, opened it and walked in, ignoring the young girl being interviewed she said. 'DS Harris can I have a word please.'

With a smile DS Harris rose out of his chair. 'Certainly boss.' Small and bald DS Harris, in his mid thirties had a smile which reached his deep blue eyes that would charm anyone. 'What's up?' he asked closing the door behind him.

'What's she in for now?' Lorraine indicated with her head

towards the interview room and the blonde girl who was scantily dressed in a sleeveless red dress that barely covered her thighs or in fact anywhere else.

'The usual, shoplifting scam, she was caught up at South Hetton this time, red handed with a bottle of gin, and two bags of crisps and two bars of chocolate...Also believe it or not, a packet of paper handkerchiefs. And still the brazen bugger is denying it.'

'Must have been planning a picnic, as well as feeling the flu coming on...Actually know how she feels.' Luke said.

DS Harris laughed. 'Now a picnic definitely wouldn't surprise me, given her track record. She's probably invited half a dozen of her moron mates as well.'

'She's turning out just like her brother that's how he started, and just look at the bastard now.'

'True.' DS Harris nodded.

'Actually I need a word with her about him, if you don't mind.' Lorraine said.

'Fine, I need a break. She's all yours.'

Lorraine nodded her thanks and pushed the door open, Luke followed her through.

The girl groaned and screwed her face up when she saw Lorraine, muttering, 'Aw no, not you.' under her breath as she stubbornly folded her arms across her chest.

'Nice to see you too Andrea.' Lorraine sat down, smiling at the girl, who tossed her head and sneered.

'Right, let's get straight to the point shall we?' Lorraine rested her chin on her hands. 'Where is it that your brother keeps the dogs he snatch's? I know he's moved his enterprise more than once. We all know that's how he got off the last time...But I'm here to tell you once and for all, that I personally will throw the book at you and see that you do hard time, real hard time, unless you get off your high horse, tell me where he is,' she leaned forward and yelled. 'NOW.'

Andrea jumped in her seat. 'I...I don't know.'

'LIAR!'

Andrea gulped. 'You can't get me locked up just for nicking a bottle of friggin gin...It's not fair.'

'Not fair!' Lorraine shook her head. 'Unbelievable. Is it fair on the shopkeeper?'

Andrea glared at her.

'Well is it?'

Andrea pouted. 'Who cares about friggin shopkeepers, got plenty of money haven't they. It's me it's not fair on 'cos it's racist so there. And you can't lock me up.'

'I beg your pardon...Racist!' Luke said in amazement. 'Good God, the politically correct brigade, have a hell of a lot to answer for.'

Andrea looked at Luke, pursed her lips and shrugged. 'Worth a try.'

Before Luke could say anything more Lorraine put in. 'So, I can't lock you up? Ha... Add the gin to everything else over the last flaming year. And the one before. And...'

Andrea screwed her face up, under her breath she muttered 'Bitch.'

'Sticks and stones Andrea, I've heard it all before...Now talk.' Lorraine banged her fist on the table.

As Andrea jumped again, Luke calmly said. 'Come on Andrea, everybody knows you and your brother don't get on, and that he's used his fists on you and other family members, more than once. Is he really worth doing time for, and don't for one minute think that in the same situation he wouldn't sing like a canary, because we all know he would...Sell his own bloody mother that one, wouldn't he?'

At the sound of Luke's gentle voice Andrea's lips started to quiver. 'If, if he finds out it's me, he, he'll fucking kill me. He will. And you know he will.'

'He won't find out.'

'Aye so you say… How can I be sure?'

'You have my word Andrea.'

'Hu, the word of a fucking copper,' she snorted. 'Are you right in the head...like a copper's words are any use to anybody?' She started to laugh. 'You're all fucking bent the whole friggin lot of you any way.'

Luke shook his head. 'No Andrea we are not.'

'How do I know it's not a plot? A plot to take both of us down. Never trust a copper. You can ask anybody that.' She folded her arms tighter.

'Enough again.' Lorraine said. Andrea was beginning to seriously annoy her. 'We haven't got time for this. You want hard time...It's yours.' Lorraine stood up.

Andrea looked at Lorraine, then for a moment she dropped her head, Lorraine glanced quickly at Luke and gave him a signal nod to carry on.

'Andrea.' Luke leaned forward. 'You know we can't really promise anything, but if you help us it will be mentioned in court and your sentence will be lighter...All we need from you is the place he is keeping the dogs, no way will it be connected to you, in the long run it's not as if he has a lot of friends who would stand by him is it?'

Slowly Andrea shook her head in agreement; she started to

chew the nail on the middle finger of her right hand as she looked up at Lorraine, when Luke went on. 'He's done the dirty on the lot of them hasn't he, family and friends?'

Andrea nodded slowly.

'That's why he moves around and recruits new scum every time he pulls a job, whatever it is.'

Andrea nodded, with a huge sigh, she said 'OK, alright. I'll tell you...But what's in it for me?'

'I've already told you Andrea, a lighter sentence.' Luke said.

'Well that depends.' Lorraine added.

'On what?' Nervously Andrea played with the bracelet on her left arm, as she looked under her brows at Lorraine.

'On whatever you tell us.' Lorraine looked at her watch. 'In the next five minutes.'

Luke smiled at her, 'Come on Andrea is he really worth your silence?'

Ten minutes later they were on their way to Great Ayton a beautiful ancient village near Middlesbrough. Just outside of the village is Roseberry Topping and Captain Cook's monument, some forty minutes from Houghton Le Spring, both were fantastic sights to see.

As Roseberry Topping came into view Lorraine remembered the very first time she had seen it, as a child on a picnic day out with her mother and Peggy, and Peggy had laughingly called it the hill with a hook.

Luke pulled up outside of Stokesley's the local butchers, in Great Ayton before Lorraine asked why, he said. 'I'm starving and Sanderson highly recommended the sausage rolls in here as well as the other stuff. Top notch, so he says...Besides the Middlesbrough squad won't be at the meeting place until one o clock. That gives us a good half hour to grab something.'

'Whatever floats your boat, if it's sausage rolls then sausage rolls it is, actually its ages since I had one,' she stared at him. 'So what are you waiting for?'

When Luke was halfway across the road she opened the window and shouted. 'Make mine two I'm starving...Oh and a can of pop.' Then she looked out of the other window and watched the ducks floating down the small stream.

Her phone rang. *Sanderson,* she thought looking at the screen. 'Yes?' she said a moment later.

'It's me boss.'

'Really!'

'Funny...ha ha...Not. I've found out that there have been at least seven other such murders in Germany over the last three years that they know of. But they suspect the count to be much higher and go back longer...So far its three men and four women.'

'Jesus Christ-Just what the hell are we up against here Sanderson?'

'Beats me boss.'

'Is there any other information?'

'Not really.'

'Shit.'

'Sorry but that's about it boss, they find the bodies often in open local places, mostly monuments or beauty spots, never any finger prints or DNA.'

'Right then, good work Sanderson, we should be back in the office before three. OK.'

'Yeah boss, see you later then...Oh I'll most probs be at the hospital, actually I'll be on my way in about half an hour to pick

Carters mother up to take her in'

'Thought Dinwall was taking her?'

'He was, but he's had to lie down for a bit, one of his flashing migraines.'

'Oh dear...Get going soon as possible, because you're way behind time. The poor bugger will think we've forgotten about him.'

Lorraine put her phone away just as Luke arrived back at the car. Reaching for her pop, she started to fill him in on what Sanderson had told her.

Between mouthfuls of sausage roll Luke said. 'Did he find out if it was just England and Germany?'

'Not sure, but I think so.'

'So we need to check on frequent travellers between us and Germany.'

Lorraine brushed crumbs off her suit, opened the door and threw the handful to the ducks. Watching them scramble for the food, she said as she picked her phone back up. 'I'll phone Sanderson back, he can deal with Interpol, he has more than one contact there.'

A few minutes later they were heading for their destination.

CHAPTER TWENTY EIGHT

When Sandra had walked into the kitchen to find her husband already there he was holding a huge bunch of flowers in his hands, pink lilies, her favourites. The flowers he always brought when he was in the dog house.

'What have you done now?' she asked, after she'd kissed him, with a smile, as she tried to sound normal.

Immediately he became defensive. 'Nothing,' he said quickly. 'Do I have to have done something wrong to bring my lovely wife her favourite flowers?'

'No, of course not I was only kidding babes,' smiling she quickly stepped forward and took the flowers from him. 'Thanks they're lovely.'

'Just like you my love.' He slowly put his arms around her; they hugged, after a moment she broke away.

'Careful you'll squash them, and they need water.'

He frowned behind her back as she went into the kitchen to get a vase before he sank down onto the settee and picked the remote up. He was flicking through the channels when Sandra came back in. 'Nowt on this bloody telly again.'

'I know load of rubbish lately, can't remember the last time there was a good murder mystery on... I know what, how do you

fancy going out for a meal tonight, that new Indian restaurant?'
She asked, thinking a night out, somewhere, anywhere, would help
take her mind off things.

'Would love nothing better my love, but don't you remember
what I told you last week.'

She shook her head. 'Remember what?'

'I'm driving down to Salford today,' he looked at his watch.
'Well actually in about an hour...It's Big Jim's bachelor party
tonight. I told you probs more than a fortnight ago than a week.
Yes it was a fortnight, on our way home from our Billy's birthday
party... Don't you remember love?'

Sandra shook her head. 'No...Not really. Weren't you at one
of those bachelor parties last month?'

'Yes, that was for the boss,' he laughed. 'Been married three
times already the prat.'

'Oh right...So when will you be back.'

'Well that's just it love I've been called in to cover a couple
of drivers on sick leave with this sickness bug that's going around,
what could I say, the boss says I'm his right hand man. So I'll be
leaving Salford in the morning, and straight back to work, got a big
load of goods to deliver to Germany. Sorry love I know you had
plans, but its good money and could lead to promotion, and in the
long run if I'm bumped up, it'll mean less time on the road,' he
nodded. 'Wont it?'

Sandra sighed. 'I suppose...But do you really have too? Go to
the bachelor party I mean.'

'Sorry love. He is my best mate...And I'll only be gone for a
couple of weeks.'

'Weeks!'

'Yes but the good news is the boss is on about opening an

office up here, which I just might be in charge of, if I keep my nose clean, just think of the benefits to be had, home just about every night, no more, or very few long journeys, now that won't be bad will it?'

'I suppose...'

He rose and put his arms around her, for a moment she nearly broke down, then sighing deeply she decided again not to tell him, knowing he would only worry and on a long haul trip that was the last thing he needed.

A few minutes later after Sandra refused all attempts to be lured into bed, and John had changed his clothes, they went downstairs. John wearing his black leather jacket matched with his black jeans and jumper which she had bought him last Christmas, and what she loved to see him in; was ready to leave. He kissed her good bye. She watched him walk up the path to his car and waved.

Sandra closed the door sat down on the stairs and sobbed her eyes out. *Stop it.* She told herself. *The doc said it's more than likely just a cyst, so stop going on like this being nowt but a big baby.* Pulling herself together she decided to have the clearing out she'd been promising to do for ages, she glanced at the clock, *plenty of time before Darren's football game starts.*

In her three bed roomed home the two oldest boys shared a room between them, as did the two youngest. One now lived and worked in London the others at various stages of university, also in London. Her only consolation was the fact that they were close enough to each other to help if it was needed.

She walked into the first room, looked around and didn't know where to start. Both beds were made and changed regularly even though it had been more than two months since either had been slept in, pale blue matching quilts, went with the darker blue walls, and curtains, the left wall covered in pictures of young girls mostly in bikinis, the right one covered with pictures of motor bikes and flash cars.

Silly idea...Why would I want to throw anything away? None of them has really left home yet.

Shaking her head, she went back down stairs, checked the clock on the kitchen wall, found she had enough time to fill the washer and clean the kitchen and to make a cup of coffee. Staring out of the kitchen window, her mind jumped back to her husband. *Just when I need him the most,* she thought. With a sigh her mind skipped again, this time from her present problem to the son she had given away at birth, and the events that had happened just a few months ago.

CHAPTER TWENTY NINE

An hour after setting off for B&Q at Washington to collect Len's soil bags, Danny, Jacko and Len were parked in Danny's van outside of the snooker club in Houghton Le Spring, eating a bag of chips each from the Silver Grid on Newbottle Street, next to the council offices and opposite Recreate Print.

Len was busy picking the batter off his chips and dropping it onto a paper napkin, when between mouthfuls of chips Danny asked. 'Have any of youse two seen Adam lately?'

'Aye.' Jacko said, 'Couple of weeks ago, it was weird he practically ran out of the shop as if he was trying to ignore me, when I caught him at the top of the aisle he said he hadn't seen me, didn't believe him then, and don't now. And he had a hell of a black eye as well. To tell you the truth I think that's why he was trying to ignore me.'

'Again?' Danny, asked as he crunched his chip paper into a ball, opening the window he aimed for the bin five yards away. 'Yes.' he shouted as it landed in the bin.

'What do you mean again?' Jacko frowned at Danny.

'Well he's had a few black eyes lately, and his ribs were really sore last month.'

'What the hell off?' Jacko asked.

Danny shrugged. 'Say's he fell down the stairs. His other black eye he said he walked into a fucking door, don't know about the latest one though, 'cos hardly see him these days, now that he's got that new girl friend.'

Len and Jacko looked at each other, as Jacko said. 'He's kept that one quiet, every time I've given him a bell to see if he wanted a pint or two, he's said his mother's not well and he had to stay at hers to look after her, though I'm sure I saw her getting into a taxi with a suitcase the day before I last rang, and she looked alright...So who's the new girl friend like?'

Danny shrugged. 'Well you can't really mistake his mother Old Kath can you? So it must have been her you saw,' he grinned. 'Still dying her hair blonde at over seventy isn't she...Though never call her Old Kath to her face, 'cos she'll murder you as she reminds you that she still does Karate...And as for the girl friend I've actually never really met her, though I have seen her around a few times.'

'I know, isn't she that one he went out with before and they kept splitting up, bossy little bitch she's lived on the Seahills for about three or four years.' Len nodded his head. 'Didn't you meet her Jacko?'

'Aye if it's the one I'm thinking about, Christina doesn't like her at all, can't remember her name though.'

'Oh, wonder why she doesn't like her?'

Jacko shrugged. 'She said the woman's pure nasty, calls people behind their backs, that sort of thing. Always gossiping about one person or another, Christina says she's never heard her say a good word about anybody.'

Not risking aiming for the bin and missing, Len screwed his paper up, and reached for Jacko's as he got out of the van and walked over to the bin; depositing them, he then got back in the van and said. 'You come up with any ideas yet for a bit of cash mate?' He looked at Danny.

'Well actually.' Danny rubbed his hands together. 'That's why I was asking after Adam 'cos we gonna need him.'

'Oh oh,' Jacko looked at him then at Len, as Danny grinned at them both. 'Come on then,' Jacko went one. 'Spit it out mate... And may God help us.'

'Well alright just fucking chill.'

Jacko and Len stared at him. 'OK, alright, what do youse think of this...You know how these new fangled craft markets are springing up all over the place now, the ones that sell homemade stuff, fancy bread and stuff like that?'

'Aye,' Len said with his usual frown, 'I know what you mean, fancy craft things. I've heard there's a really good one going at the Shotton Hall, and the Hetton centre, actually there's quite a lot of people into this crafting thing.'

'Not just there mate, like I said, they are honestly springing up all over the frigging place.'

'And?' Jacko said.

'Well...' Danny grinned. 'I thought we could get a meat stall going like, you know sell it cheaper than the shops, before we know it the word will spread they'll be queuing right round the bloody block.'

'Are you for friggin real, where the hell we gonna get the money from for that sort of venture?'

Danny tutted and pulled a face at Jacko. 'Well that's just it, so listen man, will you?'

'Whatever.'

'Let's hear him out.' Len put in.

Jacko shrugged as Danny went on. 'Aye man put a sock in it and just listen...You know the supermarkets at the end of the day when they sell stuff off for next to nowt?'

Jacko and Len nodded, looking warily at each other, as Jacko said. 'Aye, what about it?'

'Well what we do is, we go in about five o clock when they've reduced things to next to nowt, take all the cheap labels off, stick them on the fresh stuff and take it through the self check out tills, it's a doodle, some of the stuff's knocked down to a pound, we can get fresh joints worth a tenner or more for next to nowt. Ching ching...Joint of pork, fifty pence...Shoulder of lamb one pound and so on. Quid's in.'

'What?' Jacko exploded.

'Come on man think about it, we can make ourselves a bloody fortune.'

'Maybes so, but a fortune's no good behind bars.'

'We'll not get caught daft sod.'

'Huh, says you.'

'We won't get caught 'cos we'll spread ourselves around, different super markets by a different person every time. We could do four or five a night, even more, probs a hell of a lot more if we just keep rotating.'

'I see you've friggin well thought this through all right.' Jacko frowned at him.

'I have that.'

'But, what about the assistant?'

'What assistant.' Danny looked at Len. 'Why in my whole life have you always rained on my parade?'

'What parade?'

'For fucks sake.'

'He means the assistant who stands there most of the day.' Jacko put in. 'I've seen them looking around all the time watching for anything dodgy.'

'Aw that one, sorted. We go to the till that's not near to him, as far away as possible. And don't, whatever you do make eye contact, 'cos that always looks suspicious... In fact we could go in two's; one of us can distract him while the other is shoving the stuff through.'

'How?' Len asked.

Danny thought for a moment then grinned. 'Easy, just get a couple of tins, beans or something cheap, act like you don't know what you're doing, while he's busy helping you, then we can whip the gear through double quick. Actually we really do need Adam, or we gonna waste time.'

'Hmm, it's still thieving.' Jacko frowned.

'Aye but it's not your ordinary folk we're hurting is it? And the fat cats can afford it for fucks sake, any idea how much waste there is in a supermarket? Greedy twats throw stuff away at the end of the night. You'd at least think they would give it away to the homeless...And you know our rule, never nick off our own...Plus our lot will be getting cheaper Sunday dinners 'cos of us. See that way we're helping our own.'

'Oh my God,' Jacko looked at Danny. 'You've lost the frigging plot; you think you're fucking Robin Hood.'

Danny laughed, picturing himself dressed as Robin Hood. 'Aye why not?'

Shaking his head Jacko said. 'Tell you what, I'll give it a think, and let you know.'

'Aye me an 'all mate.' Len said, as Danny looked in his mirrors when he started the van up. 'Also we could resell the tins of beans couldn't we?' Len added.

'Why would we do that?' Danny asked.

'Well, because youse do know that it's gonna cost a fortune in carrier bags, don't you?'

'Unbelievable!' Jacko said, looking sideways at Danny, who burst out laughing.

They drove up passing Table rock and headed toward Grasswell. Just about to indicate left at Grasswell fish shop, Danny changed his mind and instead headed up towards Newbottle, as it made very little difference in reaching the Seahills, whichever way he went. Neither Jacko nor Len said anything, until he carried on through the lights, crossed straight over the roundabout, took a quick left and stopped the van outside of Newbottle club.

'What the?' Jacko looked sideways at Danny.

'Bloody well nearly forgot didn't I, that I had to flaming well meet old uncle Trevor in here to pick some veg up off his allotment. I'll only be a minute.'

'His veg might be good but I know for a fact, his tomatoes are nowhere near as good as mine.' Len said.

Danny looked at him sideways and shook his head.

Ignoring Len, Jacko said. 'What you talking about you'll only be a minute, might as well have a pint while we're here.' Jacko got out of the van quickly followed by Len.

'Why aye,' Len smacked his lips hurrying in front of Danny and Jacko. 'Wash the fish and chips down a treat, won't it lads.'

CHAPTER THIRTY

Finishing his rare steak he wiped his lips with his napkin, folded it neatly and placed it by his plate, with a smile and a wink for the young waitress, who he gathered was quite taken by him. He rose from his chair and made his way up to his room.

Opening his laptop he found another message, and with a satisfied smile he started communicating with the sender. After a few minutes he closed the connection and frowning reached for his map of the north east.

Folding the map five minutes later and with the smile back on his face because it was most certainly do-able.

Tonight was going to be a good night. And a very busy one.

He checked his phone for messages. *Hmm...Three.*

CHAPTER THIRTY ONE

Frecks was standing near to the open gate, watching the dogs run free in the enclosed field, they were all friendly with each other, and the latest one seemed to be making friends with the others. Elsa the white American bull dog could get a bit over excited if more than one dog got too close to her but she was usually alright. It was the sheer weight of her that the other dogs needed to be wary of, not her teeth.

Thinking of teeth, he rubbed his forefinger over his. 'Must remember to pick some toothpaste and brushes up.' he said to himself.

His mind went back to the dogs. And the thought of just how dangerous the lovely gentle Elsa could become, because of the greed and lack of compassion by some lousy rotten human beings, sickened him.

Frecks chewed on his bottom lip as the events of earlier prayed on his mind, he had stood up to the nasty creep who after taking his spite out of the dog by kicking it, had quickly left when he saw the look on Frecks face, and Greg had jumped up to stop him following him, by just managing to lock the door and refusing to hand over the key.

His thoughts jumped quickly to his army days and the things

he had seen, the things he had done in the name of King and country; the savage cruelty that people doled out at each other, as well as the animals.

Then his earlier conversation with an old army colleague came into his mind. He shuddered and quickly tried to get rid of the thoughts and the pictures they conjured up.

Slowly he shook his head, and tried some deep breaths to calm himself.

But the more he watched the dogs, who had no idea of their fate, playing happily in the field the angrier he got.

How can they, how the fuck can they do something like this? Bastard creeps.

He punched the gate, his heart beat faster, and his eyes filled up as he watched the dogs playing. 'Fuck it.'

A look of angry determination now covering his face, he whistled and one by one the dogs looked back at him. 'Come on guys, here, here. Come on come on.' Happily wagging their tails, they turned and headed towards him.

Clipping their leaders on, he took them to his car, opening it up he shoved them all in, managing all six even though they were squashed, he was determined that he was not going to leave one behind.

Amidst the growling and yapping, which soon stopped as they all found a place and happy that Elsa didn't seem to mind one bit that Joe the Border collie was lying on her back, and licking her ears, Frecks shouted for Greg.

A few seconds later Greg appeared at the doorway, 'What the?' He stared in the back of the car window as three of the dogs, a Lakeland terrier, a Collie cross and a dog Frecks had named Jessie which looked like a black Retriever and an Alsatian cross.

stared back out at him. He shook his head, for a moment his mouth was wide open as it dawned on him just what Frecks was planning to do.

'Jesus Christ...Hope you know what the hell you're doing mate.'

'Oh, yes I fucking do...I'm getting them all outta here right fucking now and taking the lot to the fucking coppers, you coming or what?'

'They'll eat us alive.'

'No they fucking won't soft shite.'

'I don't mean the fucking dogs.'

'I know who you mean Greg, but I can't do this,' the American bull dog licked at Frecks hand. Looking up from Elsa he said simply. 'Can you?'

Greg stood still for a moment as he looked into Frecks eyes, 'Not really,' suddenly he ran for the car. Jumping into the front he said. 'So what we waiting for mate?'

They had just turned right at the bottom of the track and were on the road just beginning to pick up speed when two police cars passed them.

'Shit.' Greg said. 'Looks like the buggers are onto the fucking arseholes.'

'Aye it also looks like we made it out just in time, 'cos bet your life we would have been dragged right into it. Much better we do it this way mate, than them catching us red handed, cos they would never have believed we were gonna hand them in now, would they?'

Greg breathed deeply before saying. 'Well, all I can say is, I hope you've got a plan.'

Frecks glanced sideways at him. 'A plan for what?'

'For what we do for cash when we've dumped this lot.'

'Well there's something come up, but I'm not sure about it.'

Gregg looked interested. 'Come on then tell me.'

'Just an old mate I was in touch with this morning...I'm not sure, I'll tell you more when I've had time to think about it.'

Staring straight in front of him, Greg frowned; he had also been in touch with an old army buddy, with a sort of promise of a job, and one he had never liked at all.

CHAPTER THIRTY TWO

Totally out of plan, something he hated to do and be, he was a stickler he liked everything to run as smooth as silk, but this one had sounded really desperate and the money on offer was definitely not to be sniffed at.

How could I refuse a cry for help?

He closed the boot of his car with a victorious slam.

Not too bad really. Less than twenty minutes this one had taken, from the beginning of their first hello and their last goodbye. It still amazed him the different ways that some reacted to the drugs he gave them, some were nearly out of it in minutes, then there was that one last month who had taken nearly fifteen minutes, now that had taken some role playing on his part until she finally succumbed. Shame she had actually been a lot stronger than she thought when the end was actually in sight.

Full of apologies he had sadly told her that it was way too late to change her mind now.

With a smile he looked fondly at the boot. With this one the main part was yet to come. He shivered with anticipation.

Getting into his car he drove off, in his rear view mirror he could see the large private house looming behind him, alongside the lush gardens.

'Guess it's true what they say, money isn't everything.'

Maybe's I should write a book about it.

This thought pleased him, as the house disappeared when he turned right and headed for his hotel. 'So much to do.'

He shook his head. It was going to be a long night. Not sure if he should fit this one in before or after the one he had booked, he nevertheless drove on with a smile on his face.

CHAPTER THIRTY THREE

Vanessa was making her way up the street towards Sandra's house, suddenly half way there she froze.

'Shit!' Turning she hurried back home. As she opened the front door she sniffed the air. 'Thank God.' She muttered making her way into the kitchen. She heaved a sigh of relief when she saw the iron plug was out of the wall and resting innocently on the ironing board.

'I'm going round the bloody bend.' She said, making her way back out and locking the door behind her, she headed back to Sandra's house.

'Sandra.' She yelled as she opened Sandra's front door. 'You ready yet?'

Sandra appeared a moment later, and looked Vanessa up and down. 'Well I was.'

'What do you mean?'

'Come on Vanessa look at us, we look like the bloody terrible twins.'

Vanessa looked at what Sandra was wearing, then down at her own nearly identical red blouse and cut off blue jeans then burst out laughing. 'See what you mean.'

'One minute.' Sandra disappeared back into the kitchen while

Vanessa went outside and sat on the step.

Leaning against the door post Vanessa smelled the yellow roses which were still flowering in large blue pots at each side of the door, then looked up the street, she watched as Mr Skillings weeded his garden for the second time that day, he stopped for a rest as Doris Musgrove came up her path next door. Vanessa smiled to herself as she watched them. Both of them had been so good to her and her kids.

I'm so lucky to have such good people around me. For a moment she closed her eyes, picturing what could have been, what would have been without them and Sandra. Her body shuddered. *With true friends and a bit of determination so much can be done.*

She smiled. And I'm living proof of that, who would ever have thought that I would come out the other end and life would be as good as this.

She had been thinking for a while about how she could help people who were in the same situation as she had been, but without the support that she'd had and decided that yes, she would go and see how she could help, there was a woman's refuge not far from the Seahills. *I'll go there tomorrow. Definitely.*

'Come on then.' Sandra's voice startled her.

Vanessa jumped up. Noting that the red top had been changed to a pale blue, she said. 'Nice one, very nice.'

'Yes I know. Come on then, we haven't got all day.'

Vanessa frowned behind Sandra's back, but knowing the reason why Sandra was so short tempered, she kept quiet and followed her to the gate.

They had just stepped out of the gate when they saw Dale and a girl they didn't know walking towards them.

'You alright Dale?' Vanessa asked. She would rather hear

what happened from Dale himself than trust anything Tracy Brewer had told them.

'Not really.' Slowly Dale shook his head, then started to tell Vanessa and Sandra everything that had happened as they headed up to school.

'The horrible nasty gits,' Vanessa said when he had finished telling the story. 'And you have no idea who the bloody hell the stinking rats were?'

'No, their faces were covered up.'

Sandra put her hand on his shoulder. 'I'm sure they'll get your dog back love.'

Dale nodded. 'Thank you, I hope so...Bye.' He hurried ahead with Abby in tow.

'Poor bugger.' Vanessa watched them walk on. 'He's always so polite that kid.'

'He is an 'all. Anyhow let's get a move on.'

Sandra picked her pace up, and as usual they were first on the football field.

CHAPTER THIRTY FOUR

Dinwall's Ocular migraine had cleared up in five minutes, so pleased that it had gone so fast, because sometimes it lingered for twenty minutes or so, he had been able to collect Carter's mother and take her to the hospital. 'Here,' he handed the remains of a bag of popcorn to Sanderson as he walked in. 'I know you like this shit, just make sure you don't eat it all at once, can't do with you having a sugar rush.'

Sanderson looked inside the bag. 'Where did you get this from then?' Unable to resist a nibble his hand crept inside the bag, coming out a moment later with a handful which quickly found its way to his mouth.

'Carter's mother when I dropped her off. Went into see him for a couple of minutes, told him you would pop in when you pick his mother up at four.'

'What?' Sanderson nearly choked on the popcorn. He'd thought he'd got a lucky escape from taking Carter's mother to the hospital earlier when Dinwall's migraine had cleared up, now it looked like he had not.

'Well you said you were going in later and apparently Mrs Carter's cousin is in the next ward, so she's visiting him as well, and she's quite happy to wait around for you to collect her... No doubt she'll tell you all about her cousin when you do pick her up, because I feel like I know the whole friggin family tree from top to bottom now.'

Between coughs, Sanderson muttered. 'Thanks.' He pulled a face behind Dinwall's back as he walked over to the water fountain and filled a plastic cup to the brim. On the way back to his desk the cup slipped from his hand and hit the back of Dinwall's neck, totally soaking his ponytail before completing its downward spiral and spilling the remaining water over his desk.

'What the?' Dinwall yelled.

'Sorry.' Sanderson bit his lip and looked the other way.

'I just fucking bet you are, I'm drenched here.' Dinwall grabbed some tissues and swabbed the back of his neck, as he glared at Sanderson's back.

Having slowly sat down at the desk in front of Dinwall's, Sanderson smiled to himself, as he picked up his phone to answer the incoming call.

'Come on,' he said a moment later . 'We're needed up at the Blue Lion, apparently all hell's broke loose and it's in danger of escalating onto the street.'

Dinwall frowned. 'Where's all the PC's?'

Shrugging Sanderson headed for the door. 'Ask the fucking government...All out on duty presumably...Been another incident on the A19 just outside of Newbottle...Plus even more cuts I guess. Anyway they're sending some as soon as possible.'

'Bet you it's that Miller family at the bottom of this. They usually are.' Dinwall shrugged his black leather jacket on and followed Sanderson out of the door.

When they reached the Blue Lion they found that it definitely was not the Miller family involved in a standoff, rather that it was Graham Bailes, brother of Christie Bailes, holding Jamie Barret cousin of Wayne Barret hostage with a knife to his throat, while various members of each family looked on. The families, distantly related through sharing the same great grandmother had been feuding ever since she had died more than twenty years ago leaving her money to one side of the family only. At the time the gossips had said that the old witch knew exactly what she was doing by causing a huge rift in the family.

'Shit.' Dinwall muttered under his breath, as he and Sanderson hurried through the open door.

'OK,' Sanderson stepped forward. 'Put the knife down.'

'No the bastards finally gonna get what's coming to him, dirty fucking creep.'

'Not this way Graham, he's not worth it. You know this, come on hand the knife over, and we'll talk.'

Graham looked at Dinwall, they knew each other well, had done since they had been kids. Dinwall had been surprised to see Graham as the aggressor, knowing this was totally out of character for Graham, and he also knew how much grief the Bailes had been giving them, especially lately as it seemed to have got worse since Christie and Wayne had become partners. Plus Graham also suffered from depression, had done most of his life.

'Come on Graham man, just hand it over.' He moved a step closer.

'No the bastard's gonna get what's coming to him.'

Jamie Barret, a known loudmouth coward, and a suspect in two rapes one of them family, had uncontrollable frizzy brown hair he screamed as the knife nicked his neck. Dinwall froze, his eyes meeting Grahams and seeing a man on the edge. 'Please Graham put it down now.'

But Graham was mesmerized by the trickle off blood running down Millers neck.

'Graham,' Dinwall said softly, as he slowly moved a step closer. 'Put the knife down.'

Sanderson, standing just behind Dinwall, was impressed by the way Dinwall seemed to be handling things; he stepped backwards towards the door they had come in. Just in case Graham decided to make a run for it.

Which is what he did a moment later, he pushed Jamie towards Dinwall, and as Dinwall shouted. 'Wait Graham we can sort this out.'

Graham shouted over his shoulder. 'No I have an important appointment.'

He ran through the opposite door to where Sanderson stood and jumped on his motor bike which he had parked as close to the door as he could, and was heading towards Newbottle in moments.

CHAPTER THIRTY FIVE

After making sure he had locked the car boot, for the third time, he walked into the hotel and smiled at the receptionist as he passed the desk, knowing he looked good in his black gear.

And that's what death wear's, isn't it?

Casually he winked at her, and again was pleased when she blushed.

Wonder what time she gets off?

But will I have the energy?

Hmm, 'Why aye,' as they say in these parts.

Suppressing a grin he doubled back, looked at her badge and said. 'Hello Tanya. Can I ask what time you finish work tonight?'

She blushed again right to the roots of her blonde hair. 'I...Err...Six o clock.' She slowly, her eyes capturing his, ran her tongue over her lips.

'Would you care to have a drink with me? I should be back by seven, at the latest I'm sure.' He read the badge on her chest and added. 'Tanya.'

'Well...Well yes I would...Where?'

He looked towards his left. 'Here's fine by me...The cocktail bar?'

'Yes that would be good.'

'Cheers, see you then.' He walked away with a smug look on his face, a look she couldn't see as she watched him leave.

Her friend came out of a side door. 'So, why such a happy face?'

'Make sure your phone is charged.' Tanya grinned.

'Another one already?'

'Oh yes.'

Her friend a dark skinned Asian woman called Rula, rubbed her hands together. 'So bloody easy, told you didn't I. Soon we'll be able to run for the hills and live the life that the rich and famous do. The life we deserve.'

'Oh yes.'

'Still can't understand how you can practically blush on demand though. But it gets them every time.'

'It's all in the head and what I think about.'

'Dirty bitch.' They both burst out laughing.

CHAPTER THIRTY SIX

Lorraine and Luke, followed by the patrol car containing three police officers from Middlesbrough, which had met up with them outside of Great Ayton, pulled off the road and headed up the farm track. The farm house, set against a back drop of green fields and gentle rolling green and brown hills, was built of solid grey stone and was obviously a couple of centuries old, it also looked strangely deserted. The once, which probably had been well kept flower beds, were now overgrown with weeds. A for sale sign which looked easily a few years old, lay crumpled and dirty next to the wall. One of the filthy mud encrusted windows had fuck you in fresh white paint, sprawled across it in large capitals.

When they got out of the cars, Lorraine said. 'Do you think that message is for us?'

'Who knows?' Looking at her Luke shrugged.

The three policemen got out of their car, and one of them pointed at the writing on the window, the other two laughed, then waiting for instructions looked towards Lorraine.

Lorraine studied the front door for a moment, and taking in all the rubbish that was sprawled around the two steps in front of the door, from empty carrier bags, glass bottles, dead leaves and take away cartons, said. 'Ok let's try the back, because this door doesn't look like it's been opened for years.'

At the back they found the door swinging open in the stiff breeze that had sprung up a few hours ago. Lorraine ordered one of the police men to check the grounds while she, Luke and the other two stepped inside.

After shouting, 'Hello.' A few times and receiving no answer, Lorraine turned to the policemen. 'Youse two up stairs, give the place a good search. Come on Luke.'

They turned right as the policemen rushed past them and pounded up the stairs. Lorraine and Luke found themselves in a dark dismal kitchen in desperate need of a good clean, very little light came in through the two narrow dirty windows, and the once white net curtains were filthy, torn and nicotine stained, there was also a heavy smell of Marijuana in the musty air.

Luke walked over to the cooker, resting on the hobs along with a few dirty pans was a kettle; he felt the kettle with the back of his hand. 'Well someone's not long gone, still warm.'

'Hmm,' Lorraine said from the sitting room as she pushed a newspaper from the small coffee table pressed against the wall, exposing an ashtray full of cigarette ends and two hands of cards plus a small stash of silver and copper amounting to less than two pounds.

Picking the paper up she checked the date. 'Yesterday's paper. Reckon they plan on coming back?' She looked across at Luke, as he walked into the sitting room.

Luke looked at the money on the table, and shook his head. 'Hmm, doubt it... Depends how skint they are though.' He smiled at Lorraine, who pulled a face at him.

A tiny bit of more light than was in the kitchen exposed a fire place covered in dust and ash, a once cream carpet and a tatty brown settee and matching chairs which belonged sometime in the fifties. The chairs were pushed together facing each other and a dark blue sleeping bag was stretched out, a matching sleeping bag was on the settee. As Lorraine surveyed the scene the two officers came from upstairs.

'Nothing up there Detective Inspector Hunt, only dust and plenty of that.' The first one said, PC Garmont tall and thin looked at his shorter thickset companion for confirmation.

PC Jarvis gave a swift nod, before saying in a high pitched voice. 'The place looks like no one has set foot up there for years,' He nodded again as he scratched his ear. 'Never seen so much dust lying about, the place is well and truly filthy.'

'Alright then, it looks like whoever is living here got wind that we were coming and legged it.' Lorraine said as they both nodded their heads in agreement.

'And without going outside,' Lorraine went on. 'I'm guessing that there isn't a dog in sight, because we would have heard them well before now.'

The officer who had been sent to check outside came in just then. 'All clear out there, although there is plenty evidence of quite a few dogs being kept here up to at least an hour ago, plenty fresh turd's lying about.'

'Guess that's it then.' Luke looked at Lorraine. 'It's the only lead we have.'

'Shit...What the hell can we tell Scottie?'

'That we tried.'

'He's not gonna be too happy,' she looked at the policemen. 'Right then guys, thanks very much for your help; guess we'll have to call it a day.'

After another quick look around, they headed out to their cars, the patrol car left first. Jumping into the passenger seat Lorraine tossed the keys at Luke.

'Not in the mood?' Luke asked as he started the engine.

'Far from it, thought for once we might have had a bit of good news for people, but not meant to be,' she looked at the fields around her as they sped past. 'Where the hell are they? I mean it can't be that easy to hide a bunch of dogs. For fucks sake somebody somewhere has got to see them, and be suspicious of a pack of strange dog's, and a stranger in control of them, cos that arsehole never pisses near his own pond that's for sure.'

'At a guess?' He looked at Lorraine and shrugged.

'Damn it. Just drive to Scottie's see what's going on there, fingers crossed we've got more luck and some lead or another to catch this latest creep.'

'Don't hold out much hope there either, it's very strange the way he arranged the body, there's just something I can't put my finger on.'

'Yes, it's nagging at me as well.' She rubbed her shoulder.

'Is it still hurting, perhaps you should have left the sling on a bit longer?'

'It'll be fine just a bit stiff. The doc did take it off remember just like your neck collar.'

Luke frowned, wondering why she had snapped at him, he decided to let it go, there was something bothering her and it wasn't to do with work, he was certain of this. He'd seen her staring out of the window with a blank look on her face more than once over the last few days.

'Actually just starting to realise how lucky we bloody well are,' she suddenly said. 'I mean poor Carter.'

'You can say that again.' Luke saw her shoulders shake as she tried to keep a laugh in.

Taking a right turn a minute later, Luke drove down a couple of small narrow roads, with sheep in the fields on either side, through a small hamlet of half a dozen houses then another minor road, before heading up the A19 towards Sunderland.

Lorraine remained quiet as she stared out of the window lost in her thoughts.

The recent murder of the young girl was needling at her, she needed time, time to think, time to wonder why it had happened at all, in her experience there was mostly a reason and most reasons were family or friends.

Why...Why...Why?

Such a waste of life.

And then she thought of her own life, where it was going and where it had been. She knew it was sheer hard work and determination that had got her this far. She glanced over at Luke, knowing that she really adored him- she then wondered just how far this really was.

Is it truly forever?

Will he eventually want to get married?

This thought froze her for a moment; she already had one disastrous marriage behind her. How big of a fool had she been over that, if only he had been honest with her from the beginning, and what a relief when the divorce had finally come through. From this she jumped to the night a few months back when Luke had slipped and accidently gone down on one knee, what a shock that had been.

And kids!

What if he wants kids?

Me a mother!

No way.

Panic stricken, she sat bolt upright.

'You alright love?'

'Who me? Yeah I'm fine, just err, I was thinking about the latest murder. And why, why her?'

Actually, she fanned her face with her hand; thinking about kids is the closest I've ever come to a panic attack.

CHAPTER THIRTY SEVEN

'Hurry up,' he shouted up the stairs, 'I've just watched her go into the house. We need to get out of here now.'

He heard a banging sound in answer.

'You alright?'

'Yes,' came the reply. 'Just dropped the case off the bed, I'll be down in a tick.'

'Need a hand.'

'No it's fine.'

'Alright.' He looked at his watch and impatiently tapped his foot.

He felt shaky inside as he wiped the sweat off his brow. *Come on, come on.* He walked to the window looked up and down the street, *deserted* .

'We have to go now.'

She appeared at the top of the stairs, her makeup thickly applied, her lipstick the same colour as her hair. Black leggings, and a long pale blue blouse her favourite colour, with strawberries running around the bottom and the cuffs, the blouse was open at the top revealing most of her breasts. 'Keep your hair on, I'm ready,' she shouted down at him. 'Don't want to forget anything important do I?'

'About friggin time,' he ran up the stairs and grabbed the suitcase. 'You sure this is everything, because there's no coming back.'

'It's everything I need. I double checked, that's how it took a little longer. Like you said, there ain't no coming back.' She leaned forward and kissed him.

Together they walked down the stairs and out to his car, all the time both of them kept looking around. The street was still empty. But nothing on the Seahills goes unnoticed as more than one curtain flicked.

Quickly they jumped into the car and sped off, turning the corner on practically two wheels, just as Mr Skillings was crossing the road.

CHAPTER THIRTY EIGHT

'Put that away for God's sake man.' Greg said, as panicking he stared at Frecks. 'Jesus, sometimes you just make me want to pull my friggin hair out.'

Frecks looked in puzzlement at Greg. 'What for, I don't want to be seen mate.'

'You can't walk into a fucking police station with a mask over your face, especially not these days man, Jesus they'll think you're a fucking terrorist, and shoot you on the spot, you daft fucking bat.'

'No they won't.'

'Yes they will.'

'So clever shite what do you think we should do? Eh, just let them loose to run all over the place and get ran over by a fucking car?'

'I don't know man,' Greg jumped out of the car and paced back and forth. They were parked in the Rugby club grounds opposite the police station. 'Anything but that for fucks sake, I'm not ready to be shot dead on sight. Remember one of the reasons we left the fucking army for.'

'That was in Bagdad this is fucking Houghton le spring, you for real or what?'

'It's a cop shop; God knows what they've got in there. Do you really think they tell the public everything?'

Frecks sighed, 'So what we gonna do then?'

Just then one of the dogs started barking, within seconds they were all at it.

'Shit,' Frecks jumped into the car and tried to calm them down, which in the confined place wasn't easy. 'Come on,' he yelled at Greg. 'Before somebody clocks us.'

Greg ran to the car and Frecks sped off before he had a chance to close the door. 'Hang on man, you trying to kill me off or what?'

Frecks grinned at him. 'Just had an idea.'

'And what the hell might that be?'

'Well you know that copper Lorraine Hunt?'

'Not really well, you were more friends with her than me before she went off to Uni. See her about now and then, said hello a few times, that's about all.'

'Well like you said I've known her for years and my nan lives next door to her mother and Lorraine walks her mother's dog every day, so she's obviously a dog lover, we could pop the pooches in her mother's garden.'

'Watch it.' Greg suddenly shouted as he grabbed onto the edge of his seat.

'Fucking hell,' Frecks swerved just in time to miss a van heading towards them. The van driver piped his horn, but kept moving. 'Shit was that Jacko sitting in the front?'

'Don't know Frecks, but it defo looked like Danny Jordon's van to me.'

Frecks tutted. 'Aw fuck. The gob shite will have something to say next time we're in the club.'

'Aye well, forget about that, just turn round and go to the cop shop, now.'

'What!'

'You heard.'

'No way.'

'It's the only way.' Greg was adamant.

'But what about leaving them in the garden like I said, easy way out, that way we all win, us and the dogs.'

'It won't friggin work mate, guarantee we'll be seen anyhow. So the best way is, we just pull up at the cop shop and say we found them on the road.'

'Like they gonna believe that. Even the coppers aren't that fucking stupid.'

'Or...We tell the truth.'

'Then we hide for the rest of our lives.'

'The cops will keep their gobs shut.'

Frecks laughed. 'Will they now?'

'Right, I've got it. Is that phone box in Houghton still working?'

'Why?'

'I'll phone them from there, tell the exact truth and see what they have to say about keeping us out of it.'

'Worth a shot I suppose.' Shrugging Frecks shoved the American pit bulls nose out of his ear and drove past the park and round to the back of the White Lion.

Ten minutes later Greg was back and waving a pack of dog chews, he handed a chew to each dog as he patted them.

'Righto mate, what did they say?' Frecks snarled impatiently, as he pushed Greg's hand out of the way, curling his nose up at a dog chew he was offering him as Greg laughed.

'All good. We have to meet them in a lay-by outside Of Offerton. And if it goes to court they have promised we won't have to be there, they'll say it's an anonymous tip off.'

'You sure?'

'Aye. They're over the moon to catch the bastard. Makes them look good, see.'

'Did they offer a reward?' Frecks eyes twinkled.

'No they fucking didn't.'

'Fair enough I suppose,' Frecks shrugged, 'but where the fuck is Offerton...And say what you fucking well like, the twat is still gonna know it's us.'

'Not if we say we saw the cops coming at the farm, and we did a runner.'

Frecks screwed his face up. 'For fucks sake.'

'And, by the way, Offerton is the other side of Penshaw Monument.'

Frecks looked puzzled for a moment. 'Oh right, so it is...Guess we're gonna have to brazen it out mate. OK. We'll go for it.' He started the car and headed for Penshaw.

CHAPTER THIRTY NINE

Adam finished cleaning the bathroom tiles, blue and white her favourite colours, then sitting back, looked at it with satisfaction. *She won't find any fault there...I fucking hope.*

He made his way down stairs pondering the blue carpet, he hadn't really taken it in before but just about everything in the house was blue or white, he frowned, hearing his phone ringing, quickly he got it out of his back pocket.

'Hello...Oh hi Danny, what can I do for you mate?'

Danny went on to explain their latest money making scam, and finished with. 'So we'll see you in Newbottle club this afternoon about half three OK.'

Adam looked around, he still had the hoovering to do, and she will be expecting her tea to be ready by four o clock. *Aye but if there's money involved she'll be alright about it, wont she?*

Defo. He nodded to himself.

But will she?

'Well,' he pondered for a moment, she's *been going on for ages about a spa break.* 'Right that's great see you later then mate.' He put his phone away and got the hoover out. As he bent down to plug the hoover in he noticed something lying on the floor behind the settee, scrabbling for it his fingers came up with one of her favourite lipsticks, bright red, she had been looking for it for months, making his life hell every time she thought about it.

'Brill, 'he muttered. 'That'll put a smile on her face.' With a contented smile on his own face, he put the lipstick on top of the mantel piece so she would see it as soon as she came in.

He wondered what sort of mood she'd be in tonight and if she might have to stop out at her aunts again. Her aunt Judy who he had never met was dying of cancer and needed company a lot of the time which meant Tracy had to stay overnight quite a lot lately it was really sad, but the lipstick would smooth things over.

He looked up from the lipstick to his reflection in the mirror above the fireplace. The black eye from last week was beginning to fade now, he wondered if the lads would believe he had walked into the door or take the piss.

The latter, he guessed sadly as he started to hoover.

CHAPTER FORTY

Lorraine and Luke were walking towards the hospital just as the sun disappeared behind a dark cloud and the first drops of rain were starting yet again. Lorraine was looking up at the sky when her phone rang. 'Hi Sanderson, what you got?' She stopped at the entrance and pulled on Luke's arm, tilting her head to the left for him to follow. They stopped for a minute under the side shelter of the main building.

Luke quickly stepped to one side to avoid a young woman pushing a buggy. Lorraine couldn't help but look inside and the occupant a gorgeous little one year old boy with dark brown eyes and a mop of black hair smiled up at her.

For a moment she was distracted. *Don't go there.* She told herself.

On the other end of the phone Sanderson asked if she could hear him. 'Yes, sorry.' He then told her about the dogs and the story behind them.

'Sorry Sanderson, can you start again must be something wrong with the phone.'

Sanderson repeated what he had said and Lorraine gripped Luke's arm as she told him. 'Brilliant news, of course we'll keep them out of it...Just pleased that we'll see some happy faces for once... I'll leave it to you and Dinwall to finish off...Anything on the other front?' She listened for a minute, said goodbye, then looked at Luke as she closed her phone.

'His contact is away and won't be back till tomorrow, and he's apparently not answering his personal phone,' she shrugged. 'Let's hope Scottie's found out a bit more...But in the case of his nephews missing dog, he's been found along with five others.'

'Well that's something to be pleased about. Now all we need is a way of connecting them to you know who.' Lorraine nodded her agreement and together they walked through the entrance turned right and headed for Scottie's morgue.

'Ah,' Scottie said as they walked in, he was sorting stuff in one of the many drawers, looking over his shoulder at Lorraine and Luke he went on. 'Just this minute finished. And I'm afraid it's not looking good guys.' He closed the drawer and the sound of metal instruments rang loud in the room.

Lorraine felt her heart sink, 'Shit.' She mumbled, wondering what was coming she walked over to the slab, staring at the body shape under the sheet then looked up at Scottie who was now standing on the other side.

Slowly he pulled the sheet down, his eyes flicking from the dead girl to Lorraine.

It was Luke who broke the silence. He gasped loudly then said. 'My God!'

Loraine was locked in her own mind, the carnage that had been done to the girls lower body was unbelievable. She had been cut open and the entire contents spilled out as if on display.

'We found traces of semen, so I'm certain she was raped before this happened.'

'This.' Lorraine snapped. 'This is not a happening. It's a

butchering.' She shook her head sadly as she stared again at the girl's body.

'One very depraved bastard alright.' Luke walked to the far wall, looking for something to punch, finding nothing he paced back and forth, in his years on the police force he had seen a lot, but this! Silently he vowed to find the person responsible who one way or another, would definitely suffer an accident before he made it to police custody.

Scottie moved around to Lorraine, gently he patted her arm. 'One point, she was definitley drugged, with enough to make her immobile, but sadly the poor girl was most probably still awake when this happened.'

'Shit.'

'Also, whoever he is, he's forensic aware, because there were no fibres or anything to be found on the body, nor on the silk sheet...What I'm saying is there is a tiny bit of semen is all, whither there's enough to make a match,' he shrugged. 'I think the reason her body is like this was an attempt to destroy all evidence... Really Lorraine, I'm just not sure.'

Lorraine was silent for a moment, then looking across at Scottie, said. 'Right then, thanks Scottie,' she sighed deeply then went on. 'We'll leave it to you to run the tests, and tomorrow hopefully, Sanderson will find out a bit more of what's gone on in Germany...Until then I guess there's nothing at all we can do, no leads or anything. This is some clever bastard we're dealing with here alright.'

Luke's face was grim as they ran through the heavy downpour to the car. Even in the short distance they had both become soaked through. Lorraine shook her head again as she fastened her seatbelt, scattering raindrops over the dashboard.

'Guess its home first.' Luke said as he navigated the car through the already deep puddles of water.

'Yes because I'm bloody well soaked through. Then tea at mams. God only knows what concoction Peggy's brewing up, she sighed. 'Then back to work for a couple of hours.'

Luke was quiet for a while as the rain, showing no sign of easing off lashed at the window then his sudden outburst startled Lorraine. 'God, I feel so friggin useless.' He practically shouted.

'Yeah me too, I've gone over and over in my head for a reason but can't come up with anything concrete. I mean why suicide notes when it's obviously murder?'

Luke shrugged. 'Yes, I know where you're coming from alright, and while we have nothing to go on; the bastard's free to carry on.' Just then her phone rang, looking at Luke she said. 'It's Sanderson.'

'What, oh my God...We'll be there in five.'

'What's up?'

Slowly her smile turning to a grin she said. 'We've got the bastard.'

CHAPTER FORTY ONE

Dale waited at the corner of the school for Abby, as far as he knew the bully's had left her alone this afternoon, probably because their maths teacher Mr Canstana was fairly clued up as to what went on in schools, unlike some of the teachers who it seemed to him, had their heads in the sand.

Trying to shelter behind the post from the rain which was finally easing off, and fretting because his mother had not phoned the school to say his dog was home, all he could see in his mind was his lovely dog sitting at the window waiting for him to come home. *Only tonight he won't be at the window waiting for me.*

He wiped a tear out of his eye in case anyone saw that he was crying. He knew if they did without doubt some nasty creep would poke fun at him.

His friend came through the gates. Smiling when he saw Dale, Jac asked him if he was going home as he passed with a couple of other boys. 'No Jac, not yet I'm waiting to see somebody.'

'Right then, skateboard tonight in the park?'

'No.' Dale shook his head. 'Doubt it.'

Jac, who knew about Dale's missing dog, said. 'OK mate, hope the muttly turns up. See you tomorrow.' He turned and hurried up to catch the other boys.

'Yeah, see you tomorrow.' Dale sighed.

Just then Abby hurried out of the gates, relieved that she had made it out of school without running the usual gauntlet, she smiled at Dale, but Dale was looking behind Amy at the group of girls who were sneaking up on her.

'Hey, scruffy ugly little cow.' One of them suddenly shouted as she pushed Abby in her back, and laughed as she turned to the other girls, wanting praise for her actions. The others laughed with her, spurring her on.

Abby stumbled and would have fallen if Dale hadn't caught her in time. Another reached for Abby's hair, but Dale quickly brushed her hand away. The other girls laughed and started shouting at her.

'Go away.' Dale shouted back at them.

'Found a friend have we?' The ringleader a small thickset girl with short mousy blonde hair, pushed her face into Abby's before turning to Dale and sneering. 'Or is she your girlfriend? Been kissing have you?'

Dale blushed and the girls laughed.

'Been doing more than necking on if you ask me.' One of the other girls put in.

'Yeah, getting it on youse two?' Another girl said, as again they all laughed.

'No we haven't and yes she has a friend...Me. And what's it to you?' Dale asked, he could feel Abby trembling at his side, just like next door's cat had trembled one day last month when he had found it tangled up in some barbed wire. He so wanted to put his arm around Abby, like he had the frightened cat, but he knew this lot would make something out of it, and also make big lies up as they went along.

One of them, a tall thin girl with dyed black hair, marched up to them. 'You fancy her or what, you fucking creep?' She poked Dale in his chest, as she sneered at him.

Suddenly they were all waving their arms about and shouting 'Creep.' at him. Then, surprising the girls as well as Dale, and herself, Abby jumped in front of him.

'Leave him alone.'

For a moment there was silence then one by one, the girls started to laugh, apart from two at the back who started to edge away.

'What you gonna do about it?' the dark haired girl said. 'Punch us all, come on then ugly let's see you try, rotten smelly bitch.'

She moved to the front advancing on Dale and Abby, until Emma Lumsdon came round the corner.

'What's going on here like?'

They all spun round at the sound of Emma's voice. Dale who had told Emma all about it, felt a huge relief, the last thing he wanted was to hit any girls, he knew it was wrong, though the way things had been going he might have had to, just to defend himself.

The girl with the dark hair sneered at Emma as unknown to her, the rest of her friends began to back away, and one by one they made a run for it.

'None of your business,' she said. 'So fuck off.'

'Nice.' Emma replied.

The girl moved forward. 'Gonna take us all on like?' she laughed. 'Clever shite aren't you, even you can't do that.'

'No you'll do nicely for the time being.' Emma laughed right back at her.

The girl became suspicious and quickly glanced behind her.

When she spun back her face had gone pale. 'I was only kidding Emma, you...You know that.'

'Do I?'

'Yes course you do.' She smiled, even though her body was starting to tremble.

'Well guess what.' Emma moved forward and with a stiff finger poked the girl in her chest the way she had poked Dale. 'You should know this, these two are my friends. So if I see you or any of your friends picking on them again, you know what's gonna happen...Got it?'

'Yes, sure no bother, we was just having a bit of fun.'

'Yeah right and what you did was funny, how?'

The girl stood for a moment fear all over her face, then like most bullies turned and ran after her friends.

Dale gulped. 'Wow, thanks Emma, didn't know what to do there.'

Abby staring wide eyed at Emma, nodded. 'Yes thanks. Thank you very much.'

'It's alright, Dale's helped me out before, just keep away from those waste of spacers, like all bully's, really soft as shite. Don't think you'll have any more bother with them. If you do just let me know...See you.' Emma gave a small wave before turning and going in the direction of the Seahills.

'Yeah, see you an 'all Emma,' Dale turned to Abby. 'Told you it would be alright, didn't I.'

Abby smiled. 'Yes you did.'

Suddenly Dale felt awkward he loved to see her smile, but couldn't understand why. 'I'm going home now.'

'Do you want me to walk down with you?'

'No, no than-thanks?' He could feel himself blush as he

stuttered. 'I...I'm gonna run OK.'

Quickly he took off, leaving Abby standing watching him, wondering what she had done wrong.

He spotted the police car outside of his house when he turned the corner. Gasping with delight he speeded up hoping praying that he was right and they had found his dog.

The tall police woman was coming out of the door when he reached it. The smile on her face said it all.

'Oh thank you, thank you.' He sobbed as he heard the dog barking, quickly he ran into his house.

CHAPTER FORTY TWO

Although Dinwall and Sanderson had quickly left the Blue Lion and jumped into their car, by the time they reached Newbottle there was no sign of Graham Bailes.

'Damn.' Dinwall yelled as they reached the crossroads. 'Which way? Which friggin way?'

Sanderson shrugged. 'We could try right, but there are so many roads he could take.'

'OK right it is.' Dinwall spun the wheel and with sirens blaring they headed through Newbottle village, drove down and round the roundabout and coming back on themselves headed towards Durham.

'So you know Graham Bailes don't you.'

'I do, he's about five years younger than me, but our paths crossed now and then. Actually I knew his sister Maria better she was in my year, for a wee while we had something going but it petered out. Graham always suffered from depression even as a small kid, just one of those things I guess...Never seemed to be a reason. Well not one that Maria ever knew about.' Dinwall sighed.

They reached the outskirts of Durham. 'Might as well turn back and head home.' Sanderson said.

'Guess you're right.' Dinwall drove round the roundabout

towards Houghton.

'Just had a thought, I'll phone in and see if there's any one knows what the bike reg is.' Sanderson pulled his phone out. In minutes he had the reg, and it was put on the air waves.

'So what now, back to the Blue Lion or what?'

'Well,' Dinwall screwed his face up. 'Not much point, if the other bloke needed an ambulance there was plenty there to get him one.'

'Yeah right. Any idea what it was all about?'

Dinwall shook his head. 'Could be anything, they've been warring against each other for years.'

'OK, back to the station it is.'

CHAPTER FORTY THREE

He double checked his e-mails, disappointed that work seemed to have slackened off this afternoon, although maybe's just for today. Not that he was seriously worried his diary was still fast filling up. 'And remember,' he told himself. 'I've got unfinished business tonight.'

He closed his laptop, stood and went to his window. Peering through the raindrops running down the pane he watched as the young receptionist got out of her car where she had been smoking along with another girl who worked there, and they both ran towards the hotel entrance.

A slight smile chased away his depressed look of a few minutes ago.

He felt his excitement rise at the thought of an unwilling victim.

'This will have to be seriously plotted.' He muttered as he imagined her screams.

'It's been a while.' He suppressed a giggle.

His whole body shivered in anticipation as he turned his laptop page to houses to let in the area.

He scrolled down and found one he felt would suit.

'Hmm.' He reached for his phone.

In minutes he had an appointment to view a property in Houghton Le Spring.

'Well that's sorted.' He said a few minutes later as he closed his laptop.

'What to eat for tea. Must keep my strength up.'

He grinned as he went to look out of the window. 'And there she is again, smoking her head off.'

'Really not good for you girl, in fact they just might be the death of you. Although.' His grin turned to a laugh. 'Something or somebody might get there first.'

CHAPTER FORTY FOUR

The football match was over and just in time as the heavy black clouds bursting with rain, which had been frequently occurring on and off in the North East most of the day were quickly coming back their way. A very happy Vanessa, because Darren had scored three goals, and she had seen at least two football scouts writing in their notebooks after each goal, walked down towards home with Sandra and Christina, Jacko's soon to be wife. Shivering Sandra looked up at the sky, about to remark on how nippy it had become, she was beaten to it by Vanessa.

'God I'm so bloody freezing.'

'Me too, hang on a bit.' Christina stopped walking, pulling her green wool cardigan out of her bag and passing her coat to Vanessa to hold, she shrugged into her cardigan and taking her coat back she put it on top and fastened the zip up to her chin. 'It really shouldn't be this damn cold.'

'You're right there...So anyhow, is the date set?' Vanessa asked.

'Well, we're thinking about late May next year, or probs early June.'

'June would be nice.' Sandra said. 'The sun should be out by then...I hope.'

'Yes I know, I think we'll probably go with that. I always wanted to be a June bride ever since I was little.' She smiled happily at them both.

'Yes, me an 'all, and especially since all those years ago when I was a kid and saw Seven Brides For Seven Brothers. Remember that Sandra?' Vanessa turned to Sandra.

'Sure do,' she smiled. 'We were eight and watched together in my aunt's, remember?'

Vanessa nodded. 'Yes that tiny little screen...I think it was an old film even then. Anyhow, am I a bridesmaid?' Vanessa asked, her eyebrows raised in a question.

Christina laughed. 'Sorry but the jobs already taken by Melanie who is really excited to death.'

'Bet Doris is over the moon as well.'

'She is now. At first she was a bit worried that we would be living somewhere else, but no, we're staying put. We've told her that she has a home with us forever.'

'Aw nice...Bet that was a relief for her, anyhow she makes fab pies, especially the corned beef ones, so youse won't go hungry.' Vanessa laughed.

'I know aren't they great, love her roast beef and Yorkshire puddings as well.'

They reached their street and saw the ambulance parked at the curb near to Mr Skillings gate.

'Shit what the hell's going on?' Vanessa yelled. Her heart pounding, she quickly, with the other two dogging her heels ran towards the ambulance.

They could hear a voice protesting loudly as they ran to the open doors at the back of the ambulance.

'What's happened?' Vanessa panted, as she looked into the

ambulance fearing the worst.

Mr Skillings eyes opened wide when he saw Vanessa. 'Thank God...Tell them I'm alright Vanessa, don't let them take me- don't need to go to no hospital, nowt wrong with me. But this bugger won't listen.'

Vanessa looked at the ambulance man.

'He's had a nasty fall love. In my opinion he needs to go for a check up.'

'I didn't fall; I told you twice didn't I. 'Cos I was bloody well knocked over.'

'Where did it hit you?'

'Not exactly hit, managed to fall outta the way, else he would have, and the bastard had to see me fall but he just kept going. Nice bloke, eh.'

'But who was it?' Sandra asked.

For a minute Mr Skillings eyes narrowed as he stared at Sandra, then slowly shaking his head he said 'How the hell do I know, the bugger was going too fast, friggin maniac.'

'Please Mr Skillings can you calm down, please. You're not doing your blood pressure any good.' The ambulance man said, as he climbed into the back. Mr Skillings tried to get up, still demanding that he didn't want to go to the hospital.

Vanessa, who hadn't missed the look Mr Skillings had given Sandra, looked at Sandra and shook her head. 'I think you best go with Mr Skillings, while I go home and sort my bloody lot out. I'll phone in half an hour to see what's going on and if youse can come home, don't worry I'll get somebody to pick you up. If he has to stay I'll come in.'

'Sound's like a plan.' Sandra agreed. Looking at the ambulance man, who smiled at her, and mouthed 'Thank you.'

Mr Skillings sat back down and slowly nodded, he gave a small wave to Vanessa as Sandra climbed into the ambulance and the doors closed, just before they did the ambulance man turned and winked at Vanessa, then the ambulance pulled away.

Vanessa turned to the small crowd of neighbours, spotting Doris and Dolly, she said with a puzzled frown. 'Did anybody see what really went on here?'

Dolly shook her head, it was Doris who answered. 'Don't think anybody did, I just came to the gate and saw him lying on the path. He said it's his back, he's adamant that it was a car speeding up the street...Poor old sod.'

Vanessa looked at the other eight or nine people standing there, they all shook their heads.

'It's a bloody shame when you can't cross your own flaming street for bloody boy racers thinking they own the place.' Doris moaned, as the small crowd started to disperse. Most of them muttering and agreeing with Doris.

'And I just bet they don't even live here.' Dolly put in.

'Stupid idiot not the first time I've seen drivers treat this road like a racing track.' Christina shook her head.

'I know what to do Christina, I'll pop over Trevor's and see if he'll take me to the hospital to pick them up, either later on or tomorrow if they keep him in.'

'You do that and I'll come back to yours later, see what's what. And if they keep him in Sandra will still need picking up, and if Trevor can't do it, I think Jacko will sort that out.'

'Yeah I did say, but if you're gonna ask Jacko that's fine by me love.'

'OK, see you in a bit. Oh there was something else I wanted to ask you,' Christina turned back to Vanessa. 'Is Sandra alright?

Only she's been very quiet today.'

'Yes she's fine,' As much as they both liked Christina, Vanessa knew it wasn't her place to tell what was really wrong with Sandra.

'Good.'

'Right then I'll catch you later Christina, got the animals to feed they'll be descending like a bunch of vultures any minute now...Oh Oh, here comes the rain again.' Both of them quickly made their way home.

Vanessa glanced up the street to Sandra's house. With a frown she went through her own front door, deciding it had to be something quick which was looking like it was going to be, egg, beans and chips for tea, which she guessed the gang would most likely be quite happy with.

Tough if they're not. She dug the chip pan out and started peeling the potatoes.

CHAPTER FORTY FIVE

Frecks and Greg, had both been nervous but the police had kept to their word and didn't even ask for their names as they handed the dogs over. They watched as the dogs were put in to a van, the American pit bull, the last to get in, looked back at Frecks and wagged her tail.

Frecks sniffed and looked away.

Greg elbowed him in his ribs as he said. 'Don't go all soft on me now. We did the right thing.'

'I know...I know.'

And with Greg now feeling really pleased that he had gone along with it, they decided to treat themselves to a pint or two up Newbottle club.

Passing Adam on his way out of the club, they said hello and walked into the bar. Frecks heart sank when he saw Jacko and his mates sitting at a table near the dartboard.

Leaning on the bar and pretending that he hadn't seen them. Frecks asked for two pints, before leaning towards Greg and whispering. 'Shit, look who's sitting over there. Think we should down these and do a runner mate?'

'No...Anyhow I saw them when we walked in. Thought you had as well?'

Frecks shook his head, the next minute he jumped in shock when he felt someone tap his shoulder. 'Who's that? Jesus man, you frightened the friggin life outta me.' He turned to see Danny looking at him.

'Got a minute mate?'

'Aye...Why aye mate.'

'Good, would both of you come over here for a minute, where we can talk eh?'

Frecks dreading what was about to come, sat down heavily next to Jacko, while Greg parked himself next to Len. 'OK,' Danny sat down, 'here it is lads, we really need you to work with us, fancy a bit of extra cash?'

Frecks and Greg's interest perked right up. Frecks thinking with relief that Danny must not have realised that it was him driving the car, they nearly crashed into leaned forward. 'Oh, aye, what you got then?'

Five minutes later Danny had filled them both in on their latest scam, sitting back with a grin on his face, Frecks over the moon that Danny hadn't mentioned once that they had had a near miss with a car, and praying that it was because they hadn't recognised them, said, 'Wow, I'm well up for that lads we'll make a killing, how about you Greg?'

Greg nodded. 'Yeah I'm fine with that.'

'Good, the more people we have, the more markets we can do.' Danny said with satisfaction, as he leaned back in his seat and gave a knowing nod to the others.

Suddenly frowning, Frecks looked at them all. 'Oh bloody hell. There's something I've gotta do guys.' He jumped off his seat and took off with speed towards the doors. The others looked at

Greg who shrugged.

A few minutes later Frecks was back. 'Jesus,' he wiped his brow as he sat down and picked his pint up. Letting out a huge sigh, he said. 'I've just downloaded half me fucking colon.'

They all laughed except for Len who said. 'What?'

Looking at each other they laughed even louder.

Standing up Danny shook his head at Len. 'Not to worry Len, I'll explain it all to you later.'

CHAPTER FORTY SIX

After leaving the club, and promising to be ready when they came for him, Adam cycled down to Houghton and called into the flower shop in the main street. Looking around at the selection, he wondered which ones to get, then his eyes fell on the flowers she loved the most.

White roses, that's her favourite, got to try and keep her sweet. These and a nice lovely dinner should make her happy...Well, they should! He handed the money over to the old woman behind the till, checking his change with a smile, he said goodbye and quickly headed home.

He wondered for a moment as he rode past Dale's house if the lad had got his dog back, glancing at his watch he realised that there was no time for to pop in and see, her ladyship will be wanting her tea on time. *I'll phone later.* He decided, then felt quite happy knowing he would be able to afford the Spa break she'd been going on about for a while now.

That'll put a smile on her face.

YES!

He was surprised as he walked his bike up the path and looked in the window, to not see her sitting watching the telly. She had said earlier that when she came back from her aunts she was going to dig a few of her favourite films out and just chill out all day. He knew for a fact that one of them would be Steve McQueen in 'The Great Escape.' His heart sank for a moment, knowing how many times recently that he'd wanted to escape, the constant screaming, the slaps the punches, scalding tea thrown over his legs, rows springing up from nowhere.

But I love her.

Don't I?

Course I do.

Having to spend some nights with her aunt certainly took it out of her, he knew this. From what she had told him the old lady certainly needed a lot of looking after.

She doesn't mean it, when she goes off on one.

Course she doesn't.

Things will get better. I know they will.

Locking his bike in the shed he went through the back door, and shouted. 'It's me love...You in?'

Receiving no answer he walked through to the sitting room, feeling the radiators on the way and finding them cold, he went back to the kitchen to switch them on. With a shiver he then crept silently up stairs. If she was asleep the last thing he dared do was wake her up, he'd found that out the hard way.

Frowning he looked round the room then at the empty bed, his frown deepening, he slowly moved to the spare room, which she sometimes crashed in.

'Where the hell is she?' he muttered, looking at another empty bed.

Going back down stairs he walked into the kitchen, wondering if her aunt had maybe's took a turn for the worst. With a shrug he started to prepare their meal. Suddenly he put the peeling knife down and went into the sitting room, she usually left a note of the fireplace if she was going to stop over, or she'd had to rush off somewhere.

No nothing. He stared at the fireplace.

Deciding to give her a ring, he took his phone out. After letting it ring for five minutes and receiving no answer, he put his phone away and went back to the kitchen. Where he continued to peel the potatoes, but somehow could throw the feeling off that something was wrong.

CHAPTER FORTY SEVEN

Lorraine and Luke pulled up outside of a large private house near Ryhope. The house secreted away behind other fabulous but not so large houses, was more than impressive. A long winding drive led up to the house where six huge white pillars, three on each side were holding up a stone canopy with a huge stags head on top, below the canopy there were double red doors. On Lorraine's instructions the two police officers, whom they had picked up at Shiney row, quickly moved to the back of the property. As Lorraine lifted the large brass knocker, Luke sneezed.

Lorraine, her hand still holding the knocker looked at him with disdain. 'Please don't say you've really gone and caught a cold.'

'What do you expect driving around in wet clothes?' He sniffed and sneezed again.

Lorraine pulled a pack of paper handkerchiefs out of her pocket and tossed them over to him, 'Here...And your clothes are just a bit damp, same as mine, bloody soft shite, not fresh out of a friggin washer.' She let the heavy knocker drop against the door and did it four more times before she could hear someone unlocking the door from the other side.

Opening the pack, Luke muttered, 'Thanks for the sympathy.'

Ignoring him Lorraine concentrated on the door. 'At last.' She said as the door opened.

Holding her badge up she stared at the tall dark haired man wearing a white fluffy dressing gown, who frowned down at her.

'Disturbed you have we?'

'What do you want?' He sneered down at Lorraine.

'You.' Lorraine put her foot in the doorway, as she smiled sweetly at him. 'Strange I thought with a house this grand you would at least have had a footman to open the door for you.' She pushed the door hard when she saw his knuckles turn white as he gripped the door even tighter, and stepped inside before he had a chance to slam it. The man's eyes were narrow angry slits as they flickered from Lorraine to Luke who was close behind her.

'This is private property,' He stated angrily, as a young blonde woman in a scarlet silk dressing gown, came mincing down the stairs. 'And you're not welcome.'

'Tough.' Luke said.

'What's up darling?' The woman drawled in an America accent as she smiled at Luke, and flashed her eyelashes at him.

Ignoring her Lorraine said. 'OK enough pissing about, get dressed, you're going to the station. John, David, Gerry or whatever you're calling yourself these days.'

'In your dreams.'

'Cuff him.' She said to the two policemen who had quietly came up behind him.

'What the?' He tried to spin round but one policeman had a tight grip on his arms while the other slid the handcuffs on him, as Lorraine read him his rights.

The woman gasped, as she quickly moved to the side. 'What the hell's going on Simon?'

'Simon now is it?' Lorraine smiled at him.

The woman glared at Lorraine. 'At least have the decency to let him put some clothes on.'

Lorraine shrugged. 'Doesn't bother me whichever way he comes,' she turned her attentions to the still glowering man. 'You have five minutes.'

'We'll go up with him.' Luke gestured with his head for the two policemen to follow as he took hold of the man's arm, ignoring the man's tensed up muscles, he began to lead him towards the stairs.

'But what's he done?'

Lorraine looked at the woman. 'How long is your arm?'

'What do you mean?'

Groaning inwardly, Lorraine said. 'That's how long the bloody list is.' She stopped short of adding. *You friggin thick twat.* When the woman turned and rushed up the stairs.

To Lorraine it was obvious that the woman, wife or girlfriend had gone to get dressed, she took the opportunity to look around the large hallway.

On a desk holding a large blue vase, full of white roses there was a telephone and a couple of letters, picking the letters up she saw that they were both addressed to a Mr Simon Compton. *Hmm that's a new one alright.* Quickly she phoned the station.

It was Dinwall who answered. 'Get me everything you can on a Simon Compton, double quick.'

She read out the address and Dinwall answered. 'On it now boss.'

Quickly she put her phone in her pocket and hearing shouting from up stairs she walked over to the wide staircase, it was the sort of staircase you would expect royalty to walk down, the carpet was red and the banisters were painted gold. *Wonder how many dogs died to pay for this, or how many kids lost their mind, and their life, through the drugs the bastards peddled.*

'What's going on up there?' She shouted.

'He's refusing to let us dress him.' Luke shouted back.

'Bring the bastard the way he is then, who's bothered.'

'You'll pay for this bitch.' The now Simon Compton yelled.

'Yeah right, just move it creep.'

There were more shouting and banging noises, but after a few minutes they all appeared at the top of the stairs. Compton was wearing jeans and a purple shirt.

'About bloody time.' Lorraine snapped. Turning she headed out of the door and went to the car.

At the station, Lorraine handed him over, when he was locked up and out of sight she said to the desk sergeant. 'We'll be back later to interview him, for the moment the nasty git can stew.'

The desk sergeant smiled and nodded, as Lorraine and Luke left.

CHAPTER FORTY EIGHT

Jacko, Danny and Len, up front and with Frecks and Greg in the back of the van, arrived outside of Adam's just as he was walking up his path with his bike, with a full carrier bag on the right handlebar. He'd decided that with no time to do the dinner, he'd planned to just make a ham salad instead. And not really knowing when she would be in, he had rushed back out to the shops.

Danny bipped the van horn; getting a shock Adam spun round. 'Daft sod,' he said as all five of them laughed.

'You're early.'

'Yeah early bird and all that,' Danny said. 'Come on then get a move on.'

'Two minutes, just had to run back to the shop. Forgot a few things.'

'Make it quick then mate.'

'OK, got to take these in first and put me bike away.' He wheeled the bike round to the back gate, and went into the house through the kitchen door, half expecting to find her sitting there, but no after a quick look the house was still empty. He quickly put the ham and the things he'd bought for the salad in the fridge. Grabbed two plates and the cutlery and set the table. So it would at least look like he was ready to prepare the meal.

Five minutes later they were still waiting.

'What the fuck's he doing?' Danny looked at the other four.

'God knows.' Jacko said, as Len tutted at him.

'Probs having a quickie.' Frecks grinned as Len looked down his nose at him.

About to slam his fist on the horn again, Danny stopped as the front door opened and Adam came out.

'Alright, so, where we going?' Jacko asked when Adam had jumped into the van.

'Sorry lads just had to sort a few things out. Adam fastened his seat belt.

'Washington Galleries for us four, you and Len do Asda, while me and Adam do Sainsbury. Then we swap over.'

'What about us?' Frecks asked.

'I'm dropping youse two at Tesco's in Durham first, before we go to the Galls then, when we come to pick youse two up, we'll go in.'

'Sounds like a plan.' Jacko nodded.

Danny grinned. 'So it does.'

Len walked up to the till next to the store attendant, trying to look puzzled, which really wasn't hard, he held out his two cans of beans. 'Can you give me a hand here please; I've never used one of these before?'

'Of course,' she smiled, this is what you do.' She took a can and put it through the scanner and waited for Len to do the same with the remaining can.

After a moment Len looked at her, after another awkward few moments in which he was still staring at her, she picked the other can up and shoved it through.

'You put your money in there.' She pointed to the coin slot.

'Oh OK. But does it know that if you buy two cans they're on special offer?'

'Yes.'

'Will it give me the right change?'

She looked at the pound coin in his hand. 'Certainly.'

'Clever things these machines aren't they.'

'Yes, they certainly are... Do you want a bag?'

'Not if they're five pence.'

'OK.' Looking away she hid a smile, as his five pence change dropped.

Seeing Jacko quickly walk past with three heavy laden bags. Len grabbed his five pence, thanked the assistant and quickly followed Jacko. His tins clutched to his chest, the receipt trapped between his fingers and flapping about like a flag, he quickly passed Jacko and spotted the van in the car park. He was sweating when he got there. Danny jumped out and opened the door for him and Jacko.

Len heaved a huge sigh. 'I'm well pleased that's over mate.' Putting the cans on his seat, he took a perfectly folded white handkerchief out of his pocket he shook it open and wiped the sweat of his brow.

'Wow mate,' Danny said to Jacko, 'Looks like you've done very well indeed.'

Jacko heaved his bags into the back. 'Aye man, seven joints of pork, four beef and four lamb, plus half a dozen packs of steak and a couple packs of sausage.'

'Beats us mate...Three beef, two lamb, half a dozen packs of pork chops, and five packs of the best bacon.'

'Wonder how Frecks and Greg have done?' Len said as he put his cans of beans into the carrier bag next to the two cans Adam had got.

'See you wasted money on a carrier bag Adam.'

Adam groaned. 'What the hell did you expect me to do Len, carry them with my teeth?'

'It's alright Len we need the bags for the customers,' Danny said. 'Anybody got a stash at home?'

'Oh, never thought of that.'

'Aye, me mother's got a stash, she throws nowt away. I'll sort them out later.' Jacko winked at Danny.

'We've got some an 'all.' Adam said, as Danny drove off and headed towards Asda's to drop Len and Jacko off, while they returned to Sainsbury's to repeat the action.

Forty five minutes later, they pulled up outside of Tesco's Durham.

'Get in!' Danny said, as he spotted Frecks and Greg standing outside with two full carrier bags each.

'Good haul mate?' Jacko asked as they reached the van.

'Why aye man, half a dozen joints, loads of sausage and bacon, it's a doddle.' Frecks said, as they climbed in the van.

'Where should I put these cans?' Greg asked.

'Give them to me.' Len reached for them and dropped them into the bag with the others.

'Right, youse two wait here, while we go in.'

'Hang on,' Jacko said, 'I think we might have been making a mistake.'

'How's that?' Danny frowned at him.

'Well, don't you think it might look a bit suspicious if four blokes walk in together?

They all looked at the doors and watched as a lot of women by themselves went inside, a good few couples, two men together, and just the odd lone man.

'Aye you might be right there,' Danny said. 'I'll go first, then after a few minutes, youse follow one by one. Sort of mingle with the crowd.'

Back on the road again with no mishaps and a massive haul, the crew were very happy until Jacko said. 'So where we gonna put it all, till we do the markets tomorrow?'

'Shit.' If Danny hadn't been driving he might have froze, luckily there was a parking sign coming up.

Having pulled over he turned to them. 'Why the hell did I not think of that. Shit fuck shit!'

'Oh dear.' Len said.

Danny glared at him. 'Not helping Len.'

Len pulled a face at Danny.

'Guess we'll all have to take a couple of bags home each. And put them in the fridge.' Danny said.

Len shrugged. 'Good job I've got a large separate freezer as well. Really you should have thought about this.'

'Yes Len.' Danny glared at him. 'I think we all know that now, alright.'

Greg looked quickly at Frecks, before turning to the rest and saying. 'We won't be able to do that guys.' He looked again at Frecks.

'Why?' Len looked suspiciously from one to the other, as he brushed imaginary dust off his trousers.

'We em, 'cos we both in digs like,' Frecks answered, unable

to meet Len's eyes. 'Don't think the landlady will be too happy about us filling her fridge up, she'll probs have a hissy fit, she's a right miserable git to start with.'

He didn't tell them that their digs were now in Hetton park on a bench each, because some clever shite grassed them up for sleeping on his grandmothers floor, and she got into all sorts of trouble with the council and was landed with a heavy bill that they were doing their best to pay off. Neither did they tell them that their bathroom was Hetton baths, and that the landlady was Mother Nature, as is the lot of many an ex soldier.

'OK, we'll manage somehow. It will only be for a little bit, 'cos we're gonna sell like hell, aren't we lads. So what markets you got booked then?' Jacko looked at Danny hoping that he had at least done that.

'Well...I thought we could sell from the van on one of the lay-bys first. Just to see how things go, you know what I mean. I've seen loads of vans doing that.'

'No Danny I don't know what you mean. You told us it would be markets. For fucks sake.'

'Well lads,' Danny looked at them all in turn. 'You know that was before I found out you had to have a friggin licence to sell foodstuffs on the markets, so I thought...'

'You thought we would just pull up somewhere and start to sell food from an unrefrigerated van. You right in the head or what?'

'So I made a friggin mistake, thought people just pulled in and set up shop.' Danny's fingers were tapping nervously on the steering wheel.

'Fucking hell!' Adam looked open mouthed from one to the other. The only thing on his mind was if this blew up in their faces there would be no spa day, and hell to pay. He groaned inwardly, just when he thought this job would keep her sweet.

'I know,' Len grinned and clapped his hands. 'We could go round the clubs tonight, remember when the fish man used to come selling crab sticks and things.' They all looked at Len in amazement.

Danny was the first one to slap him on the back. 'Well done mate, brill idea.'

'Anybody got any of those straw basket things, you know like the fish man used to come round the clubs with?' Danny asked.

'Aye got half a dozen on me allotment.'

'Cheers Len, you saved the day.'

Len preened himself like a strutting cockerel, as the others grinned and patted his back.

CHAPTER FORTY NINE

Vanessa's phone rang, the caller ID said it was Sandra. 'Hello love what's happening?'

'He's fine, sprained a couple of muscles in his back, but he can come home now. They've gave him loads of painkillers, should be back to his usual self in a few weeks.'

'That's great I'll see if Christina's sorted Jacko out for a lift. Be there as soon as.'

'OK love. We'll be waiting out the front, 'cos we're both going crazy for a ciggie.'

'Thought you were packing in?'

'Well I was...I am...Just not yet.'

'OK.' Vanessa said goodbye and closing her phone, shouted up stairs to put an end to the row she could hear brewing between Kerry and Claire. 'Right youse two, zip it now.'

'It's not me Mam.' Claire yelled down the stairs. 'It's her, lady muck, our Kerry.'

'Not it's not, bitch.'

'Enough the lot of you.' Vanessa shouted back, she could hear Emma laughing. 'Robbie, sort those two out, and Emma get your nose out...I'm off to pick Sandra and Mr Skillings up.'

'OK Mam.' Robbie groaned, as Vanessa closed the door

behind her.

Shaking her head Vanessa crossed the road and went over to Jacko's house. *Friggin teenage girls, who would have them. Give me lads every time.*

She was about to knock on the door when it was opened by Christina. 'Saw you coming love. I'm sorry but Jacko won't be able to pick them up, he's out on a job, unless it's a couple of hours or so, cos I don't know exactly what time he'll be back.' She looked at her watch and shrugged.

'Damn...Never mind, it's alright though Christina, I'll ask Clive up the street 'cos I saw Trevor passing in his car ten minutes ago he must have gone out as well. Clive will probs do it. He sometimes plays bowls with the terrible trio.'

Christina laughed, knowing she meant Dolly, Doris and Mr Skillings.

Five minutes later Vanessa was on her way to the hospital and being serenaded by Clive, white haired and thick set he considered himself a better singer than Tom Jones, as he belted out, Green Green Grass Of Home, in a deep grating voice.

Sandra and Mr Skillings were waiting outside of the entrance as Clive pulled up. Vanessa jumped quickly out of the car, to help Sandra with Mr Skillings.

'I'm fine.' Mr Skillings kept repeating as they manouvred him into the back seat, pulling a face at Vanessa, Sandra took the wheel chair back to reception.

For the next fifteen minutes, the journey made longer by catching every red light there was- they were treat to just about every song Tom Jones had ever sang.

Relieved to give their ears a break, it was hard to tell who jumped out of the car first when they arrived outside of Mr Skillings house, Vanessa or Sandra.

'Thanks Clive,' Vanessa said, we'll take it from here love.'

'No bother at all.' Clive grinned. 'I'll help you in to the house with him.'

'No.' Sandra quickly replied. 'We can manage him, cheers love. You've done your bit.'

'It's no bother, the old bugger needs a bit of help, so I'm your man.'

'I am here you know.' Mr Skillings said. As Clive got out of the car and took his left arm.

Vanessa pulled a face, behind his back, and mouthed to Sandra. 'One more bloody Tom Jones song and I swear to God I'll fucking kill him.'

Sandra laughed, together the three of them with a struggle, managed to get Mr Skillings up his path and sitting in his favourite chair by the fire.

'Right then I'm off now,' Clive said. 'Gotta feed the hounds.' Clive had two racing dogs that he adored, and regularly raced them at Sunderland dog track.

'Thank you very much for your help. But what about the petrol money, how much do I owe you?'

Clive backed away holding his hands in the air. 'No worries I've got it sorted. In my book if you can't help a mate out, then you ain't no mate.'

'Thank you very much.' Mr Skillings replied with a big smile, as Clive turned to go.

Vanessa and Sandra also both thanked him for his help, turning to Mr Skillings, Sandra said. 'Tell you what Mr Skillings, how about I go to the fish shop grab a fish lot each for our tea, cos

I'm bloody starving.'

'Yes, that'll be great I'm hungry as well.' He felt around his jacket pockets for his wallet.

'No, Mr Skillings, this one's on me.' Quickly Sandra left before he could argue with her.

Watching out of the window as Sandra walked down the path, Vanessa then turned to Mr Skillings. 'Ok, what's up with the nods and looks?'

'It was him.'

'Who?' She held her hands out palm up, with a questioning look on her face. 'What was him?'

'The bloody bloke who ran me over silly...It, well it was Sandra's husband.'

'What!'

'Yes, he was definitely driving, and that nasty Tracy Brewer person was in the car sitting next to him.' He looked down at the table by his side, saw his cigarettes, heaved a sigh of relief as he took one out of the packet. He thought he had lost them at the hospital and had fretted that the cash he had, wouldn't run to another pack for today.

As he lit one of his twenty a day habit up, Vanessa stared at him, in shock, and said 'No way.'

'Yes, and trust me, they were in one almighty hurry to get some bloody where.'

'But what the hell was she doing in the car?'

Mr Skillings shrugged. 'Don't know. She was looking very smug though.'

'Are you sure it was her?'

'Oh yes.'

Puzzled Vanessa went into the kitchen, looking for something to do. Her eyes fell on a couple of plates and a cup in the sink. 'I'll just wash these up for you.' She said over her shoulder.

'There's no need love.'

'It's no bother.'

'Em, Vanessa.'

'What love?'

'I was wondering, if you or Sandra would draw my pension for me tomorrow. Oh and cancel that doc's appointment till next week. Please.'

'Consider it done.'

Waiting for the sink to fill up she stared out the window into the back garden, her mind on Sandra's husband.

She had never been keen on John, since the day she had met him, even though he had actually turned out to be a good husband to Sandra and a good father to the kids. But there had been something there from day one, even through the alcoholic fuzz all those years ago there had been something she couldn't quite put her finger on.

Surely he's not cheating with Tracy Brewer of all people.

He wouldn't.

That'll kill Sandra.

No way...He'll have just been giving her a lift somewhere. She must have stopped him in the street and asked for a lift.

There'll be a legitimate reason.

She shook her head, as she muttered. 'But why didn't he stop when he knocked Mr Skillings over?'

Shit, Sandra must never find out it was him, she's got enough on her plate.

Going back into the sitting room she sat down opposite Mr Skillings. 'Please tell me that you're not going to let her know that it was John who nearly ran you over?'

'What...No way...But what do you think he was doing with her in the car?'

Vanessa heaved a sigh. 'Probs just dropping her off somewhere.'

'Do you think.'

'Why aye.'

CHAPTER FIFTY

He was just about to pass a lay-by when his phone rang; quickly he pulled over as the car driver behind him pipped his horn. He piped back and opening the window, he thrust his arm out and stuck his middle finger up, shouting, 'Fuck off twat. Do you know who you're dealing with? Prick.' As he brought the car to a halt.

He pulled his phone out and checked the caller ID and smiled.

'Hello there, how are you?'

'Fine. How's business?'

'Couldn't be better, picked quite a few clients up. Actually I'm thinking about moving up here, it's not a bad place at all- for the time being anyhow.'

'Good anything to show me?'

'Oh hell yes. I'll be posting a couple later on tonight, how about you?'

'Did a fantastic one last night, the fool, oh my God you won't believe what she wanted me to do.'

'Show me.' He could feel himself becoming exited.

'Show me yours first.'

He laughed. 'Come on you've already seen it.'

'True,' it was his callers turn to laugh. 'OK, I'll tell you a bit but not enough to spoil it for you.'

'Come on then.'

Five minutes later smiling and breathing deeply he pulled out into the traffic, knowing that he had taught his trainee well.

He reached his destination with a few minutes to spare. Quickly he whipped his comb out and ran it through his hair.

One has to be smart for these occasions. He thought.

Getting out of the car he walked up the drive and rang the doorbell.

CHAPTER FIFTY ONE

After calling back home to change their clothes, because of Luke's insistence, they were finally finishing their meal at Mavis's house. Peggy with frequent flicks of her bright red hair picked up everyone's plate and made her way into the kitchen.

'I really don't think Lasagne is an Australian dish...Do you?' Lorraine looked at Luke.

Luke grinned. 'Yeah I was thinking pretty much the same thing. Definitely not from Australia.'

'Hmm, nice though mind.' Mavis said. 'And please Lorry, put her out of her misery with that bloody hair of hers. I fear she's gonna break her neck if she flings it to one side again.'

Lorraine laughed, 'OK Mam.'

Peggy came back in carrying a huge dish of Pavlov. 'Here it is guys my Australian dish.' She put the bowl on the table with a flourish.

Lorraine laughed. 'Looks good but we thought that you meant the lasagne was Australian.'

'No.' Pulling a face at Lorraine, Peggy did another flick of her hair.

'Isn't Pavlov a New Zealand national dish?' Luke asked. His spoon poised in his hand

'No way.' Peggy glared at him.

'Just thought I had read somewhere that the two Country's were claiming it as their own.'

'Nonsense.'

'Whatever Peggy, it looks lovely, nearly as nice as your hair.' Lorraine smiled at her.

Peggy nearly did a pirouette. 'I know,' she flicked her hair again. 'Don't I just suit it?'

'Course you do Peggy. It takes years off you.'

'Really!'

Lorraine picked up her spoon, tentatively she tasted the Pavlov. 'Oh yes I mean it,' she smacked her lips. 'And this is fab.'

'Well,' Luke patted his mouth with his napkin, a few minutes later. 'Don't care who the hell claims it, Peggy that was simply lovely.'

'Thank you kind sir.' Peggy flirted with her eyes.

'It really was.' Lorraine and Mavis said together.

'I'm well stuffed.' Luke rose from his chair and stacked the bowls ready to take them into the kitchen, but Peggy grabbed them off him.

Looking at Lorraine she said. 'I've told you before this one's a keeper pet. You listen to me I know about these things. Keep tight hold. But you know if you ever get sick of him.' She winked at Luke.

Lorraine rolled her eyes, 'Yes I guess he is. A keeper, so jog on Peggy.'

Grinning Luke patted his stomach. 'Now ladies please. And we gonna have to take the mutt for a walk, probs put on a half a stone with that really fab meal Peggy.'

'Yeah me too,' Lorraine said. 'Duke,' she shouted. 'Come on, walkies. Be back in half an hour Mam.' Duke appeared a few seconds later with his leader in his mouth and tail wagging hard, Lorraine patted his head.

Good.' Peggy said. 'Cos believe me I've got loads of pics to show youse both, and you Mavis. Because I've been keeping them till we're all together.'

Mavis pulled a pained face behind Peggy's back, as she said. 'Oh can't wait.'

Looking at Luke, Lorraine groaned inwardly, while Luke tried not to grin.

They walked up the Burnside to the beck, where Lorraine let Duke off the lead, Duke was both human friendly and dog friendly, and always obeyed his return whistle, so they had no qualms on letting him run. They passed a young man who was out jogging; Lorraine couldn't help but notice his pale blue trainers.

'Not another one.'

'What do you mean?'

'It seems just about everyone I've seen today is wearing the same trainers.'

'You're over-thinking my love, not everybody is rogue, maybe's they are the latest thing.'

'Hmm maybe's.'

Lorraine whistled for Duke. A few minutes later when he had not put in an appearance, she whistled again. 'Where the hell?'

Her heart in her mouth, she anxiously looked around, just as Duke came bounding out of the trees on their left.

Breathing a sigh of relief, and with Luke knowing exactly what she had been thinking, they headed for her mother's house, where they spent the next half an hour looking at endless photographs because Peggy had been right, she certainly did have loads to show them.

'Right Peggy, great photos, but we've got to go now, there's Someone we have to interview.'

'Oh, is he one of the bad guys?'

'Well why would I be interviewing him if he wasn't.'

'I mean one of the really bad guys.' Peggy's eyes were wide.

'Yes Peggy a complete arsehole in every respect.'

Peggy trembled. 'Oh I so love it when you catch the real scum.'

CHAPTER FIFTY TWO

The meeting had taken a while longer than he'd thought it would have, he so hated it when his clients turned out to be fussy.

Arriving back at the hotel at six thirty, He casually strolled into the lounge, which was decorated in mostly red, from the thick carpets to the leather settees, red the lovely colour of blood. Now that was his favourite colour.

And there she was sitting near the window with a glass of red wine. His whole body tingled.

Tanya turned away from the view when he was half way across the almost deserted room. There was only one other couple in the far corner, and judging by the miserable looks on both their faces, he guessed they were not having a good time.

'Well hello there.' He said when he reached her, taking in her navy lace dress which even sitting down he could see was very short, sleeveless and cut low at the top so that her breasts nearly spilled over.

'Hello yourself.' Tanya smiled up at him.

He sat on the chair opposite so he could watch her breasts move with every little move she made.

'I thought you weren't going to make it.' She batted her blue eyes. He particularly liked the way they seemed to sparkle.

'I wouldn't miss this for the world... Your eyes,' he smiled at her. 'Are so beautiful.'

She blushed. 'Do you really think that?'

'Of course I do, you must have been told this before. Of course you have,' he stared deep into her eyes, as she blushed again. 'What would you like to eat?' He picked up one of the menus and handed it to her.

'What ever you're having.'

'Rare steak it is then.'

'Oh Sorry, but no thanks, I don't like it rare, could I have mine well done please?'

Because his face was hidden by the menu Tanya didn't see the evil look that passed over it.

When he put the menu down his smile was firmly back in place. 'Course you can, you can have anything you want. Beautiful lady.'

She continued flirting with him for the next hour as they ate their meal, until he glanced at his watch, then quickly standing up he said. 'Sorry but I have to go now.'

'What!' Tanya was amazed, she had felt that he was walking right into her trap, and she could tell he was gagging for it. 'But I thought?'

'Yes, but there will be other nights, I have to meet a client who's about to leave the country early tomorrow morning, so it's tonight or never. We can do this again because it looks like I'm going to be around for a while.'

She raised her eyebrows. 'Are you?'

'I most certainly am. How about tomorrow night?'

'Yes, of course we can.' she replied quickly as she raised her eyebrows in a question. 'Same time? Same place?'

'Fine by me, goodnight lovely.'

'Yes same to you.' She muttered as he walked away.

Tanya pulled a face at her friend Rula who had been sitting outside watching them. A moment later she was at the table, camera around her neck staring down at her.

'What the fuck just happened?'

'He had somewhere to go.'

'Damn.'

'Yeah couldn't quite believe it myself, thought he was...In fact I'm sure he was raring to go.'

'Hope you not losing your touch?'

'As if!'

'Could have sworn it was in the bag.'

'Well it's on for tomorrow night.' Tanya laughed.

'Shit why didn't you say?'Rula clapped her hands and did a little dance. 'Sunshine here we come.'

Outside he smiled to himself as he got into his car, pleased that the rain had finally stopped, he paused a moment before starting the car to gaze at the wonderful sunset.

CHAPTER FIFTY THREE

He was escorted into the interview room by a constable and told to sit at the table. It was ten minutes later before Lorraine and Luke walked in.

'So, Mr Simon Compton or whoever you are pretending to be now, I want to know exactly where you were for these dates.' Lorrain said before she sat down and pushed a piece of paper over the desk towards him.

He glanced at them and shrugged. 'Don't remember.'

She picked the paper up and folding it neatly in half, returned the shrug. 'Not really bothered, to tell you the truth. Not that you would know anything at all about telling the truth. It's a concept you never learned isn't it.'

He stared at her a puzzled frown on his face. 'So why did you ask then?'

'Just filling in time until the finger prints come back.'

'What, from where?'

'That's for me to know and you to wonder.'

He leaned forward and yelled. 'I want my lawyer.'

'Do you really need one?' Lorraine shouted as loud as he had.

'Yes. I demand my lawyer, now.'

Lorraine stood up followed by Luke. 'Demand's is it...Well

that's gonna take some time isn't it, so I guess we'll have to see you later. Take him back to his cell.' She said to the officer standing by the door.

'Yes Boss.'

'No you can't do this.' He banged his fists on the table, as he glared up at Lorraine.

'Can't I... Watch this space,' she glanced at her watch, then smiling sweetly at him, she said. 'We can hold you for hours yet. Have fun pet.'

They left him banging his fists on the table. Outside of the door they could still hear him shouting, until Luke started another round of sneezing.

CHAPTER FIFTY FOUR

Working late Scottie pulled the sheet over the latest person to arrive on his slab. A young man whose blood had shown a massive amount of cocaine, he had marked it as accidental death. But sometimes he wondered in these cases if it really was an accident or suicide. In the absence of a letter stating otherwise he really had no choice.

So sad, so young. As often in these case's he wondered if more could have been done to help.

Perhaps if the family's had been more alert at the start, he shook his head, the kids were so clever at hiding things these days, even the best parents in the world could be totally unaware, no one wants to believe that their darlings would even contemplate doing drugs. And why would they, just as many kids overdose from supposedly good homes as those from bad homes. He looked at the body once more and shook his head.

'The government needs to do more in the schools. And on the telly.' He muttered. 'To warn them, instead of concentrating on all this PC shit.'

He switched the light off on his way out and decided to call in on Carter. Taking the lift, he was surprised to see Sam in the lift, looking red faced Sam said, 'Hello.' As Scottie walked in and pressed for the floor he wanted.

'Bloody hell, thought you went home hours ago?'

'Well, I err.' His face flushed even more.

Scottie grinned guessing rightly that Sam had been visiting with a certain nurse.

When Sam said no more, Scottie shrugged, 'Well?'

Just then the lift stopped and Sam did a quick exit, saying. 'See you tomorrow.' Over his shoulder, as he hurried away.

Scottie sighed as the lift doors closed. 'Very best of luck young'un.' He muttered.

Carter had been moved onto the main ward, Scottie smiled when he saw him staring intently at his lap top.

'How you doing mate?' Scottie asked in his booming voice, when he reached him, startling Carter.

Carter answered with a huge smile as he said. 'Guess what, I can go home tomorrow.'

'Great news son. Soon have you back at work.'

'Doc says, not till next week.'

'Well you know what they all say, don't run before you can walk.'

Although he couldn't wait to get back to work, Carter cringed at the thought of walking, never mind running. Opening the drawer on his bedside table he took out a miniature chess set. 'Fancy a game.'

'Don't mind if I do.'

Scottie left an hour later, having been beaten by Carter. On his way to the car park he suddenly remember he had said he would call in and see how his nephew was doing. Glancing at his watch and thinking it was probably too late he took his phone out of his briefcase and rang them.

'Hello, I'm sorry can't get over tonight, I'll call in the morning on my way into work OK.'

A few minutes later he said goodbye and noticed four missed calls from Edna.

'Shit.' He rang her as he watched a couple of drunken men dragging a young woman into the emergency entrance.

'Hello Edna I'm on my way.'

'Well its cold fish and chips for you, 'cos I'm not warming them up.'

'That's fine love.' Smiling he got into his car and headed for home.

CHAPTER FIFTY FIVE

After dropping Lorraine off at home, Luke had driven down to the Shiney Row Co-op for some parocetemol, on his way back out of the shop, he spotted two youths hanging around a white sports car outside of the vets across the road. Silently he watched them through the windows of the four by four parked on his side of the road, which hid him from their sight. The pair were dressed in black jeans and black hoodies with the hoods pulled over their faces, both were wearing blue trainers. As the taller of the two raised a base ball bat over his shoulder with the intent of smashing the car window, Luke ran across the road.

The smaller one saw him coming, too late to run away he faced up to Luke and raised his fist, turning Luke used his elbow with a sharp jab and caught his nose, the youth screamed and his friend raised the bat above his head.

'Fuck off bastard.' He brought the bat down aiming for Luke's head. Luke did a quick side step, lunged towards him and brought his knee up between the youths legs. A second later he was sprawled on the ground, his hands between his legs and screaming louder than the other one, his friend, hand over his nose to stem the blood, ran away.

Luke phoned for a patrol car and read the youth his rights.

Sitting up the youth said. 'Who the fuck are you anyhow?'

'You my friend are about to find out.'

'You're not my fucking friend.'

'What's your name?'

'Fucking Bat man. What's yours?'

Luke groaned. 'Yet another arse hole.'

'Funny name that.'

'Leave the comedy till you get to the station.'

It was then that it dawned on him that Luke was a policeman, his face drained of colour as he stuttered. 'I wasn't doing anything. Really I wasn't.'

'Yeah, tell that to the judge.'

The patrol car pulled up, and Labuki got out, holding a pair of handcuffs. Quickly she slipped them on the youth while Luke explained what had happened

'So take him in and we'll sort it in the morning.'

'You can't fucking well keep me in all night. 'The youth yelled.

'Oh I assure you we can.'

Luke helped Lubuki to get the struggling youth into the patrol car, said good bye then as they drove off he crossed back over the road to where his own car was parked. Once inside he got the paracetamol out of his pocket and swallowed two of them, after putting the lid back on the bottle of water he kept in the glove compartment he headed home.

Sitting by the fire Lorraine reached for the television remote. Luke had gone up to bed half an hour ago even though it was only half past nine, after telling her what had gone on outside of the Co-Op sneezing his head off and moaning about a headache.

'Man flu.' Lorraine had shouted after him.

'What ever.' Luke had replied.

Now staring at the screen, she declared. 'Boring shit.' As she pressed the button and flung the remote down- which landed on top of her mobile. Getting up she went to her bookcase and sorted the latest Stephen King out, hoping that it would take her mind off things.

Half an hour later she closed the book, and sighed, great as she thought he was, even the King couldn't stop her mind from going into overdrive.

What if he does want kids?

Actually he will, of course he will it's only natural, even though he's never mentioned kids before.

Of course he will...Shit.

Do I want kids?

This was the root of the problem, until now Lorraine had never even thought about motherhood, now she couldn't stop thinking about it.

But what about my work?

I love my job, and worked damn hard to get where I am.

I love Luke!

What if he leaves me if I say no to kids?

What will I do then?

Ah, but he does have one daughter. Selina.

He might not want anymore.

She blew air out of her cheeks, and decided to do some ironing, which she always found calming. Too soon with nothing left to iron, she switched the iron off and going into the kitchen grabbed a can of coke out of the fridge, sitting back down she switched the news on.

'More doom and gloom,' she muttered. Shaking her head she finished her pop, killed the television, and went up to bed.

Ten minutes later unable to get to sleep she was back down stairs again.

Her mind going over and over the picture of the dead girl, she put the television on again and channel hopped, finding no interest in anything she went back to the news, bored of hearing and seeing the same thing repeated, she again tried different channels, finally settling on a true murder programme.

Fifteen minutes in she sat bolt upright in her seat. 'Friggin hell!' she stared at the screen.

Quickly she phoned Sanderson.

CHAPTER FIFTY SIX

'Your turn to get them in.' Jacko said to Frecks.

Having sold two baskets full of meat, they had put the rest in different freezers, hoping for a good day tomorrow, all of them were very happy at the profit they had made so far.

Frecks looked around at the others, then back at Jacko. Slurring his words, he said. 'Who me?'

'No that friggin old wife sitting in the corner...Of course you, thicko.'

Greg looked at Frecks. 'He's right, its defo your turn mate.' Greg waved his glass in the air.

'Oh, OK.' Frecks drained the dregs out of his glass, tried to stand and slipped back into his seat, grinning at them he tried again, with a bit more success and a helping hand on his elbow from Len.

Fully upright he said. 'Right guys, same again?' They all nodded in unison.

He made his way to the crowded bar amidst cry's of 'Yes,' and 'Come on.'

Deciding to go to the toilet first as there was a queue at the bar, and thinking the cheers were for him, Frecks grinned at everyone he passed. Totally forgetting that it was race night at the

Beehive, and the punters were cheering on their horses.

Somehow he missed the toilets and ended up outside. Staring up at the starry sky he yawned and muttered 'Guess it's time for bed.' Slowly a little unsteady on his feet, he crossed the road, weaved his way past Sunnyside, and crossed over into the Burnside.

His park bench bed in Houghton Park calling to him, he suddenly had a creepy feeling like he was being watched, he stopped and looked around and was very surprised to see that somehow he had missed his way and was down the beck, and on his way to Fencehouses.

'How the hell?'

Shaking his head he turned round, and still weaving from side to side headed back in the general direction of the Burnside, he reached the small bridge over the beck and stopped when he saw someone standing at the other side.

Fear penetrated the alcoholic fuzz in his brain. It's him; fucking hell...Knew we shouldn't have trusted the coppers, for fuck's sake. I'm dead meat here.

Slowly the figure came towards him.

Wondering if he should stay and fight or run as fast as he could, he blew air out of his cheeks when the figure's face, drawing closer became clear.

'Jacko! What the hell are you doing here?'

'Following you, bloody idiot.'

'Who's the idiot, me or you?'

'Funny sod. Come on.'

'Where? Frecks frowned.

'My house, Greg's stopping at Danny's tonight. You should have told us youse were on the street for fucks sake.'

'You sure about that.'

'About what?'

Next to Jacko now, Frecks went on as they started walking. 'I mean that I can stay at yours?'

'Course you can.'

'Great, thanks mate; does that mean I can have a bath?'

'Don't push it.'

'Oh, well that's alright...Breakfast in bed then?' He asked hopefully, leaning to one side as he smiled.

Jacko stopped walking and shaking his head said. 'First off there ain't no bed, it's a sleeping bag on the settee. And you better not piss on it.'

'Who me?'

'Yes you.'

'Never pissed on the park bench...Yet...And me friggin back's starting to seriously act up. And I honestly never pissed on the bench that was Greg.'

Jacko shook his head, trying not to laugh he went on. 'Secondly, course you can have a bath,' he stopped walking and looked at Frecks, 'In fact I insist on it... And I'm sure we can find something for you to eat in the morning. Probs just cornflakes though.'

'Aw thanks mate, you're a star.'

They headed towards the Seahills, neither of them taking much notice of the car; contain two passengers as it passed by them.

'So how long you been on the streets then?'

'Too fucking long mate.' Frecks replied.

'Why did you leave the army?'

'What's this twenty fucking questions?'

'Just interested, that's all.' Jacko opened the gate, and Frecks followed him through.

'Do you smoke in the house? Frecks asked, as Jacko put his key in the door.

'No, no smoking in the house, you'll have to have one out here.'

'No bother mate.' Frecks sat on the step and fished in his pocket for his baccy tin, finding it he started to roll a ciggie. Jacko sat down beside him.

'You want one?'

'No, it's been a few years since I packed in.'

'Good on you, might try it one day but, you know where I've been for the last five years, well they sort of helped.'

'Rough was it.'

Frecks paused, with his cigarette half way to his mouth, for a moment he stared ahead of him, turning to face Jacko he said, 'Rough doesn't cut it man, and when you come home after everything you've seen. Nobody cares.'

'That bad.'

'For most of us, yes. Some it's even worse, what they saw, what they had to do...It changes you forever.' Again he stared into space, thinking of a very brave man who had saved not only his life but that of five others in the unit. And what that man had now become.

He rose from the step followed by Jacko. 'Bed time mate?'

'Whatever.' Jacko said as he opened the door.

CHAPTER FIFTY SEVEN

Arriving back at his hotel, he smiled at the night manager, a tall slim man wearing a tight gray suit, on his way across the foyer, the manager smiled and said goodnight. Buzzing with energy he took the stairs two at a time, taking a liking to the deep red and black embossed wall paper on the walls and the polished mahogany stairs. Slightly out of breath he reached the third floor.

He had failed to see the smile turn to a frown on the night manager's face as he had stared at the large stain on the right leg of his jeans.

In his room as he was taking his clothes off he noticed the stain, he squeezed the material between his fingers and they came away red with blood.

'Shit!' He wiped his fingers then threw the jeans across the room.

Did anyone see?

No, too dark.

The manager?

No.

Shaking his head he walked over and picked the jeans back up, going into the bathroom he put them into the sink to steep. Stripping the rest of his clothes off he thoroughly examined them, one tiny spot on the cuff of his shirt which might or might not be blood caused him to scrub the cuff clean just in case.

Naked he walked into the sitting room, picked up his lap top, sat down and rested it on his knees, in a few moments he was through to his friend in Germany.

'Good night?' his friend asked.

'Very good. He got everything he asked for and more. You know the rules, always aim to please.'

An hour later he closed his laptop, got dressed and quietly left the hotel.

Finished with the job in hand he drove to the Seahills.

CHAPTER FIFTY EIGHT

On the Seahills the lights went out one by one. As they settled down for the night; no one was aware of the danger that walked among them, especially not the two young women, who staggered home after a late night out.

The man all dressed in black was in the shadows as he watched them.

So this is where you live, good to know.

The urge in him was strong, even though it had already been offered to him on a plate, but he resisted as there were two of them.

'Only one of you would have been a different story.' He whispered to himself.

Oblivious to him Tanya and her friend Rula, giggled and lurched their way home, as they rehearsed their plans to enrich their purses in the coming days.

Smirking he sauntered back to his car.

'Things to do, places to be.' He sniggered as he drove off into the night.

CHAPTER FIFTY NINE

Just gone seven o clock in the morning and Jan Emmerson in the early peace and quiet, was walking with her dog along to Nose's point in Seaham Harbour, on the site where the old Dawdon pit had stood. A spot she always loved to visit, and a place where she knew the history well. Near to the edge of the cliffs she stopped and breathed in deeply as she looked out to sea. After a few minutes she turned and walked in land.

She especially loved the story about the unsung hero. And read it just about every time she walked past the boards depicting the history of Nose's Point. Once many years ago a crew were stranded off Hawthorn Hive, they were rescued with the help of a dog who swam out to the stricken vessel with a rope, a life line to the shore.

Her own dog Zack, a Boxer, suddenly started barking, and agitatedly running round in circles. Frowning she shouted of him, but Zack just kept on barking.

She fastened the top button on her red coat the collar making her short silver hair stick out at the back, and quickly headed towards the dog, which was now behind one of the wooden information pillars, and really going crazy.

'Zack, what's the matter with you?' She yelled as she reached him, quickly she crossed round to the other side of the pillar and bent down to grab his leader. As she started to straighten up, her eyes fell in line with the pillar. 'What's the...Oh...Oh...My dear God!' Screaming she sank down on her knees. She stared at what was in front of her, her heart began to race. Slowly her hand clutching at her chest, she staggered back to her feet.

Sensing her distress the dog barked even louder.

For a minute unable to move, she stood there and stared in shock and horror. At the young man who was nailed by his hands and feet to the pillar. On his head was a crown of thorns. Blood which was now stilled had left tracks down his face. The broken stems of poppy's lay on the floor at the young man's feet the crushed petals scattered there ,were the same blood red colour as the puddle at his feet.

Screaming she backed away, with shaking hands she pulled her phone out of her pocket, missing many digits and hitting the wrong ones, she finally managed to dial the police number.

'Help,' she yelled into her phone. 'There's a body, a dead body, it's...It's.' She screamed again, then unable to stop crying intermittingly screaming she went on. 'Please come quick. Hurry hurry. Please.'

It took a few minutes for the woman on the other end of the line to calm Jan, she encouraged her to calm the dog down, Jan did this by holding the dog close to her chest, and gently rubbing his head. Once the woman on the other end of the phone got the correct location out of Jan, the wheels were set in motion and help was on its way.

A few minutes later when Jan was sitting still cuddled into the dog and sobbing, a young blond man in a blue hoodie and trainers, with a black base ball cap, came striding up to her with an arrogant stance, he frowned at her for a moment before asking. 'You alright there Mrs?'

Jan stared at him then slowly pointed with her finger, the young man turned round. 'Fuck shit.' He gasped. His whole body shivering, he sat next to Jan and put his arm over her shoulder. Jan's dog licked his hand.

Sanderson, who lived the nearest to Seaham harbour and was given the call, was the first to arrive. Shocked himself by the sight of the body, he was comforting Jan and the young man when Lorraine arrived a few seconds after the ambulance, and a local police car, shortly after that Scottie and his team pulled up.

Sanderson shook his head at Lorraine, and gestured with his hand towards the other side of the posts. An ambulance man came up and took over the care of Jan, and the young man who was also suffering shock, freeing Sanderson to follow Lorraine. He reached her at the same time as Scottie did. Lorraine was staring at the flowers.

'Yes I've counted them.' Sanderson said.

'It still doesn't add up,' Lorraine looked at him. 'And I wish I knew the story behind the bloody flowers, some sort of sorry? She threw Sanderson a puzzled look.

'Unless,' he replied. 'You accept that there *is* another male body unaccounted for.'

'That's all we fucking need.'

'That's what I thought,' Sanderson stared at the body. 'Eighteen to twenty years, do you reckon?'

With a heavy sigh Lorraine nodded. 'We've got to catch this bastard and soon before the body count goes any higher. And how are we going to keep it from the public now, with two witnesses, plus the curtain twitchers, wondering what's going on?'

'I agree...It's not going to be easy.'

Turning she shook her head as she walked towards the car, and bumped into Scottie.

'Hi there love,' he said, 'from what I heard on the way here this is another grim one.'

She nodded. 'Yes Scottie it is...Have you found out any more on yesterday's case?' Her voice was full of expectation, but Scottie soon squashed any hope.

'Sorry love, but nothing, the tiny bit that we had there was no match for. It's so flaming frustrating, never known a case like it, it's as if the arrogant bastard is taunting us...' He looked around, then back at Lorraine, before saying. 'Where's Luke?'

'He's off with man flu, as if we weren't bloody well stretched enough.'

'Poor bugger.'

'He could have picked a better time though, than right in the middle of all this.'

'Lorraine!'

'I know, I know, shouldn't moan, cos the poor bugger really is poorly...I wanted to send for the doctor last night, but he wasn't having it. But if he's no better when I get in, trust me the doc's coming out.'

'Oh believe me, I trust you.'

Lorraine smiled. 'Yeah too right...And by the way Scottie, be prepared, it's pretty damn gruesome...And believe it or not, but it seems like we have a missing body.'

'What?'

'You'll soon see when you count the flowers. I've set the lads on a search, but if it's anything like the last one, I don't hold out much hope. It seems this one isn't too keen on the idea of being caught just yet.'

'I agree,' Sanderson said as he came back to them. 'Look's like this bastard intends on making a career out of this vileness. ' .

Scottie went to the posts as Lorraine took Sanderson to one side. 'Well, did you watch it?'

'I did that Lorraine, pretty gruesome. But the programme its self was twelve years old and based on a murder in the fifties.'

'Yes, which means?'

'You know what it means. We have a copycat murderer on the loose.'

'Clark is so gonna freak out when I take this to him.'

CHAPTER SIXTY

Having spent the night in a travel lodge near Manchester, they were in the departure lounge of the airport when John's phone rang again. With a heavy sigh he pulled it out, looked at the number and put it straight back in his pocket.

On her way back from the toilet where she had vomited her whole breakfast up mostly because of the vodka she had consumed last night, Tracy saw him shake his head as he put his phone away. She walked over to the shop and bought headache tablets and a bottle of spring water.

'Was that her again? She asked, as she sat down facing him, her face twisted in a scowl, as feeling only a tiny bit better, she sighed as she pulled the zip on her red jacket up. 'Damn it I so wish that fucking kid would shut the hell up... They better not be sitting near us on the plane and that's a friggin fact, noisy little git.' She glared at the baby, who looking over his mother's shoulder saw Tracy's scowl and screamed louder.

John looked over at the young woman as she tried her best to comfort the baby. Turning his head back to Tracy he said. 'Yes, that's the fourth time in ten minutes she's phoned.'

Tracy unscrewd the cap off the water, and swallowed two tablets, before saying. 'Next time just tell her where we are, and to fuck off, put the poor bugger out of her misery...Just make sure you don't tell her where you really get your money from that she's been living on for years.' She giggled. 'Actually, yes do, and make sure you tell her where the moneys come from that's bought her fancy posh ornaments, as well as her fucking fancy clothes.'

'Tracy!'

'Well she's gonna be hounding us for God knows how friggin long. Just man up and tell her we're fucking off to live a new life in Germany.'

'That's a bit harsh.'

'You having second thoughts?'

'No.' He leaned towards her and taking her hand said, 'Tracy you know it's you that I love. I can't live without you. I need you with me every single day. It's the thought of you that keeps me going, not Sandra. For God's sake Tracy, haven't I told you over and over.'

'Then fucking well tell her.' She reached for the pocket where his phone was. 'Or I will.'

'No Tracy.' He grabbed the hand reaching for his phone.

'Why?'

'Because It's not that simple, we've been together for a long time, you know this...And there's the boys to think of, it's gonna be a shock to them.'

'How come you fucking wait till now to think of all that?' She threw her holdall down and stamped her foot. 'So what, you just gonna piss off now and leave me in the lurch?' Her voice rose with each word, drowning out the crying baby.

As people began looking at them, John stood up and tried to comfort her. 'Please Tracy, it just sort of came over me.'

Just then the boarding sign came on. She picked her holdall

up and stared at him.

John slowly nodded. 'You know love that It's you that I want. Plus with all the work I've got lined up in Germany means I won't be travelling a lot of the time, just the odd job here and there, we'll be together most of the time.'

Visiously she slapped his face. 'Don't you ever do that to me again.'

For a moment John was in shock, she had never shown any sort of violence before in all the time he had known her, which it then suddenly dawned on him, was not really that long.

Realising what she had just done, she was immediately contrite. 'I'm sorry, really John, I think it was all of this happening suddenly...Really I'm so sorry.' Gently she touched his face where she had slapped him.

Sighing John nodded, taking her hand he smiled as together they walked up to the desk. Tracy produced her passport and was duly passed through. When John handed his over the woman at the desk stared at it then back up at John. He watched puzzled as her hand reached for the buzzer, in moments he was being stared at by two armed guards.

'I'm afraid you will have to come with me.' The nearest one, small with balding ginger hair said.

'But why...I haven't done anything?'

'It's that cow. I know it is.' Tracy yelled.

'You are wanted for questioning by Houghton le Spring police.'

'What the hell for?' John stepped back, shocked. Quickly he looked around, at the passing lines of people.

'Sorry sir. I don't know why. Come this way please.'

'OK.' He shrugged at Tracy, who followed them.

'Just wait till I get my hands on her, the visious nasty cow. I'll personally cut her fucking plait off.'

'Leave it Tracy.' John shook his head at her. 'We don't know what it's about yet.'

'Oh yes we do. What else could it be but that cow reporting you missing?'

They followed the security guards into a side room, Tracy complaining the whole time.

CHAPTER SIXTY ONE

Halfway through his full English breakfast that he had not expected to have this morning but which he was thoroughly enjoying, he wiped his mouth with his paper napkin and took a sip of tea. Feeling someone standing next to him, he put his cup down and looked up to see a young girl staring at him.

'Who are you?' She asked, frowning at him.

'I'm Frecks, he smiled. 'And who might you be?'

'I'm Melanie...Is Frecks a real name or a made up one? 'Cos it doesn't sound real.'

'I guess it's a made up one on account of the...'

'Freckles?' Melanie put in quickly.

'Something like that.'

'Aw right.'

'Morning Melanie pet, do you want Cornflakes this morning or a proper real English brekkie?' Jacko asked as he came in from the kitchen.

'Hi Dad,' Melanie grinned. 'Just cornflakes, ta.' she turned back to Frecks. 'Are you my dad's friend or my nana's?'

'Err...Your dads.'

'My nana's away,' Melanie pulled out a chair and sat down. 'She's in Scotland seeing her brother, uncle Tom, 'cos he's poorly and he fell over and broke his leg. They put a chalk on his leg so he can't get out much that's why nana's gone up there, to help him sort things out.'

'Nice...Not that he fell over and broke his leg like. I mean nice that he has someone to help him.'

Melanie nodded. 'I know what you mean. Nana says that's what family's are for. Anyhow she's bringing me a new phone,' Melanie leaned over and whispered. 'I'm not supposed to know about it. But I heard Dad telling her to get me one, cos my other one got nicked, and uncle Tom's friend sells phones on the markets up there.'

'Did it really get nicked?'

'Well I did have it in my coat pocket, then it wasn't there so...' She shrugged. 'I suppose I might have dropped it somewhere but me and my friends looked all over the place, so we think somebody nicked it.'

Jacko put a bowl of cornflakes in front of Melanie. 'Eat up pet else you'll be late.'

'Dad.'

'What Melanie?' Jacko sat down and looked at his daughter.

'We have sex education today is there something's I should take or?' She rested her hands palms up on table, and looked at Jacko with a questioning look on her face, as Frecks nearly choked on the last of his bacon.

Frecks bit his lip; looking at Jacko's frozen face he couldn't keep the amusement off his own face.

After a moment Jacko got his breath back. 'I, err...I don't think so love, the teacher should have everything you'll need I'm sure...'

'OK Dad,' Melanie jumped up from the table and looked out

of the window. 'Can't see Emma and Suzy, they must have gone without me.' Grabbing her school bag off the floor, she quickly left shouting her goodbyes over her shoulder.

When the door slammed behind her, Frecks slapped the table with the palm of his hand as he laughed loudly.

Jacko frowning at him only made him laugh even more. 'Your face man, when she said that...Guess that's where a mam comes in handy, do you reckon; especially with the little girls. Oh dear.' he laughed again.

Jacko shook his head, though he couldn't help but smile himself.

'OK,' he said when Frecks calmed down. 'Let's get this sorted; we've got the pubs down Chester Le Street to do today, so let's see if we can shift this lot, 'cos we did great yesterday. And we'll find some time to go to the council and see if we can try to get you and Greg some sort of emergency accommodation cos I'm sure they have something kept aside for emergencies...OK.'

'Well you would think so but we put our friggin names down months ago, heard nowt since.'

'What address did you give...One park bench Houghton Le Spring?'

Frecks scowled at him. 'We not that fucking stupid you know.'

'That's debateable. So what address did you give?'

'Me nana's dick head, 'cos that's where some nasty nosy bastard grassed us up at.'

'And the last time you checked in there?'

'Two weeks, three weeks maybes. Been a bit wary of going back in case the same nasty twat did it again, as it is, nana's in debt cos of us...We've been working, trying to get some money to give to her, guarding dogs so we slept there at the farm, till we sort of fell out with the boss man.'

Jacko raised his eyebrows.

'Long story, might tell you one day.'

'Right then, we'll check your nana's house before we go to work.'

'Sounds like a plan,' Frecks jumped up and held out his hand. 'I don't know how to thank you mate.' The next moment as Jacko reached for his hand, Frecks had Jacko trapped in a bear hug.

Hiding a smile as he disentangled himself, Jacko picked the dishes up and headed for the kitchen, over his shoulder he said. 'Come on then you daft sod, get a move on.'

CHAPTER SIXTY TWO

Lorraine, her elbows on her desk rested her head in her hands, and gave a weary sigh as Sanderson, and Dinwall stared down at her. She had just informed Dinwall of what she and Sanderson had watched on the television last night. Finally she looked up.

Dinwall was frowning as he said. 'So you're saying it's a copycat off years ago?'

'Certainly looks that way to me.' Sanderson said.

'So how did they catch him?'

'That's just it,' Lorraine said. 'They didn't, it wasn't until months after the last killing that someone reported a terrible smell coming from a flat somewhere in the middle of Chicago. When the authorities went in, it was to find that he'd been dead for months and the place was a shrine to his victims.'

'Jesus'

'They also found a stack of letters from people who wanted to commit suicide. Also there were pictures all over the walls, a sort of before and after scenario.'

'No way!'

'Way.' Lorraine sighed. 'Looks like we're gonna have our work cut out alright.'

'What did he die of?'

'Heart attack. One small consolation the fucking rats had been nibbling away at the vile git.'

Dinwall rose and started pacing up and down the room, for a moment he reminded Lorraine of Luke when something was bothering him.

'Cup of tea anybody?' Sanderson asked as he made his way over to the tea stand.

'Not for me.' Dinwall said.'

'Me neither thanks. Problem is we're lost guys, and if we take the flower count seriously, there is defo another body out there. Also what the hell is it all about, and I know I've said it before. But it's chewing me to bits this leaving flowers lark. Some sort of misguided guilt, or the sick bastard's idea of a joke, 'cos we've been here more than once.'

Both men were quiet for a moment then Dinwall said. 'Could be any of those reasons, who even knows why the murdering scum bags take things or leave things. And can we establish for certain if it's a male body that's missing or a female?' Dinwall looked at the other two.

'It's all about power. Power over the victims, or power over us.' Sanderson said, shaking his fifth bag of sugar into his cup and stirring it vigorously. 'They love that they can keep on killing while we run around like headless chickens.'

'I agree, in some cases it's a bloody sick game to them, and as we know they love to keep it going as long as possible, but in the end a lot of them glory in being caught and love having their name in the media.'

'That's true.' Sanderson said.

'Also I think the missing body is male.' Lorraine looked at them both for confirmation.

'Yes,' Sanderson agreed. 'The body definitely has got to be male.'

'So,' Lorraine turned to Dinwall. 'Any one reported missing in the last twenty four hours?'

Dinwall shrugged. 'Not so far boss, but it's still early. Oh and I had a wee talk with our doggie pal, he's only gone and admitted to everything.'

'Well done, saved me the bother of even looking at the git. And Luke had a run in with some other's wearing the blue trainer's last night. Outside of Shiney Co Op. On being questioned they both admitted to buying the trainers off Wayne Barret, who in his turn pinpointed Simon Compton.'

'That's what I thought all along boss. And when I informed him Compton confessed. Plus I think it was the fear of being interviewed by you that made him sing.'

'Well it's not like he had much choice but to admit, did he? Sanderson frowned at Dinwall. 'Not when he'd been grassed up by Barret.'

'Yes but what if he's admitting to that to hide some other activity of his?' Lorraine frowned. 'Guess I'm gonna have to talk to the twat after all.'

'Want me to be there Boss?' Dinwall asked.

'No, it's fine.'

'OK Boss.'

'Right, I think I'll take another look at the murder scenes, just in case we have missed something.' she grabbed her jacket off the back of her chair. 'I need to see Scottie anyhow...And Dinwall, get onto the passport people and try to find out if any locals frequently visit Germany.'

'Already done it boss I was in early this morning. All ports and air ports are on the lookout.'

Lorraine complimented him on her way out. When she had left, Sanderson said to Dinwall. 'Crawler.'

'Just doing me job.'

'Aye if you say so.'

'What the hell is wrong with you, lately you've been moaning more than ever?'

'Nowt wrong with me.' Sanderson straightend his navy blue tie, then shrugged, as he took a sip of his tea.

CHAPTER SIXTY THREE

Lorraine was half way to the hospital and well pleased that yesterdays frequent downpours seemed to have vanished, she pulled her sunglasses out of the glove compartment and pulled the visor down as the sun, becoming brighter by the minute played on her hands- just then her phone rang.

Cursing she dropped the sunglasses onto the floor as she pulled over to the side of the road.

'Damn.' She frowned at her phone and realised she was missing both Luke and Carter, even if it was just for the practical things.

'Hello Dinwall, this better be good.' She said as she rummaged around the floor of the car for her glasses.

'I just found out boss, we have four people in the area who regularly visit Germany.'

'Do we know any of them?'

'Well, one's from Newcastle. A woman, name of Maria Walters, she goes over once a month. Don't know why yet. And there's, you not gonna believe this but that Simon Compton, who we have in custody already, supposedly business trips four or five times a year.'

'Oh my God. Do you think it might be him? Because trust me,

I wouldn't put nowt past that nasty bastard. And like we thought before he did admit without too much prodding to the other stuff. Could be a cover up.'

'Well you did say he might be confessing to the other shit to cover his tracks. Anyhow the other is a Mr Carl Simms from Darlington who goes over once a month to visit his family. And the last one is closer to home, Its Sandra Gilbride's husband, who drives a lorry over there at least once a week.'

'Sandra Gilbride, do you mean the Sandra Gilbride who lives on the Seahills?' Lorraine was shocked, she knew Sandra quite well, though not her husband so much.

'Sorry, yes that Sandra Gilbride, it's her husband, John Gilbride. It's a good job I phoned earlier so most of them will be on the lists.'

'Hmm, tell you what, hold everything I'm on my way back. And check up on the female Maria Walters, at this stage and due to the drugs used to practically make the victoms helpless, we're not ruling out any females strength wise.'

She phoned Scottie and told him she would be in to see him later then quickly did a U-turn and headed the car towards Houghton Le Spring.

'OK Dinwall, you come with me. We'll pay a visit to those on the list.' Lorraine said, fifteen minutes later.

'Oh right, but before we go, about that business yesterday with Graham Bailes.'

'What about it?'

'He's been reported missing.'

Lorraine looked at him. 'You don't think he could be our missing body, do you?'

'Well I certainly hope not, he's never been one of the bad guys, more of a loner, keeps himself to himself if you know what I mean...His family are out looking for him now and of course rumours are coming in that they're already up in arms blaming the other part of the family.'

Lorraine dropped her bag onto the floor. 'Shit, that's all we need on top of this, a friggin family feud...Sanderson get a patrol car in the area now, and keep them there until you hear otherwise from me. Clark can shout from his friggin castle about not enough resources to police one estate constantly, as much as he wants. I'm not having blood on my hands over this.'

Both of them nodded in agreement with her.

'Right think we'll just have a slow drive around the Seahills before we do anything else. Sanderson, man the fort please. Dinwall with me.'

'Sure thing boss.' Sanderson replied, glowering at Dinwall's back as Dinwall jumped up and followed Lorraine.

Lorraine had not missed the look, on the way to the car she said. 'Is he giving you a hard time by any chance?'

Dinwall sighed. 'Well he is, believe it or not, a tiny bit more grumpy than usual...Actually he's a big bit more grumpy than he usually is.'

'Thought as much. Listen Dinwall don't take it personal, it's nothing you've done, the reason is, it's because he's retiring in three or four months.'

'Shit. I should have realised. That's why he's so bloody edgy all the time.'

'Yeah, and I'm thinking he's not taking well to the idea. We are going to have to do something for him. And I for one will be really sorry to see him go.'

Dinwall nodded. 'Yeah...And to be truthful I'll miss the moany old git as well...When you say do something do you mean like a party?'

'Actually I was thinking of having him come in part time in a sort of advisory role, I've heard it's done at other stations, very successfully as well.'

Dinwall frowned, realising that even though Sanderson could be a pain in the arse, he really would miss him. 'Hmm, do you think he'd go for it?'

'Worth a try. Also, of course we'll have a party for him, we couldn't not, could we?'

'Yeah, think his ego would be gutted if we didn't.'

'Ok, sorted. I'll check with the chief, and I'll leave the party to you. You've got four months to organize it.'

Realising he'd been conned, Dinwall frowned again. 'I guess so Boss.'

CHAPTER SIXTY FOUR

Sandra opened her curtains to see the post man coming up the path carrying a parcel. Quickly she went to the front door.

With a smile the postman, who had the longest grey beard Sandra had ever seen, said. 'Could you take this parcel for number fifty seven please?'

'That's way round the corner.'

'Yep but nobody else in the street seems to be in, or even up out of bed yet.' He grinned. 'I'll drop a card in and let them know where I've left it.'

'OK no bother.' She took the parcel and signed the black box for him.

'Thank you.'

As he walked up the path she looked at the name Tracy Brewer. 'Shit, of all the bloody people.'

She put the parcel on top of the kitchen bench, wondering briefly what was in it. Then sticking her middle finger up at the parcel she went up stairs to dress.

Before she put her bra on she felt her breast.

Still there.

Stop it, I'm gonna drive myself crazy. Vanessa's right, the doctor's right. It's nothing to worry about.

But still?

No! Don't go there.

Quickly she dressed, teaming her black jeans with a black roll neck jumper, and went down stairs.

She picked her phone up and frowned when she saw she had no missed calls.

'Why hasn't he returned my calls?' She muttered, as she slipped her tan coloured jacket on, and dropped her phone into her pocket. Grabbing her black bag she went outside and headed towards Mr Skillings house.

Knocking on the back door she opened it and went into the kitchen to find Mr Skillings enjoying a bowl of cornflakes. Devouring the last spoonful he pushed the bowl away smacked his lips and with a smile said. 'Morning my lovely.'

'And good morning to you. You're defo looking a bit better today pet.'

'Feeling better, a bit stiff like, but you know hopefully that'll pass soon.'

'Sure it will. You up for a bit of shopping or do you want to write a list and me and Vanessa will get it for you.'

'Would you? That would be good, thanks. Really don't think I'm up to trashing around yet.'

'No bother.' Sandra had thought the shops would be too much for him but knowing how proud and independent he was she thought she'd better ask.

While Mr Skillings wrote his list out, Sandra washed his breakfast dishes up. After drying her hands she picked the list up, studied it, then putting her coat on she shoved the list into her pocket.

'Right, I'll pop over and see if Vanessa's ready and we'll be back later OK?'

'Aye love that's fine,' he grabbed her hand. 'Don't know what I would do without youse two girls.'

'You know that's what friends and neighbours are for Mr Skillings. And you've been really good to us, and all of our kids...We'll be back soon.'

He watched as she walked up the path and crossed over to Vanessa's. Sighing he tried to get up out of his chair and managed on the third attempt. Slowly step by painful step he made his way into the kitchen, his heart heavy with worry, wondering if he should have told Sandra that it was her husband who had nearly knocked him over shaking his head as he filled a glass full of water, he knew he could never ever tell her because it would break her heart.

After downing the entire contents of the glass, he made his way back to the sitting room and his seat by the window. He had just made himself comfortable and reached for his paper which Jacko had kindly dropped off for him earlier, when a police car flashed past.

'Wonder where that's going?' He muttered as he leaned forward to try and see more.

His vision was suddenly blocked as a dark haired man in a black leather jacket, walked up the path next door.

'Hmm, stranger on the loose.' As if sensing him, the stranger looked in his direction.

Mr Skillings never a shy or timid man, sat back as the stranger's cold stare penetrated him. A sudden attack of the shivers made him look away for a moment, when he looked back the stranger had gone.

Mr Skillings had seen many things in his life time, the

evilness of war being only one of them, he had learned the hard way to always trust his instinct. And today it was screaming at him.

Who the hell was that?

Hope the miserable git's not moving here.

He hobbled back to his seat in front of the television, just as Dolly and Doris came in.

CHAPTER SIXTY FIVE

I already told you NO. He typed onto the screen.

So why do you still keep contacting me? Came back the answer.

It's you that keeps contacting me.

Is it?

For fucks sake.

Ha Ha. Remember Captain Philips, who used to go off it if he heard anyone swearing, the upper class twat that he was.

Fuck off and don't bother me again.

OK, keep your friggin hair on. You know where I am if you want me.

Fuck off.

Switching the computer off he slowly walked out of the library.

CHAPTER SIXTY SIX

Sandra and Vanessa were coming down the path when Vanessa spotted the police car parked outside of Sandra's house. 'What the hell are them buggers doing at yours?'

'What?' Sandra quickly turned her head in the direction of her house. 'Bloody hell.' Followed by Vanessa she ran up the road and reached her gate just as Lorraine was getting out of the police car.

'What's the matter?' Sandra asked anxiously.

'Hello Sandra, is your husband around.'

'So he's alright?' Sandra's heart beat slowed down.

'As far as we know, we just need a few words with him.'

'What for?'

'We need to talk to him Sandra, just to clear a few things up, that's all.'

'He's away at Stockport for a day or two, some sort of works do, then his regular run to Germany.'

'OK, could you give him a ring and ask him to contact me please.' Lorraine handed her card over.

'Is it something serious?'

'Just a few questions about his frequent trips to Germany. I'm sure it will sort itself out so don't you go worrying.'

Sandra nodded as she stared at Lorraine's card. 'Well he does go there quite often, but...But it's his job. Has something happened over there like?'

'It's just a few questions and a few things to clear up, nothing to be worrying about,' she refrained from saying, yet, as she went on. 'Any Idea when he'll be back?'

'Three, four days.'

'Right, we'll be off then.' Lorraine got into the car and they pulled away.'

'What the fuck was all that about?' Vanessa asked.

Sandra shrugged as she pulled her phone out of her pocket, 'don't know but I'm gonna find out.' Quickly she dialed her husbands number.

Ten minutes later after numerous calls and messages, she looked at Vanessa and said. 'Why isn't he answering?'

Vanessa stared at her; all that was running through her mind was Mr Skillings insisting that it was Sandra's husband who had caused his accident.

'Maybies he's hung over after that party he went to. Or he's already on the road?'

Sandra sighed. 'Yes that might be it, though he said it would be maybies a few days before he goes to Germany, he has something's to sort out at head office first...I'll phone again later.'

'Come on then, shopping.'

Sandra hesitated. 'Look, I really can't be bothered today.' She opened her purse and took Mr Skillings note out. 'Here, can you get those for Mr Skillings.'

'You sure?'

'Yes,' she toutched the side of her head. 'I think I've got a headache coming on... See you later alright.'

Vanessa took the note. 'Right I'll pop along to see how you are when I get back love.'

Without answering, Sandra headed up her path to the front door.

Vanessa watched her as she waited at the bus stop, wondering just what the hell was going on.

Back home Sandra closed the door behind her, she had remembered that her husband had another phone that he mostly used for work purposes, and wondered if he had wrote the number down in the note book he kept in the cabinet on his side of the bed, because he was hopeless at remembering numbers. She went straight up stairs, where she began opening the drawers on her husband's side of the bed, with each empty drawer she gasped.

Moving to his side of the wardrobe she felt a lump beginning in her throat, she pulled open the wardrobe door to find it empty of most of his clothes. She sat down on the bed and dialed his number. Again there was no answer.

'John.' She sobbed as she dropped her phone onto the bed. 'What have you done?'

CHAPTER SIXTY SEVEN

Adam made sure everything was clean and tidy; before he put his black jacket on, picking up his phone he looked at it again, still no reply from Tracy. Frustrated he put it in his pocket, then felt a twinge of guilt as he thought. *What if something's happened to her aunt?*

She might have died. Maybe that's why she's not getting back to me.

'Shit, that's it, poor Tracy.' He muttered.

About to go and wait outside for Danny and the crew, his elbow caught a glass of water on the kitchen bench as he passed.

'Aw fuck.' He felt the water running through his jeans and down his leg. Quickly he ran up stairs-pulling his shoes off and then his jeans, he opened the wardrobe door. In stunned shock he stared at the empty space.

Five minutes later he phoned Danny. 'Hi mate, I'll not be coming today, can barely get out of bed with this friggin flu.'

'OK, no bother, you sound a bit sniffy. See how you are tomorrow- little comfort I know, but you're not the only one down with it.' Danny replied.

'Yeah, tell me about it... It's doing the rounds; hopefully see you tomorrow or the next day.' He put his phone down on the side of the bed and sat staring at the wardrobe. His mind going over and over the past weeks, wondering what he had missed.

Why would she suddenly just up and go?

Yes she's a bad tempered bitch at the best of times, but I know she loves me.

She can't help her mood swings.

Can she?

Where the hell are you Tracey?

He looked at his phone again, just as there was a knock on the door. He got up off the bed and pulled the curtain along, looking out of the window he saw Sandra Gilbride standing there.

CHAPTER SIXTY EIGHT

Earlier Jacko had phoned Greg and told him to meet him and Frecks outside of the Gentoo offices in Houghton, the three of them were now sitting in the office of a young girl with black hair which she wore in a pony tail, and wearing an ice blue shirt, with a badge declaring her name to be Susanna.

'But you must have been given forms to fill in?' She looked from one to the other.

'Aye and we filled them in.' Frecks replied.

'So why is there no trace of them?'

'How the hell do we know, it's your office.'

'Excuse me.'

'Why, what have you done like?'

Jacko kicked his ankle. 'Oww.' Frecks rubbed his ankle and glared at Jacko.

'So,' Jacko said. 'You are saying that there are no forms at all?'

'Exactly.'

'But we did fill them in...You've lost them haven't you and you're blaming us.' Frecks insisted.

'We did fill them in,' Greg said, before the woman could speak. 'And it was him over there that we gave them too, that bald man with the skinny mushtach. He's just standing up now, look him over there.'

They all looked over to where he pointed, to see a young woman holding onto the hand of a toddler who was trying really hard to pull away.

They heard her say, 'Thank you.' As she stood up to go.

The woman they were dealing with jumped up and quickly went to the man, after a few minutes talking they both came back over, sitting down the man said. 'I remember youse both coming in, what seems to be the problem?'

'Well I'm pleased you remember us, 'cos apparently there's no record's of us.' Frecks glared angrily at the man.

'Give me a few minutes.' He stood up and went into the back room.

Frecks looked at the women. 'I told you we filled them in... Didn't I.'

'Alright, enough, it's gonna be sorted.' Jacko said.

'Aye well we not going to the back of the queue, that's for sure it was flaming well long enough the last time.' Frecks folded his arms across his chest, and stared at her.

The man came back with a hand full of forms, seeing them Frecks groaned. 'Not again.'

'I'm sorry but somehow the first lot have been lost in the system.'

'I knew it.' Frecks slapped the table with the palms of his hand.'

'Calm Down,' Jacko said. Looking at the woman then the man, he went on. 'So what happens now?'

'We fill the forms in again, on line.' The man replied.

'What!' Frecks exploded. 'Have you any idea how long it

took us to fill them in the first time.'

'I suspect you might have pressed the delete button by mistake.'

'Oh shit,' Greg's said. 'So are we ever gonna get somewhere to hang our heads other than the park bench or good friends floors?'

'Well, we'll fill these in again, make it legal and I may have somewhere for you later today.'

'What?' Frecks eyes opened wide.

'Four brand new two bedroom flats will become available from this afternoon.'

'Are those the ones just been done out on the Seahills?' Jacko asked.

'Yes two large semi detached houses have been made into four flats.'

'How mate,' Frecks looked at Jacko and lifted his hand in a high five, 'Looks like we gonna be neighbours.'

Jacko nodded, ignoring the raised hand.

Nearly an hour later, forms filled in and with instructions to be back at three thirty, they were waiting to be picked up at the corner of the White Lion by Danny, and Len.

'Wow, what a stroke of luck.' Frecks said. Greg nodded his agreement.

'It was that lads...Oh here's the van.'

Danny stopped the van and the three of them climbed in.

'Where's Adam?' Jacko asked as he fastened his seatbelt.

'He rang me earlier, he's got that flu bug that's doing the rounds, our lass has it as well.'

'Aye and you better keep away from me,' Len said from the

back seat. 'Cos I don't want it.'

'You actually refusing something for nowt Len?' Jacko asked. 'That's a first.'

'Funny bugger.' Len scowled as they others laughed.

'So where we off too now Danny?' Frecks asked. 'Cos we gotta be back for half three.' He looked at everyone in turn and grinning nodded at them. 'We're getting the keys for a fucking flat at last.'

'Great news.' Danny said. He was echoed by the rest of them.

'Yes, and guess where the pair of them are going to live?' Jacko put in. 'Only on the bloody Seahills.'

'Not a better place in the world guys. So today I thought we could do a couple of clubs down Chester le Street. Try to get rid of this lot. Then go shopping later...Before you ask Frecks, I'll drop you and Greg off first.'

'Thanks mate.'

'So what youse gonna do for furniture?' Len asked.

'Shit never thought of that.' Greg said.

'Well I've got a spare single bed you can have.'

'Champion, thanks Len, we'll take turns sleeping in it.' Greg laughed.

'Well we're getting a new dining table and chairs, youse can have the old ones.' Danny said.

Before they reached Chester Le Street roundabout, they had been promised table and chairs, the single bed, an iron, and an old TV which needed slapping now and then.

'Also,' Len said. 'You can have the wardrobe in the spare room. No good to me now, it's just standing there empty, since the oldest lass moved out.'

'Thanks Len.' Greg said.

'Isn't there a place, some charity or something where you can get stuff if you've never had a house before?' Danny said.

'I'm sure there is.' Jacko nodded. 'Just can't remember its name.'

They pulled up outside of the pub. 'OK, you and Greg jump out here.' Danny looked at Frecks. 'We'll pick you up on the way back.'

'Righto...See youse in a bit.' Frecks and Greg got out of the van. Together they walked into the pub their baskets on their arms fully laden, as Danny pulled away.

Two minutes later they were marched out of the pub, by two thick set bouncers and told not to come back.

'Fucking shocking.' Frecks said, as he and Greg sat on the waist high wall to wait for the others. 'A man can't earn a decent crust these days.'

Greg laughed. 'Too true, you do realise we're gonna have at least an hour or more to fill.'

'No way, the others will shift that lot soon.'

'Yeah right. In the mean time you can tell me what's bugging you.'

'What do you mean?' Frecks frowned at Greg, but didn't meet his eyes.

'I know when something's the matter with you, you've been on edge for a few days now. So spit it out.'

Frecks kicked his heels off the wall, for a moment he stared at the view, swinging his head towards Greg, he said. 'I can't tell you mate.'

'Can't or won't.'

'Trust me you really don't want to know,' he stood up. 'I'm going over to the shop for some fags.' He headed towards the grocery shop across the road.

'Thought you'd packed them in?' Greg called after him.

'Changed my fucking mind OK.' He replied, without turning around.

Five minutes later he was back, sitting down, he leaned against the wall and lit a cigarette up, drawing the smoke in he held it for a moment, before blowing smoke rings.

'Are you gonna tell me what the friggin hell's up with you or what mate?'

'Already told you, nowt.' He finished the cigarette in silence, stubbed it out on the ground, then laying his head back, he closed his eyes.

'For fucks sake.' Greg shook his head. 'You know you can tell me anything, and you usually do so what the hell is it?'

Sitting up he stared at Greg, before looking down at the ground and muttering. 'Sorry can't do it mate...Anyhow I'm probs wrong anyway.'

'Just spit it out.'

'Fuck off.'

An hour later Danny's van pulled into the car park, the lot of them were grinning until they saw the full baskets.

'What the hell happend?' Danny jumped out of the van and stood with his hands on his hips.

'They threw us out.' Greg said.

'So why didn't you phone me?'

'Got no money on the phone.'

'Me neither.' Frecks said, as he stood up.

'Shit. And those two baskets have been standing in the

fucking sun all this time.'

'Hell, never gave it a thought, sorry.' Greg picked his basket up and walked to the van.

'We'll have to share those baskets out and take it home, we can't sell them now. Anyhow we had a good one, so you'll be able to put some money on your fucking phones, and make sure you keep some on. Right jump in 'cos we're dropping youse two off for your keys, then we off to hit some supermarkets Silksworth way.'

CHAPTER SIXTY NINE

Edna, miraculously recovered from her recent bout of illness, in which time she had managed to aquire a new perm in her silver brown hair, peered over here glasses at the body of the young man on the slab, she was still staring a few moments later when Scottie came in.

'Tell me what the hell sort of depraved evil git does something like this?' She practically shouted.

Scottie sighed and held his hands out. Slowly he shook his head. 'We've already been through this my love.'

'Then I'll tell you, to do this you have to have lost all traces of humanity. And that's if you ever had any in the first bloody place...It's either born in you or beaten into you, one or the other.' She shoved her glasses back up her nose as she turned away from the slab and sat down. 'Sometimes I wonder if that's why the aliens don't show themselves, 'cos they know we are bloody horrible nasty gits.'

Used to Edna's conspiracy theories, Scottie tried not to smile as he said. 'Tell that to the detective's, though I'm guessing Lorraine will agree with you, she's that pissed off with this case, she's about to believe anything. Oh yes, and she'll be popping in later dear.'

'How the hell she deals with this sort of thing all of the time beats me,' Edna noisly scrapped her chair up to her desk. 'Then again, how the hell do we...How does anybody?'

'Someone's got to do it. Anyhow, it's great that the bairn got his dog back.'

'Yep...I phoned just a few minutes ago, all's good. I invited them over for tea tomorrow, he wants to bring a friend with him. Girl called Abby... I said that was fine and you would pick them up about five. OK.'

When Scottie didn't answer, Edna turned, he was staring at the body the way Edna had been a few minutes ago.

'What?' Edna asked.

'He looks sort of familiar, I'm sure I've seen him around somewhere.' Scottie frowned.

'You've said that before, turned out they've been total strangers...What should I do for tea tomorrow?'

'What?'

'Tea tomorrow, what should I make?'

'You know whatever it is, will be fab.' He looked back at the body, then walked over to one of the many drawers in the room, taking his phone out he rang Lorraine.

'Hello', he said, when he heard her voice saying hello back, he quickly went on. 'It's only me your most favourite person in the world.'

'How did I know that?' Lorraine said as she walked in.

'Bloody hell.' Scottie spun round as both Edna and Lorraine laughed. 'Didn't think you were that close!'

'Well I was...Hi Edna.'

'Hi yourself lovely.'

'OK,' she walked over to the body. 'Anything to tell me?'

'Well like the first one, he has been heavily drugged. When we removed the penis from his mouth, there was a note halfway down his throat.'

Lorraine feeling like she wanted to gag, breathed deeply for a moment, before she said. 'Saying what?'

'Pretty much the same as the last one.'

'But how can there be a suicide note when it's so obviously murder.'

'Well I've been thinking about that, this was a very healthy young man.'

'And?'

'The only health reason he had to want to die, must have been depression.'

'I'll go with that, so he wanted to kill himself, but why was he murdered?'

'Ah,' Scottie patted the side of his nose with his forefinger.

'What if he had help.'

'Help?' Lorraine frowned.

'Well, I got to thinking, what about this internet thing, what if he did want to die but hadn't the guts to go through with it?'

'And he went on line to find out if there was someone out there willing to help...Perhaps for a price.'

'Yes, that's it. Only the sick pervert he got in touch with, doesent do exactly what they asked.'

'Nowt as queer as folks.' Edna put in.

'You're right there Edna...Hmm, that's an interesting theory Scottie. 'I'll chew it over with Dinwall and Sanderson when I get back.'

Edna nodded her head in agreement. 'Anything's possible these's days. That internet thing has a lot to bloody well answer for, giving scope to the sick and depraved animals out there...In fact it's an insult to bloody proper animals isn't it.'

'True.' Scottie nodded.

'Actually,' Lorraine took her phone out of her pocket. 'Better get Dinwall on it now, he's our internet guy.'

When Dinwall answered she told him what they had just talked about. 'Hmm,' he replied. 'That's an interesting possibility, I'll get right onto it boss.'

'Yes, and get Sanderson to check out any strangers in the area, especially from down South.' Something clicked in her brain as she said that, but she couldn't quite grasp what her instinct was trying to tell her.

'Will do boss.'

'Sorry?'

'I'll get right onto it...What you said.' He sounded puzzled.

'Oh yeah right, sorry I drifted off for a minute there, something I said about down south sparked something... She hesitated a moment. 'Ah that's it, that bloke who was at the Angel of the North the other day taking pictures, arrogant bastard remember his name?'

'No I wasn't there, but I'm sure Carter will, or Luke.'

'OK get the name off one of them, and get him checked out.'

'Will do.'

'Cheers, bye.' Closing her phone she looked at Scottie. 'The more I think about it the more plausible what you said becomes.' She held her hand out for the note. Scottie handed it over. When Lorraine shook it out of the plastic bag she read it then looked at Scottie.

'I know what you're gonna say.'

'That it's exactly the same as the last one, the only difference being the names.'

Lorraine nodded. 'Even though we checked the last note for finger prints, of which there were none, we need to get the handwriting checked.' She phoned the office again, this time to speak to Sanderson, who was out of the office and on his way to Cara's parents with the first note before she closed the connection.

'Hope something comes of this, thanks Scottie.'

'My pleasure.'

'Oh,' Edna said. 'Where's the lovely Luke?'

'He's in bed with the bloody man flu, still managing to eat though...And he's in the huff because he can't make it to the gym tonight.'

Edna grinned. 'Well a body like his doesn't come from nowhere, you gotta work on it.' She winked at Lorraine.

Lorraine smiled. 'I guess so Edna...Well I've got to get back to the office, to run a few things past the guys, thanks for your help.'

After saying their goodbyes and Lorraine was outside, she phoned Luke, when he answered she asked how he was.

'Not good,' Luke replied. 'Cant flaming well stop coughing or bloody sneezing.'

'OK, my mother and Peggy are going to call in and check on you at dinner time, to see if you're alright and if there's anything you need.'

'Peggy's already been and took my order for lunch.'

Lorraine laughed. 'How am I not surprised.'

He yawned then went on. 'And guess what.'

'The mind boggles where Peggy's concerned, but I guess you're gonna tell me anyhow.'

'She's just flaming well gone and left me the photos off last night to look through again in case I missed any.' Just then he started another fit of coughing.

'You sure you don't want me to call the doc's?'

'No, hate the poking and prodding.'

'Friggin hell you sound like my uncle Paul. Ask Peggy she'll tell you all about him.'

Luke groaned. 'No thanks.'

'Ok, I'll check on you later. Love you.'

'You too.' He managed to say before sneezing.

'Enjoy the photos.'

Luke snapped his phone shut.

Arriving outside of Houghton police station, Lorraine spoke a few words with Labuki as they passed on the steps to the door, who informed her that it was all quiet on the Seahills at the moment and both families had been warned to calm down and that Graham Bailes was still missing.

She walked into the office just as Dinwall was putting his phone away.

'Hi boss, that's Manchester I've just been talking too. They have John Gilbride, and Tracy Brewer.'

'Oh wow that was quick.'

' Wasn't it...Apparently they were both booked on a flight to Germany, no return tickets booked. And Sanderson has tracked two of the others down, and he's adamant they aren't the culprits,' he looked at his watch. 'Actually he'll be back in five.'

Lorraine had just finished telling Dinwall about Scottie's theory when Sanderson walked in.

'No trace what so ever of a Steve Jonstone anywhere in the north east. Made a few phone calls got one of the PC's to help and he's not registered anywhere, nor is there any reference to him living in Stockport.'

'So with that I'm guessing he gave us a false name when we spoke to him at the Angel.'

'Looks like it.' Sanderson agreed.

'Now why would he do that?'

'Sounds like he's guilty of something,' Dinwall said. 'Did he act suspicious?'

'More arrogant than anything else, and he certainly didn't take kindly to Luke stepping between us, if looks could have killed Luke would be dead by now.'

'So do you reckon he's our man?' Sanderson asked.

'Until, or if, we rule the arrogant git out, then yes. We need me, Luke, Carter and Lubuki to get together with a sketch artist as soon as possible. Like now.'

'I'll see to that.' Dinwall said picking his phone up.

CHAPTER SEVENTY

Sandra forced a smile out when Adam opened the door. 'Hi love, this parcel was left at mine this morning.'

'Thanks.' He muttered reaching for the parcel.

'You alright Adam?'

Adam shook his head, as he glanced at Tracy's name staring up at him from the parcel. 'No not really Sandra, you might as well know, 'cos people are gonna be talking anyhow...She...' He hesitated a moment then blurted out. 'Tracy's left me.'

He looked so sad that Sandra didn't click on at first, and then it really came down on her. She gasped. 'What...What do you mean, she's left you?'

'Her clothes are all gone. The drawers and the wardrobe, they're...They're empty.'

Sandra's mind flashed back to John's empty drawers and his empty side of the wardrobe.

Her eyes wide in shock she stared at him for a moment then muttered. 'So...So are John's.'

Puzzled he said. 'What do you mean?'

'John's clothes are all gone as well.' She burst out crying.

Adam put his arm around her. 'Come in.' Tucking the parcel under his arm, he ushered her inside.

He sat her down on the settee and went to put the kettle on, a few minutes later he came back in with two cups of tea, he handed one to Sandra who was still wiping tears out of her eyes and sat down facing her.

'Are you thinking the same as me?'

Sandra looked at him. 'Too much of a coincidence isn't it?'

Adam nodded, staring at a recent picture on the mantlepiece of him and Tracy, both of them smiling; he felt a lump swelling in his throat and blinked. 'How long do you think it's been going on?'

'I don't know...But for a while now I've noticed she's been wearing some of my clothes that I gave to the charity shop.'

Adam punched the side of his chair. 'Damn I knew I'd seen that red coat somewhere before.' Becoming more angry by the minute he jumped up and began to pace the floor. 'I'll kill the fucking bastards.' He yelled. 'Both of them.'

Sandra who had known Adam for years and had never once seen him angry or never felt she had anything to fear from him stared at him as he ripped the paper off the parcel, then she gasped as a handbag exactly the same as she had bought a month ago, fell from his hands.

CHAPTER SEVENTY ONE

Frecks and Greg were waiting on the corner of the street, eating a slice of pizza each for their dinner; when Frecks noticed a man coming out of one of the houses further up. For a moment he froze as he recgonised him.

'No way.' He muttured, as he dropped the remains of his slice into the box.

Greg looked at him. 'What?'

'Nowt, just singing.'

'You!' Greg laughed. 'You know you've been warned about that before, wasn't it off Major Brigson, no less.'

'Funny twat.'

Greg laughed as he grabbed the piece of pizza up. 'I'll have that if you don't want it.' Without waiting for Frecks to say yes or no, he swallowed it.

Frecks screwed his face up. 'Greedy git.'

'Come on, here they are at last. Wonder where we going today?'

Frecks shrugged as Danny's van pulled up. He had other things on his mind other than meat pilfering.

'Been thinking,' Danny said as they climbed into the van. 'We best move onto Darlington way for a bit, plenty supermarkets and pubs to sell our gear. We don't want to be recognised by going in the same places all the time.'

'Sounds good enough to me.' Greg said, as Frecks muttered something unintelligible.

'What did you say?' Len asked looking at Frecks.

'Nowt, never mind.'

'Take no notice Len, he's been in a funny mood for the last few days.'

'No I haven't it's you that's been in a funny friggin mood.'

'Now children.' Jacko said. 'Thought youse would be happy today, with the new flat.'

'Yes we are you believe me. It's fab, and thanks Jacko mate.' Greg said.

'Did you all see the news, about that body found at Seaham harbour?' Len asked.

'Aye, pretty grim, the bastard who did it wants stringing up, that's if they ever find him, we need the coppers back on the beat like they used to be.' Jacko said.

'Yes I watched it just before we came out. Friggin shocking, the nasty swine.' Greg looked at Frecks.

Avoiding his gaze Frecks shook his head as he loosened his seat belt. 'Just drop me here please.'

'What?' Danny looked at him, as Greg frowned.

'I feel sick. Sorry but I can't fucking do this today.'

Danny stopped the van and Frecks jumped out. He slapped on the door as the van started to pull away. 'Cheers, see youse tomorrow.'

'Well that's two down...What the?' Jacko said as everyone looked at Greg.

'Beats me.' Greg shrugged.

As the van drove off Frecks headed back home, hand in his pockets and his head down. He had not been telling lies when he'd said he felt sick, he truly did, along with a splitting headache, he suspected was due to over thinking. But what could he do but go over and over what he suspected.

He rubbed his forehead as he sat down on the bench facing the church.

What can I do?

What should I do?

I need proof.

After ten minutes he decided exactly what to do. Rising from the bench he headed towards the Blue Lion.

CHAPTER SEVENTY TWO

Vanessa saw Sandra running up her path as she looked out of Mr Skillings window. Quickly she knocked on the window, not hearing the banging Sandra reached Vanessa's door and was about to go in when Vanessa opened the window. 'I'm over here,' she shouted. 'Sandra.'

Sandra turned and spotting Vanessa she ran across the road.

'What's up?' Mr Skillings asked as he came in from the bathroom.

'Don't know but Sandra's running around as if all the hounds of hell are chasing her.'

Just then Sandra, tears streaming down her face burst through the door. 'He...He's gone...He's ran away with her.'

'What, who's gone.'

'John he...He's ran away with Tracy Brewer.'

'What.' Vanessa gasped.

'So that's why they were in such a flaming hurry.' Mr Skillings said, as he stood there with his mouth open.

Vanessa shook her head at him, but Sandra did not miss it nor the look that passed between them.

'What.' She demanded, looking at each of them in turn.

Mr Skillings shuffled his feet, as Vanessa turned her gaze to the window.

'What?' Sandra demanded again. 'I know youse both know something so tell me.'

Mr Skillings sighed. 'I didn't want to tell you love, but it was him who ran me over, your John, he was driving the car with Tracy Brewer sitting next to him.'

Sandra collapsed onto the chair behind her.

'Youse knew all along and you didn't tell me...Why?'

'No way did we know that Sandra, we didn't honest, you know for a fact I would have said, Christ I would have knocked the nasty git out, you know that, both of them. We didn't tell you because we thought it would upset you that he was driving the car. We knew nothing about them fucking off together'

Sandra looked at Mr Skillings. 'I'm sorry.' She sobbed.

'You've got nothing to be sorry about pet.' Mr Skillings rested his hand on her shoulder.

'So how do you know that they've buggered off together?' Vanessa sat down next to Sandra.

A fresh lot of tears ran down Sandra's face as she told them about the parcel and delivering it to Adam.

'Poor Adam...Those two have a fucking lot to answer for.' Vanessa said, as she was thinking. *Of all the friggin times to pull a stunt like this when she's terrified she has cancer.*

'Do you want a cup of tea love?' Mr Skillings asked.

'Please.' Sandra sobbed.

'Make it extra hot and I'll find the bastards and pour it over their fucking heads,' angrily Vanessa stormed to the window, looking up the street towards Sandra's, she shook her head. Turning back she said. 'You're stopping at mine tonight and forever how long you want too.'

'No really...I'm alright.'

'No you're not and I'm not arguing with you, OK.'

Sandra smiled as she whispered. 'Thank you.'

Mr Skillings came in.' There's three cups on the tray Vanessa, will you bring them in please?'

'Sure no bother.'

Vanessa came back with the teas just as Mr Skillings was saying. 'You will need to go up to the dole in the morning.'

'What for?' Sandra frowned.

'Because you will need money to live on...Have you checked your bank account?'

Sandra's face drained. 'No, should...Should I?'

'Is it a joint account.' Vanessa asked as she put the tray on the small coffee table, and handed Mr Skillings and Sandra a cup each.

'Yes.' Sandra looked from one to the other with fear in her eyes.

'We'll go up to the cash point and check, soon as we've had these, no point in leaving it till tomorrow and fretting all night long, is there.'

'You're right,' Mr Skillings said. 'Best to check now.'

'But he wouldn't...Would he?'

Vanessa shrugged. 'If you ask me he's capable of anything now, I mean who would have thought?'

Fifteen minutes later they were standing outside of the cash point at Barclays bank. Sandra gasped as her bank balance came on the screen.

'Oh my God.' She gasped.

'The rotten lousy scumbag.' Vanessa said.

'There...there should be more than ten grand in there.' Sandra whispered.

'Nice of him to leave you three hundred, isn't it, the dirty rotten scumbag.'

The next moment Sandra collapsed onto the pavement.

A man they vaguely knew, waiting behind them to use the machine helped Vanessa to pick her up. 'My car's just round the corner, I'll drop youse off home if you want, or the Doctors.'

'Thanks very much, home would be good.' Vanessa said. 'Much appreciated.'

CHAPTER SEVENTY THREE

Lorraine collected the two plates of mince and dumplings wrapped in tin foil that her mother had made, said goodbye and headed home to Luke.

Reaching home she parked the car, and unaware that she was being watched, she opened the boot, collected the plates and went inside. Luke was sound asleep on the settee.

'Food Luke,' she shouted from the kitchen as she took his plate out of the microwave, placed it on a tray and made her way into the sitting room.

Luke stirred and slowly sat up.

'Feeling any better?' She asked as she put the tray on his knees.

'A little, but my heads pounding.'

'OK, had any paracetamol?' Without waiting for his answer she went back into the kitchen and put her own meal in the microwave, a minute later she was back with a glass of water and a packet of tablets

As she handed him the glass she couldn't help thinking. If I do have kids this is what I'll be doing for the rest of my life.

Seeing the strange look come over her face, Luke said. 'Are you alright?'

'What?' for a moment she just looked at him. 'Oh yes I'm fine, just thinking about   what's going on with this case.'

'Not a lot from what you've said.'

'Shit, has the sketch artist been here yet?'

Luke frowned, then shaking his head as he scratched the stubble on his chin said, 'No, is one coming like?'

'Remember that guy who was at the Angel of the North when we got there.'

'Couldn't forget the miserable git.'

'Well the name he gave us is not known anywhere, before you say it yes obviously there are a few with the same name but none fit the age group or the discripton and none come from Stockport.'

'So hence the ID pic.'

'That's the idea. Are you finished?' Lorraine looked at his still half full plate.

With a sigh Luke pushed his tray to the side. 'Sorry really not hungry.'

'You'll never get better at this rate.'

'Will do, just need another day or two.'

Just then there was a loud knocking on the door. 'That'll be the sketch artist.' Standing up she took her empty plate and Luke's into the kitchen then went to open the door.' Come in Jen,' she said to the young blonde woman who smiled at her. Lorraine had worked with Jen more than once and had found her work very good. 'Luke's through there.'

Lorraine followed her through as Jan said. 'I've been to the hospital and seen Carter...Hi Luke.' Jan sat down. 'Would youse both like to take a look. He swears it's the double of him.'

Lorraine took the paper out of her hand, for a moment she stared at it, handing it over to Luke, she said. 'That's him alright, I would say his bottom lip is a bit fatter though, sort of sticks out, a bit like a spoilt brat.'

Looking at the paper Luke agreed. 'Spot on, also you're right about the lip.' He handed the paper back to Jen.

Taking out her pencils Jen chose one and worked for a few minutes on the drawing, then handed it back to Lorraine.

'That's it! Spitting double of him...Thanks Jen, you're so damn good.'

Feeling proud of herself Jen got up to go.

'Would you like a cuppa or something stronger?' Lorraine asked her.

'No thank you. Gotta get home to my little girl.'

'Oh yes, how is she doing, two or three now?'

'She's three next month.'

'Lovely.' Lorraine walked her to the door, when Jen was on the step she said. 'So how do you find mixing being a mother with work?'

'No problem, she's in nursery three days a week and loves it, the other days my mother has her...No way could I have given up work I love my job.'

'Good...Well I'll see you then.'

'Yes, bye.'

Lorraine closed the front door and leaned against it. *She makes it sound so easy.*

But is it?

Sighing she pushed the thoughts away and went into Luke, who was now flat out and snoring.

'Oh dear, she muttered, 'Best to just leave him a note, he needs his rest.'

Rumaging in her bag she found her note book and had to

rummage deeper for a pen. Hastly she wrote.

> Have to go back to work to interview
> John Gilbride. See you later.
> Love you xxx

Lorraine put the note next to his glass of water then she quietly left the house, as she got into the car she had the strangest feeling that she was being watched. Slowly she looked around, in the slowly darkening sky all she could see was two boys about ten years old, kicking a ball about, and as far as they were concerned she wasn't even on their radar.

Shaking her head she got into her car and headed back to the station, thinking. God I'm bloody imagining things now, got to stop getting obsessed with something that probably won't even happen.

CHAPTER SEVENTY FOUR

Jacko and the gang arrived back in Houghton just after six o clock and bitterly disappointed.

'What we gonna do now?' Len wailed.

Danny shrugged. 'I'll think of something, don't worry.'

'Bastards.' Greg muttured.

'Good job I sensed something was up.' Jacko said.

'Aye, how did you guess?' Len looked quizzically at him.

'It was the way those two security people were looking at us, then looking down at the pictures in their hands. Just guessed, and had a funny feeling that it was us they were looking for.'

'Well it was good while it lasted.' Danny pulled up outside of Greg's flat.

'Aye and I guess we had a lucky escape, cos you can guarentee the other supermarket chains will have us on those camera things...Plus we got plenty lamb chops in the freezer.' Len said.

Greg shook his head as he got out of the van. 'OK see youse all later.'

'Cheers mate.' They all echoed.

Greg waved, as he walked down the path to the flat.

He was curious to see if Frecks was in and why he'd cried off sick when there was nothing wrong with him.

Opening the door he shouted Frecks's name. When there was no answer he started looking around. Everything looked the same as it had when they had left earlier. Going into the small kitchen last, he found as he had in the other rooms, that there was nothing to suggest that Frecks had been home any time through the day.

He opened the cupboard door and took down a jar of coffee, waiting for the kettle to boil he mulled over the last few days.

There is defo something up.

He's just not being right.

But what the hell is it?

He took two steaks out of the fridge, looked in the cupboards, all he could find was a tin of beans and two tins of soup.

Guess its steak and beans then.

We've lived on worse.

Stirring sugar into his coffee he walked into the sitting room, and surprised at how dark it already was he switched the light on, sat down and picked the paper up, wondering as he did so if they might have been better off staying in Germany.

A moment later he sat bolt upright when he read the headlines, about a disfigured body found at Noses Point at Seaham Harbour.

CHAPTER SEVENTY FIVE

Lorraine walked into the interview room, sat down and switched the tape on, before she could say anything. John Gilbride practically shouted. 'What the hell is going on and why have we been dragged back here?'

'You tell me.'

'What?'

'You heard.'

'Tell you what?'

'First why were you going to Germany, although,' she stared at him for a moment. 'That's pretty obvious, what I really want to know is what you do on your frequent visits there?'

'I'm a lorry driver, so I think it's pretty obvious, and do I need a lawyer present.'

'Do you?'

'I don't know, you tell me.'

'Are you a murderer, do you murder people for money, specifically people who want to die but can't do it themselves?'

John Gilbride's jaw fell open, as he stared in shock at Lorraine. 'What?' he blustered. 'You...You really think that I'm a murderer?'

'Prove to me that you are not a murderer. Tell me what you

do in Germany. And by the way we know that the haulage company you say you work for- doesn't exist.'

Still in shock and still staring at Lorraine, this time with a deep fear in his eyes he slowly shook his head as his face grew pale and he said 'I am not a murderer.'

'Prove it.'

'Where's Tracy?'

'Waiting her turn.'

'I want you to know she had nothing to do with it, and my wife Sandra had no idea, she truly thinks...Thought I worked for a haulage company.'

'So who do you work for?'

He hesitated 'Myself, I pick refugees up and bring them to England.' He dropped his head.

'You what?' Astonished Lorraine stood up and leaned over the table. 'You're telling me that you're a people trafficker.'

'Better than being a murderer...And I make sure that they are all delivered safely.'

'Delivered.' Lorraine banged her fists on the table.

CHAPTER SEVENTY SIX

'What's wrong?' Kerry asked her mother as she came downstairs dressed in her running gear. 'Is that Sandra I can hear crying?'

'It's a long story pet.'

'So shorten it.'

'OK, Sandra's husband has been playing away with Tracy Brewer.'

'What! That nasty bitch?'

'Apparently the pair of the horrible gits were running off to Germany.'

'No way.'

'Yes so Sandra's staying with us for a few days till her boys come home, I couldn't see her be by herself. And also the coppers are looking for him, they might even have him by now, but Sandra doesn't know why.'

'Poor Sandra...And have you heard the news?'

'What now?'

'There's only a murderer on the loose.'

'What?'

Just them Mr Skillings tapped his way in. 'Yes, it's all over the news, just up the road in Seaham.'

'Shit, we better make sure all the doors are locked, and you girls are not going out of this house tonight that's for sure.'

'Mam! I'm off for a run.'

'No you're not.' Quickly Vanessa ran and locked the door, on her way back she shouted up the stairs. 'Nobodys going out of this house tonight.'

'What.' Robbie shouted back.

'You heard.'

'What you on about Mam?' Claire asked as she appeared at the top of the stairs surrounded by her siblings.

Looking through the window as he passed, he saw the look of bewilderment and fright on the Lumbsons faces and knowing the reason why, smiled as he walked on.

CHAPTER SEVENTY SEVEN

Lorraine had the latest report from Scottie in front of her, she looked at her watch, eight thirty, she should have been home hours ago, sighing she rested her head on her hands, her elbows on the table as she read through it. Her face twisted with anger at what had been done to the two victims, made more graphic by the pictures in her mind. The door opened and Sanderson walked in.

'Three things boss.'

She looked up at him and nodded for him to go on.

First Gregor from Germany has finally got back, he's been off with the flu, says his throat has been that sore he couldn't even talk so he took himself off to his place in the woods. Anyhow Over the last five years there have been fifteen suspicious murders that were made to look like suicide, four of the bodies are still unidentified, and each body had flowers beside it. There have been no murders for the last four months, and they are no closer to finding the culprit.'

'Well I guess that hasn't done us much good...OK, number two.'

'There's been another body found, sadly this time we know who it is.'

'Oh for fucks sake...Who is it?'

'Graham Bailes.'

'What?'

'Sorry, but yes.' Sanderson could picture what was going through her mind, the carnage that would happen between the Bailes and the Barrets.

'Where, when was he found?'

'Just five minutes ago, the call came in just before I came in here. He's been found sitting propped up on Penshaw Monument, facing west. The entire contents of his stomach have been spilled. That's all we have for now.'

'Shit, damn fuck!' Lorraine reached for her black jacket. 'Phone Dinwall; tell him to meet us there.'

'Do I have too?' Sanderson grumbled, scrambling in his pocket for his phone.

Lorraine frowned at him, 'Come on.' Quickly with Sandersons phone pressed to his ear, and Lorraine struggling with the left sleeve of her jacket, they ran out of the building towards the car.

They reached Penshaw Monument in less than five minutes. The Monument, a folly built in 1844, is a replica of an Athens temple. Built on a large hill the Monument could be seen from miles in all directions.

'Well thank God its flood lit.' Lorraine said as they started the steep walk up the hill. She heard Sanderson breathing deeply as he gamely tried to keep up and slowed her pace down; just before they reached the base of the monument, Dinwall caught up with them.

'Hi boss.'

Lorraine looked sideways at him. 'What the?'

'Sorry boss, it's all I could grab.'

Dinwall was wearing black jeans, and underneath his brown jacket was a red and white striped pyjama top with a sunderland badge on. His ensemble was finished off with a pair of red slippers.

'It's all I could grab.'

Sanderson laughed and pointed at the pyjama top. 'Go to bed early round your way don't you.'

Dinwall screwed his face up at him. 'It's called relaxing after a heavy day...You should try it some time.'

The scene was taped off and two police men were standing guard Lorraine walked up to the first one. 'OK, who found the body?'

'A group of teenagers, just having a drink up here, reckon they were stargazing.'

'Where are they now?'

'On the way to Houghton station.'

'OK, did you get anything out of them.' She moved closer to the body and saw for herself that it was indeed Graham Bailes.

'Not really they were all in shock, couple of the girls were screaming, and one of the lads. He was the first one to reach the top and find the body.'

Lorraine was staring at the body which was covered in blood. Bailes throat had been cut, as well as being sliced open from his throat to his navel, the cut was in the shape of a cross.

'OK, I've seen enough, there's nothing we can do until Scottie gets here. We'll have a look around.'

When they reached the east side of the building Lorraine stopped and faceing Dinwall and Sanderson said. 'What did you notice?'

'No flowers.' Sanderson got in just before Dinwall, much to his satisfaction.

Lorraine nodded. 'Why?'

'Perhaps he's sick of playing games.'

'That could be true.' Dinwall said. 'He is some arrogant git that's for sure.'

'Aye, and an arrogant git that's running rings around us, no finger prints no nothing.' Sanderson replied.

'Well the identikit on that Stockport bloke goes out tonight,' Lorraine spotted Scotties van approaching. 'Maybies someone might recognise him.'

'Well if they do let's hope he's the one we're looking for. In the mean time there's not a lot we can do until Scotties finished his work, is there?'

'You're right Sanderson. Let's get back to the station see what these teenagers have to say...Shit it hasn't took them bloody long to get here.'

Sanderson and Dinwall looked in the direction Lorraine was facing and spotted, the Sunderland echo van approaching followed by the Tyne Tees television guys.

Both of then groaned and quickly followed Lorraine down the hill, half way down they bumped in to Scottie and his crew.

'We're getting off now, we've got the kids who found the body to interview. I'll phone you later OK.'

'No problem, another gruesome one I'm guessing.'

CHAPTER SEVENTY SIX

Unable to sleep again Lorraine decided to go for a run. It was exactly two o clock in the morning when she closed the door behind her.

Heading down the road she failed to notice the man who had been watching the house for the last hour. She ran up to the Burnside and decided to head through the beck and double back towards home through Fence houses.

There was something that John Gilbride had said that didn't quite ring true, and so she had not ruled him out yet, although the time line made it more than likely not him. And as for Tracy Brewer, as far as Lorraine and Sanderson were concerned the woman was a born liar. And this new death, well the kids were so obviously telling the truth, and had just stumbled across the body, it was something they would have to live with for the rest of their lives.

As she was nearing the burn a wind seemingly from nowhere sprang up whisking her hair into her face. Suddenly she felt something touch the back of her neck, spinning round with her fists up, she was surprised to see nothing there, spotting a few large leaves swirling around and realising what had happened she blew air out of her cheeks in relief.

Having watched her go, and waiting for five minutes in case she had forgotton something and came back, which she had done before, he slowly crossed the road.

Luke turned over and struggled to sit up. Realising that he couldn't hear Lorraine breathing he looked over to her side of the bed to find it empty.

Where the hell?

Straining his ears, he heard a noise coming from the door down stairs, then a low bang as if something had knocked into the wall. Thinking it was probably Lorraine coming in or going out, because the door stop had mysteriously disappeared a few months ago, and since then the door banged against the wall.

Feeling weaker than ever and slightly dizzy he slowly lay back down, hearing the bedroom door open he looked towards it expecting Lorraine to walk in.

He gasped a moment later as a man holding a knife above his head burst into the room.

'Get out.' Luke managed to yell.

'NO...No one talks to me the way you did and gets away with it, do you know who I am?'

Recognising him Luke slowly nodded.

'Good because tonight you die.' Grinning he moved towards the bed, still holding the knife menacingly above his head.

Luke struggled to get out of bed and slipped onto the floor, in a moment the cold steel of the knife entered his back.

Lorraine saw the distant flash of lightning to the South and decided to cut her run short.

No point in me getting soaked and catching the flu as well. She thought as turning she headed for home, a few steps later she stopped as her phone rang.

'Hello.'

'It's me Sargent Wilks , we've had a Miss Tanya Sunly report in that she recognised the man on the photokit as a resident in their hotel up until yesterday.'

'Does she know where he went to, did he leave a forwarding address?'

'No sorry.

'Ok, not much we can do tonight, we'll be on it first thing in the morning.'

'Cheers boss.'

After saying goodnight Lorraine closed her phone. Another flash of lightning accompanied by a low thunder sent her running for home.

He grinned, pleasure spreading over his face as he raised his arm savouring the moment he paused as he watched the blood already pouring from the wound in Luke's body; just as the knife was about to strike again, the arm holding it was grabbed and pulled back with such force that the knife was dropped.

Frecks raised his fist and hit his old army colleague with such force that it broke his jaw, and knocked him unconscious. Quickly he ran into the bathroom and grabbed a towel. Back in the bedroom he pressed the towel over the wound and phoned for the police and an ambulance. Dropping his phone he felt for a pulse.

CHAPTER SEVENTY SEVEN

Labuka, working nights this week was shocked to find that a report of a disturbance requiring immediate responce, was at her boss Lorraine Hunt's house.

Quickly she and two other police men were in the car and heading for Lorraines.

Reaching the address they jumped out of the car ran through the open door and hearing a noise from upstairs they took them two at a time, seeing the open bedroom door to the right Labuka was the first in.

She saw a man leaning over Luke his hands covered in blood and pressing a towel on Luke's back, in the corner another man with blood dripping from his mouth and his hands tied in front of him, sneered up at her. Quickley she took her phone out to ring for an ambulance.

'I've already sent for an ambulance.' Frecks said.

'Good,' Labuka nodded. 'So what happened here?' She asked, her heart trembling, as she put her phone away and knelt down beside Luke and felt for a pulse.

Ten minutes later Lorraine jogged into her street and was shocked to see an ambulance and a police car outside of her house, for a moment she froze, then gasping ran towards the stretcher that was being carried into the ambulance and also taking in the fact that the man they were looking for was being put into a police car.

'What...What's going on?' She yelled.

Labuka grabbed her arm. 'Please boss.'

'What the fucks happened?' Lorraine yelled.

'It's Luke, he's been stabbed.'

Shaking Labuka's hand off, Lorraine jumped into the ambulance.

CHAPTER SEVENTY EIGHT

One week later

Sandra closed her door walked down the street to Vanessa's, on the way she said hello to Dolly, Doris and Mr Skillings as they headed for the bowling green. After assuring them all that she was fine, she turned, her face changing to show she was far from alright. She went into Vanessa's house.

Vanessa was at the window and smiled at Sandra when she came in. Sandra held a white envelope out, as she said. 'I darsent open it.'

'Give me it.' Vanessa took the envelope from Sandra. Tearing it open she hastily read what was written, looking up at Sandra, she grinned. 'Told you everything would be alright, didn't I.'

Sandra heaved a huge sigh of relief. 'Oh,' she clutched her chest. 'Thank you God.' She started to cry, as she looked at Vanessa, and knew she would never have got through this last week in hell without her.

'So you ready for our plan?'

'You bet. And fuck him.'

Vanessa grinned. It had been hard those first couple of days and she feared Sandra might do something silly. She knew they weren't out of the woods yet, it would take months even years for Sandra to get over her cheating husband, but taking each day as it came was good, and today was the best day yet.

They had decided, Vanessa's idea and mostly to keep Sandra occupied, to take a catering course, hopefully the outcome being that they would rent a shop out in Houghton and turn it into a cafe. Having never worked a day in her life, Vanessa was excited, already she had a money pot on the table which her family and friends had added contrubuitions too, and they were hoping to be in a position to open up next spring.

Vanessa ran a brush through her hair, pulled her blue blouse down, faced Sandra and said. 'This is it kiddo, the first day of the rest of our lives.'

Lorraine stared at the car park from the doors at the entrance of the hospital. She was waiting for her mother and Peggy, along with Sanderson, Dinwall and Carter.

Apart from dealing with Simon Compton who was now looking at a long stretch behind bars, and the murderer they now knew as Jake Freeman, who was looking at life; she had hardly left Luke's side for the whole week, he had lost so much blood and had been in an induced coma the whole time until an hour ago.

She spotted them arriving and waved, when they got out of the car she could see Dinwall carrying two black plastic sacks. She bit down on her lip to stop herself from screaming, but could do nothing to stop the tears running down her face. When they reached her, her mother flung her arms around her and whisperd in her ear. Lorraine nodded and gave her mother a small smile. For once Peggy with tears in her eyes, was lost for words. In turn they all hugged Lorraine, then together they headed for the lift.

Lorraine took deep breaths as the lift reached floor six, the doors opened and they all stepped into the corridor. Waiting half way along, outside of Luke's room, Scottie, Edna and Clark waited for them, soft smiles on their faces, Sam who Lorraine had not seen as he was standing behind Scottie, leaned to the left and waved at her.

'Thanks for coming,' Lorraine whispered as she opened the door, flinging it wide she shouted. 'Happy birthday darling.'

Luke sitting up, but resting on the pillows grinned as they all poured in the room. Dinwall opened one of the sacks and the happy birthday balloons escaped. The other sack was filled with cards and presents.

Luke was overwhelmed. 'Really you shouldnt have.'

'Oh yes we should have.' Clark entered the room and moved to the front as Lorraine took hold of Luke's hand. 'So when can you expect to be back to work?'

For a brief moment the room was silent, then they all burst out laughing.

THE END

For Now